"It's an excellent   eant remarked.

"*Imitation!*" O'Brian snapped. "I'll have you know this is the real thing! 'Twouldn't do to have no fake around our necks." Her left hand went to the gem and held it up defiantly to him, still on the neck chain. "You see? It's *real*."

Maslovic reached out and turned the sparkling emerald-colored gem so that its slightly flattened face was towards him and stared into the darker area.

The darker area inside was a green so dense and deep it seemed like some sort of liquid, swirling and going down much farther than the gem itself was deep. And in that dark area, pictures began to form.

Maslovic couldn't decide if those pictures were in fact real and emanating from the stone or somehow in his mind, but they nonetheless seemed very real if also very surreal, as if actual shapes and places were being viewed through some dense liquid lens.

The images were strange, bizarre. Human figures twisted into grotesque shapes, creatures very nonhuman twisting and writhing and swarming, all superimposed against alien landscapes, distorted scenes of a swirling hell of intense storms and volcanic fire; and, finally, a barren, dark landscape with structures, structures clearly not in current use but rather the remnants of ancient cataclysm.

Slowly he became aware, in the dark world of wreckage, that the point of view was resolving on some sort of eerie cavern. He felt himself pulled down towards the cavern, and then, just inside in the darkness, there was . . . *another*.

He let out a sharp, short cry and dropped the gem, backing away. It took him several seconds to regain control of himself. Irish O'Brian had a smirk on her face that was almost unbearable.

"So you met dear Tad, didn't you?" she asked with a sense of total satisfaction.

KASPAR'S BOX

JACK L. CHALKER

KASPAR'S BOX

Copyright © 2003 by Jack L. Chalker

A Baen Books Original

Baen Publishing Enterprises
P.O. Box 1403
Riverdale, NY 10471
www.baen.com

ISBN: 0-7434-8843-1

Cover art by Bob Eggleton

First paperback printing, August 2004

Library of Congress Cataloging-in-Publication Number
2002043994

Distributed by Simon & Schuster
1230 Avenue of the Americas
New York, NY 10020

Production by Windhaven Press, Auburn, NH
Typeset by Bell Road Press, Sherwood, OR
Printed in the United States of America

For all those who
look at the world
crumbling and despair,
maybe a little kick
in the pants.

"If the Universe is full of advanced civilizations, where are they?"

I:

MELCHIOR: SURVIVING THE FIRE

"The trouble is," Gail "Lucky" Cross griped, "even after all this time marooned on this pest hole, I *still* haven't lost any weight!"

Jerry Nagel looked up at the sky. "I think you're gonna get the chance real soon. Looks like we're coming around the big planet and into the sunlight. If not today, then tomorrow for sure."

They had been dreading that moment since they'd been marooned on this hot, horrid Hell of a world. It was bad enough as it was.

The entire planet was an active volcanic zone, so far as they could tell. Every mountain, large and small, seemed to be slightly conical and had smoke rising either from the top or from fissures along the sides. Even the flat plains were nothing more than magma

1

flows, recent and not so recent, with soft spots that could crack or invert or turn into pools of magma without notice. The air, heated partly from the proximity of the great gas giant that was a barely failed proto-sun, was further warmed by convection from the large number of hot spots. Since the environmental suits had been put away in case of severe emergency, there was no air conditioning or other comforts, either. The thermometer built into Jerry Nagel's watch said it was a comfy thirty-two degrees Celsius, and the perceived heat was much greater thanks to the tremendous and constant humidity that varied between ninety and a hundred percent. That it rained—a lot—was the only positive about the place. It cooled them off and drained some of the humidity from the air, at least for a short period.

There was also a constant haze: dust particles from the countless eruptions that went on around the planet in a near continuous cycle. They had small nasal dust filters in the survival kit, but it seemed like they were always getting clogged. Three, four hours and you had to wash them out and clean them. They at least allowed breathing, but they were all covered most of the time by fine chalky dust or, when it was wet, a light gray mud.

And yet they were surviving. The rainfall was easily captured and provided a steady supply of drinking and cooking water, and the lush vegetation on the oldest, thickest plains contained plants that proved to be almost made for them. The fruit, while not anything to write home about, was nourishing and had vitamins as well as sugars, starches, and fibers. Their kit told them they could live on it, and they'd been doing so.

There were creatures, both the flying and crawling kind, that served the purpose of insects to the plants, but they didn't seem to be in unmanageable numbers, nor did they seem to be on the prowl for some fresh human. In fact, the things tended to avoid them; either they lacked what the creatures needed or maybe they just smelled wrong.

Jerry Nagel was an engineer by trade. The red and purplish fronds provided huge surfaces for cover and seemed quite tough; other plants resembled bamboo and similar plants that could be depended upon for some structure. With help, he'd managed to fashion a couple of shelters, which allowed them to store the salvaged equipment and some spare materials, and which also provided shelter from the elements to an extent. After the shelters were up, they were able to keep some harvested wood dry, and Lucky Cross had fashioned a crude kiln from lava rock and the nearby fires. She'd already made some large amphora-like jars as well as small cups and trays. Water could be stored before it got fouled by the dust, and they could eat and drink off something other than lava rock.

They had made no attempt to contact or in any way even alert the neighbors that they were around. The nearest creature colony, stranded aliens like them—or the descendants of stranded aliens—was about fifteen kilometers away and they wanted to keep it that way. The things might well be smart, but something that had a giant sucker for a face and clawed appendages clearly designed for ripping and tearing by some violent evolution were not likely to be easy to talk to, and they did not want to become a new taste treat. The alien colony was oriented towards the ocean shore, not inland. For now that was all right with them.

Nagel saw Randi Queson sitting on a rock under a giant fern and thought she looked like a gnome or some other fairy creature from the old children's books. She had average looks and figure, and was putting on a little weight, as they all were with this heavy sugar and starch diet, but she could afford it.

Spacer crews generally took what the doctors called "lust abater" drugs subcutaneously to keep things from getting out of hand in the close quarters of interstellar space, but because people didn't want them to last forever, they tended to wear off after a set period of time, at which point they could be renewed if need be or let go. It was long past the six-month period since those last implants and, as the only man left alive out of the crew, marooned on a planet with three women, he could hardly hide that fact sometimes, but he tried. It wasn't like any of them could have kids; *that* was abated as a matter of course until undone by a medical science long out of reach somewhere in those vast starfields beyond. Not that any of them wanted kids, particularly on this hellhole, but it was certain that they weren't going to be like the holy commune over on Balshazzar. There would be no human colony on Melchior.

In a way, that made it a lot easier here. They were responsible only for themselves and each other, not anybody else, and the future was pretty much now.

He went over to Queson and sat beside her. "You've been thinking again," he kidded her in a mock scolding tone.

She smiled. "It's an occupational hazard."

"We don't have occupations anymore. We're castaways on a desert island with no hope of rescue. Food, shelter, little more, and always afraid the sucker-faced pirates will find us."

"You had a broader education than most engineers," she noted.

He shrugged. "Broader interests, maybe, or maybe just broad-minded parents. My mother was a literary historian who made hand-colored pottery in her spare time. Dad was a mathematician with a passion for playing the piano in an age when few even knew the term except as a digital sound. Both throwbacks. I think they met somewhere in the old Combine, maybe even on or near Old Earth, when he was trying to find a robotic program that could tune a piano and she was working in the library that day on the restoration of ancient live performances. She was actually an expert on children's literature in an age when nobody had to be literate any more and few were or are, I guess, so she got drafted for all sorts of shit like that."

She looked over at him. "That's interesting. I never knew that. Maybe we haven't all talked ourselves out yet. At least we haven't started killing each other. Truth is, I never paid much attention to that sort of thing before, but what I'd give for books and recordings and complinks now. My *god* I'm bored!"

He sighed. "Yeah, well, there isn't much to do here, that's for sure. I've been thinking, though, that it might be time to see if there was anything at all that we *could* do." He looked up at the always bright sky, now dominated by the gas giant. In a few hours, rotation would bring them back into the light of the great sun beyond and the temperature would rise to unbearable levels and they would have to seek shelter, shade, and whatever protection they could. He had worked out a system where they collected rainwater from the frequent, violent thunderstorms in rock basins, over which they'd built a thatch and leaf roof. In the worst of the heat they got into the pools and just stayed there until it was over. It wasn't great—often the water temperature was almost too hot to bear on its own—but, usually, it helped. The fact that there was always a breeze from either the inland or ocean sides helped, too. But you didn't live through midday on Melchior, you just survived it.

"Six more days and we'll be out of the sun," she noted. "At least it'll make things bearable."

"Uh-huh. For fifteen days. But it's still fifteen days of nothing much, just improving our area so we can survive the next fifteen days' exposure to the sun. I don't know about you, but I'm just not the type to live like this."

She looked up at the great gas giant that lit the huge moon even when it was away from the sun and shook her head. "At least the Reverend or whatever he is up there has *something*. Friendly aliens to learn from and about, a large mixed population, probably the books and entertainment we miss in his wrecked ship. Hell, we don't even have *that*. Just what we salvaged."

He paused a moment. "Well, I've been thinking about them. Particularly on the night side, when you can see them, almost think you can reach out to them, high in the night sky when Balshazzar approaches. They're farther out—it's hot as hell there, too, at midday, but I bet they have a better or more comfortable time. Maybe caves that aren't lava tubes that may or may not open up again at any moment."

"I've been thinking about those. They *are* cooler, and there are some that collect a fair amount of rainwater. We've seen two or three whoosh out, but most of them are long dead and plugged. Temperature's gotta be, what? Ten, fifteen degrees cooler in there at midsun? I'm willing to take the chance on that just to not have to turn into a boiled dinner for hours every day."

"We can move. I can't see any reason not to. Not now, anyway. If one of them *did* give way it would be a quick death, not a slow one like *this*. The Rev might not be trapped in heaven like it looked, but we're sure stuck in Hell."

"Li's claustrophobic," she reminded him. "That's the only problem."

Nagel shrugged. "I'm not sure we can do any good by making ourselves martyrs to our problem child. I keep thinking that, if the situation was reversed, the old An Li wouldn't have hesitated a minute if it was her comfort against somebody else's misfortune. She doesn't have to come if she can't hack it. We'll be back over here when it's a little cooler—like now."

"Yeah, can't be more than thirty-five Celsius," she commented. "Not like midday."

She was being facetious, but it wasn't far off the mark. They had some instruments salvaged from the shuttle before it went down in the lava and the midday sun at this latitude had reached as high as fifty degrees, enough to kill any of them if they were exposed for any length of time. Only the countless storms saved them at all.

"You're not just thinking of the lava tubes, are you?"

She shook her head slowly. "No, not really. Just a first step to doing *something*."

"You're thinking of Magi stones again, aren't you?"

She nodded. "I know, they're probably just a natural phenomenon, an emitter of some kind of radiation that causes hallucinations, but we've compared notes. Even in that horrible overdose, you, me, Lucky—we all had the same hallucinations. And even with the ones and twos, that sense of observing and being observed, of an *intelligence* out there, looking back at us, aware of us, but in a way that is alien, possibly malevolent, possibly just indifferent or removed, like some Greek god looking down on a peasant village. I can't shake the idea that there's something more to them."

"They're definitely natural. We saw where they were formed."

"Yes, there were several such, but all localized, all seeming to *extrude* from the hard volcanic basalt. It was almost like . . . like they were being somehow *manufactured* in those spots. I know it's crazy, but I can't kick it. It's probably the heat and the hopelessness, but what the hell can I do?"

The sameness of the hallucinations had gotten to him as well, almost as if they either were one collective mind at that point or were all receiving the same very strong signal, a signal directly to the brain.

"But it destroyed Li's mind," he reminded her. "She's like a little child. Trusting, not thinking very much, just sort of existing. Almost like a lobotomy. Almost like everything that was there came out in that hallucinatory session and in that butchery of Sark. Little An Li, maybe forty, forty-five kilos, beating up and taking apart a man half again her height and more than twice her bulk."

"And she might do it again, if she got close to the stones."

He nodded. "I've always been afraid of that. I could take the old An Li coming back, but I'm scared of that monster that came out of her. I want to know it left her rather than went back into hiding."

"I think that monster's in all of us," Randi told him. "Except maybe no more in her. In all this time here I've seen no sign of any change. Have you?"

He shook his head. "No, none. Maybe that frenzy killed it, but it makes the point even more. If it's also inside you and me, what's to keep *us* from winding up letting it out, or letting it run away?"

She shrugged. "After a lot of thought, I've decided that it doesn't matter. If we can learn something by studying the stones, maybe use them, then great. If what was buried deeper in us than in her gets out and one of us dies, so what? Beats living endless years like *this*, at least to me."

"And if it escapes and runs away?"

"Then we'll be like poor An Li. We'll happily sing little songs and pick flowers and not even care if we crap as we walk and we'll die sooner, but we won't feel a thing."

He looked over at the shelter. "You talk to Lucky about this idea?"

She sighed. "No, but I think we should. Either way, I'm going to try it. You feel like going cave shopping with me?"

He chuckled. "I thought you'd never ask. Our first date. And if we happen to have to go far afield and find an extrusion of Magi stones . . ."

"Then," she said, "we'll see what develops."

Lucky was divided on the idea, but decided to come along anyway. It was better than being stuck back here as nursemaid to An Li. As for Li, she either came with them or she stayed. She didn't seem capable of too many decisions, and that was one she might hate but was capable of making.

They decided that it was best to simply lay it on her as they were going to leave. There was no use in bringing up anything in the future, even a few days in the future, with her, nor giving her any time to go into hysterics or childish rants. They would simply go. She would come, or not, and that would be that.

The scout who had first discovered and named the Three Kings system had never mentioned that the planet-sized worlds he named after the Magi were moons, so there was no name for the huge planet that loomed over them half of each day. Queson thought of naming it Jerusalem, since Bethlehem seemed too modest for such a monster of a failed star, but Jerry Nagel had nixed that idea. "*Next* year in Jerusalem," he said. "Jerusalem is hope, the destination we hope to reach. I'm more inclined towards Pharaoh, since it holds us unwilling captives."

"I was thinking more of Babylon," she commented. "Or maybe Egypt?"

"No, not Egypt, nor Babylon, either. There's a *will*

here someplace. The Holy Joes on Balshazzar felt it, sensed it, and warned us of it. The will that traps them there. Pharaoh was the stubborn captor; Egypt was just the place. And not Babylon, surely, and not just for the same reason. Nebuchadnezzar would be a fitting name it's true, but Babylon, and Assyria, and Persia are where the Three Kings came from, right? And we don't know which conqueror is lurking here someplace, making the rules. No, we've got Alexander or Cyrus somewhere in the shadows playing games with us, but not up there. Pharaoh, I think, will do."

"What're you guys talkin' about?" Lucky asked, already breathing hard from the long walk, carrying, as they all were except An Li, supplies for several days on their otherwise bare backs. "All them names nobody can pronounce. They sound like those names a Hindu guy once spouted trying to explain his charms to me when we was offloading freighters back in the old days. Never got that right, either."

"Well, they're from a religion," Randi Queson responded. "Judaism and Christianity, mostly. But the places were real, and historical."

"You study all that shit?"

"Some of it," she replied. "A lot more I picked up, and some was from my own family. Mostly, I think I just looked into things because I found them interesting and I got curious."

"And I'm pretty much the same," Nagel told her. "Not much on the family side—they were about as religious as you are—but from other people I worked with or got to know. You weren't curious about the Hindu fellow's beliefs?"

"Not really. Sounded pretty silly to me. So does all this shit. Fancy names from folks too long dead talkin' about places that probably don't exist no more if they ever did and old fairy stories. What good does it do to know any of that? Does it fill your belly or get you a job or make you well when you're sick? Just stories, that's all. We're all the way out here in the middle of who knows where, a zillion light-years from anything or anybody 'cept the others stuck here, too, and we ain't bumped into no gods yet."

"I wonder," Randi muttered.

"Huh?"

"Somebody once said that if we ever ran into a race so advanced that they were as far ahead of us as we were of bugs and germs they'd be supernatural to us. Maybe that's what God and the angels really are." She paused a moment, liking the idea. "And maybe Satan and his demons, too. A lot of our myths and legends and core beliefs came from real events and real people at some point, even if they got twisted or misinterpreted. Certainly those monks who scouted the known and unknown universe were devoted to looking for God. That's how we got these names for these moons."

Lucky Cross looked over the blasted volcanic landscape and coughed some dust and sulphur from her lungs. "And you think God's hiding around here playing with us now or something?"

Randi Queson looked around at the same landscape and shook her head. "No, not God. Definitely not God. . . ."

There was a darkening above and the sounds of rumblings in the distance.

"Going to rain soon," Jerry Nagel noted. "We ought to find some shelter while we have time."

"Great!" grumped Cross, in a singularly bad mood this day. "So we'll be stuck in mud and wrapped in mud and slip-sliding the rest of the day."

"It'll cool things off for a bit," Queson noted hopefully.

"Make us human mud-pies, that's all," Cross responded.

"Where's An Li?" Jerry asked them, looking around. "*Li! An Li!*" he shouted.

"You two go find us a shelter," Randi told them. "I'll find An Li."

The former leader of the salvage team that employed them all wasn't far away; she'd simply gotten distracted by something and that became the only thought in her mind. She was sitting there, dusty and stark naked, staring at something she'd found in the volcanic ash and humming a little tune from some distant point in her childhood.

"Li, honey, you can't go off by yourself like this," Randi scolded. "You have to stay with us."

An Li didn't seem to hear, but she was certainly aware that the older woman was there. She turned, looked up at Randi Queson, and smiled a vacant, little child's smile, and held out whatever she had to show the team geologist what she'd found. "Pretty," she said.

Randi squatted down and took an object from An Li's hand and looked at it. It wasn't very large, but it was definitely no volcanic oddity. It was a bright, shiny, golden color, so polished that it reflected a distorted vision of whatever image it captured. It was certainly not heavy enough to be pure gold—a hundred and fifty grams, no more. It had a pentagonal base no more than fifty or sixty millimeters long with a series of pentagonal brackets, a half dozen or so, running down its length. Why it wasn't sandblasted or bent and twisted was as much a mystery as what it was or whose it might be. The only thing she was sure of was that it couldn't have been dropped very long ago from the looks of it, and whoever lost it just might come back looking for it.

They were in strange territory now, and needed to

tread softly and carefully. She wasn't sure whether to take it or leave it, but An Li made up her mind for her by grabbing it out of her hands and clutching it to her. "Mine!" she said. "Pretty!"

Randi sighed. "All right, you can keep it, but we have to go and find the others. It's going to rain. Get very wet. Can you hear it?"

As if on cue, loud rumblings of thunder sounded far too close to ignore.

An Li got up and took Randi's hand, clutching the strange artifact in the other, and kept pace as much as she could with the larger woman striding off towards where the other two had vanished.

The golden artifact wasn't the first such strange, small, manufactured alien object they'd come across on Melchior, and such things had been reported even in the original scouting reports. It seemed at times as if some alien machine was shedding parts, but it was more likely some minor tool of one of the stranded alien creatures they'd spent time avoiding. No two that they'd found had ever been alike, almost as if each were from a different creature or civilization, but that meant little. It was why the term *alien* had been invented.

They often had wondered if Doc Woodward up on the paradise-seeming moon of Balshazzar stumbled over these things. Maybe he even found out from his alien friends what they were and why they were scattered all over the place. Still, it would make more sense if *he* found them on the relatively static garden moon than them finding such things here, on volcanic Melchior, where everything was constantly in motion from dust, quakes, volcanism just under the surface and sometimes on top of it, and violent rainstorms. Things like these should be mostly melted or worn away by now. Most instead looked almost new, like this thing.

Even the aliens shipwrecked along the coast had been here long enough to have pretty much exhausted what they'd salvaged and they surely didn't have the kind of technology to make whatever this stuff was. It made no sense at all.

Rocks that stimulated your emotional centers and maybe spied on you and exquisitely manufactured pieces of junk that did nothing. Parts of the puzzle that they'd all love to solve, but which they had about as much chance of solving as they had of flying off this hellish world. Still, they occupied the mind, even Li's.

They came up over a rise and looked for Jerry and Lucky. A fumarole nearby spouted loud white noise and steam from venting the result of rainwater hitting something far too hot and not very far below. All of them had learned not to go too near those roaring holes in the rock.

The storm was really coming towards them now; you could see its darkness creeping towards their position, blotting out the sky and landscape. If they didn't spot the others quickly, it would be necessary to find someplace else to ride out the fury that was clearly unavoidable.

Randi spotted an oval opening about a meter high and perhaps two wide that looked promising. Hoping that it opened out a bit, she headed for it, letting Li get down and back in, then doing the same, but the childlike woman got to the edge of it and suddenly shouted "*No!*" over the noise of the storm.

"Come on! You've got to! Otherwise you'll be out in the open!" Randi yelled back, but Li shook her head, twisted, broke away and began running off in the direction they'd been heading. Realizing that the only choices were between getting caught outside and staying put, the older woman decided not to chase the other. The gods had a strange protection for the mad.

She backed further in as the storm hit with all its fury and, feeling a bit more room, she managed to get back so that she never lost sight of the opening but could roll over if necessary or crawl on her elbows and knees. She didn't want to get too far in; there would be nothing but absolute darkness not far from where she was now.

Lying there, though, she first appreciated the cooler feel of the cave rock against her bare skin. A little bit of rain made it in, and there was a tiny rivulet now coming in and going around her which also felt quite nice. It wasn't enough to fear flooding the cave, but she kind of rolled in it, wetting herself down some more and thus cooling off all the better, and she used a little of it to wet her lips. After that, she just lay there, waiting for the fierce storm to abate.

For a while there was nothing but the roar outside, the slight wetness of the pencil-thin leakage, and the smell of damp rock but, as she lay there, she suddenly began to get the impression that she wasn't alone.

There wasn't much in the way of wildlife on Melchior to fear; everything dangerous seemed to come from worlds even more distant than her own. Still, might not one of those have taken shelter from the storm just as she was doing now?

The thought unnerved her, particularly when coupled with Li's adamant refusal to take shelter there.

She reflected that, since they'd been marooned here, she'd never really been alone nor, for the most part, had she wanted to be. Not even the kind of privacy that you got from going to your cabin on board ship, or doing the most private of things. They'd all stuck very close together, at least in pairs, even when there was nothing to do but lie around and brood. Now she was feeling that sense of being alone, of being apart from other human company, and her mind was playing the usual games with her. She knew that, but she also couldn't shake it. She didn't *want* to be alone, and the idea that she might well be, and that she might well *not* be but with something she didn't want to meet, started to eat at her.

The fear was becoming overwhelming; a sense not so much of claustrophobia as of being cut off, utterly, completely defenseless and alone, and she felt panic rising in her. The storm was still going, and it was still a very dangerous storm, but she fought a building compulsion to wriggle forward, to run out, to get away. . . .

There *was* something there! She couldn't hear it nor did she have any physical evidence of it, but she could sense it, just back there, looking at her, studying her. . . .

She managed to turn slightly, to look back into the darkness, to make one last stab at conquering her insanity and, after a moment, she began to see what was back there, what was causing all the fear and distress.

The Magi stones were there, embedded in the cave wall, and they were softly glowing. . . .

Radiation! she told herself. *It's just some form of radiation! They're nothing but a geophysical phenomenon!*

But the operative word was "physical." It was a real effect, and knowing that it was an effect of the stones did her no more good than realizing that a knife was a knife when the important thing was that the knife was stabbing you.

She could feel it going right through her, right down to her soul, the feelings of fear and danger and menace.

"*It takes practice*," said a man's voice, and she almost jumped out of her skin.

"Who's there?" she shouted, backing towards the cave opening.

"It's kind of like piloting. You can crash. It can even kill you. But if you can get the hang of it, it will change you in amazing ways."

The Magi stones seemed to pulse at the man's words, keeping a throbbing action in between that beat at the inner corners of her mind. She wasn't sure even now if she was hearing anything at all or if she was simply overwhelmed by the radiation of the stones and on her way to Li's land of insanity or worse.

"Calmly. If you know any meditation it helps," the voice said. Now she was certain it wasn't a physical voice, but speaking directly to her mind. *"The stones were not designed for minds like ours. They grow them for themselves, we think."*

"'We'? Who's 'we'?" She was trying to focus just on the voice, breathing in a steady manner, and trying to put out of her mind the emotional pulses that rushed to the core of her being every time the other spoke.

"My name is Robey. John Robey. I'm on station today and I was attempting to see what came in when I sensed you. We should not talk more now. Can you leave? Get away from the stones?"

"I—I'm not sure," she responded. "There's a storm. . . ."

"Go if you can. It takes a lot of practice. I am holding off the effects as much as possible, but I'm not the most gifted at this. You are now tuned to this batch. Were I to lift my mental shield it might well steal your mind or your very soul. Come back. Any outcrop will do. Return for a few minutes each day. Alone. Slowly we will teach you."

"Who is 'we'?" she asked again. "And why should I believe I'm not already having a conversation with myself?"

"We are the Arm of Gideon. On Balshazzar. Make sure that Balshazzar is in your sky before you try again. The kind of power required to go through the big planet would fry your mind. Someone, often many, are always on duty. We will be watching for you. We've been wondering how long it would take before this happened. Now go if you can. If the storm will not kill you, you must go into it. Even with help, I'm losing it. Go!"

She backed out of the cave even as she felt first a sudden release in her mind, then almost immediately a return to a building attack on her last emotional defenses.

The rain was still falling but the worst of it was past, and the electrical activity was now intermittent even though occasional claps of thunder, echoing against the barren landscape, could still deafen her.

She started to run. Not in any particular direction, just away, away from the cave. She didn't think, she *couldn't* think. It was as if her mind was totally blank leaving only emotion, a desire to flee, to just go anywhere but there. She ran through the rain, wild-eyed, more animal than human, until finally slipping, falling, she lost consciousness altogether in the remnants of the storm.

She came to, rather than awoke, trembling, and she looked up into the concerned face of Jerry Nagel. "Randi! Come on! Snap out of it! Are you all right?"

Slowly her senses flowed back into her mind, but they didn't make things any easier. She trembled as if she had contracted a serious palsy for several minutes, then choked on something, began having a coughing fit, and eventually she threw up over and over until there was nothing left for her stomach to give.

She felt—weird. That was the word that came to

mind, and it fit, even though she was having trouble defining it further. She felt detached, as if her mind, the thinking part, the personality, was somehow disconnected from her body but floating just beyond it. She could barely feel the body, nor did it fully respond to her commands. Still, when she could, she gasped, "Jerry!" And then for some reason she just began to break into uncontrollable sobs, grabbing and holding on to him with a viselike grip.

He let her go for a little bit, but when he finally tried to break free and get her some water she couldn't release him.

"Please! Please!" she managed, breathless. "Just— humor me for a little bit. Just hold me. I need—I need to bring myself back."

So, for as long as he could, he just held her there and let her calm herself and gather her wits.

Lucky Cross came up with a boot in her hand. It was one of Randi's, and it was last seen on the woman's foot. Now it was not only not being worn, it seemed to have been yanked, pulled apart, ripped half to shreds. "Pack's back there as well," the pilot commented. "Straps are broke but it's still okay. We can probably mend it. She's barefoot from now on, though. Musta been real wild to have had the strength to rip them things like that. Them boots are rated for industrial units!"

Nagel looked down at Randi, who seemed half lost in some other mental place, but she was still awake, still staring at him.

"You want to tell us what happened?" he prodded gently.

"I—I needed to get out of the storm. The cave I picked had the rocks."

He gave a low whistle. "You're lucky you didn't go Li's route," he noted. "All comes clear now. I wonder just how common those damned things *are*?"

"Very, I think. And there's more, but even I can't tell you if it was real or not." Slowly, between gasps and occasional reflexive gags, she managed to tell the other two about her ethereal conversation with John Robey up on Balshazzar.

Lucky cross-checked the sky, which was already clear after the storm. "Yep, it's up there, all right. See it? 'Bout two hands up from the horizon to the west and maybe, oh, five o'clock."

They had discovered almost from the start that the other moons were readily visible when all were in the same part of the sky, and that Balshazzar, being so relatively close, was quite prominent. A blue-white world about the size of a gaming token in one of the bars back on Marchellus, it would have dominated any sky it was in save for the even larger gas giant that loomed over them and trapped them both.

Kaspar, much farther out and smaller than either of the other two, was harder to spot, but hardly invisible in the night sky. There was just too much of a light source for reflection for anything of any size to remain hidden out there.

"You think it was real?" he asked Randi.

"I—I think it *might* have been. I think you and I both had an idea it was more than just a mineral. I wonder, though. Do they also have outcrops of them on the other two moons?"

He smiled. This was the old Randi coming back, slowly but surely. "I think they might. At least on Balshazzar. Who knows about Kaspar?"

She sighed, but made no move to get up or break physical contact from him. "He said it took practice. Like learning to fly. And that it was just as dangerous. Do you think maybe he really *was* real?"

"Well, it ain't like we got a computer with a roster handy," Cross noted. "Still and all, mind-rotting rocks

I can see, but mind-reading radio rocks, well, I got to say you'd hav'ta show me."

"Well," Nagel said, "remember that horrible night when those rocks took us over? I can't help remembering that when those of us who survived, one way or the other, compared notes we found we all had the same nightmares. Pretty strange alien nightmares, too. Ones I never got out of my head, and I don't think you two ever got out of yours. Suppose we were actually seeing something real? Some real places, real events? Something so horrible, so traumatic, it stuck in the minds of the entire alien race that created these things, assuming that they are artifacts, not natural. Maybe, just maybe, our minds don't work like theirs so we don't process the information right, but it's nonetheless real. If these things could in fact be controlled . . . Think of it! Two-way telepathic broadcasting! And they—the Holy Joes up on Balshazzar—they've been stuck there a lot longer than we've been stuck here, and with more contact with other alien species who might have been there longer. It's possible. It just could be . . ."

"Then you think—maybe . . . I wasn't losing my mind?"

He gave a wan smile and shrugged. "You might well have been at the brink of insanity and *still* heard just what you heard. Who says they're mutually exclusive? One thing's sure, though. All of us—one at a time, anyway, with the others ready to pull them out—have got to experience this, maybe, if it's learned, all get taught how to master the damned things. It may be the only chance we got of ever getting off this hole."

"Or it may just drive us all nuts like Li," Cross noted.

"If it isn't real, what's the difference?" Randi asked her. "And if it is, and even one of us manages it even if the price might be madness for others, then to me it's more than worthwhile. I'm scared to death, and all I want to do is run and hide and sleep for a year," she added. "And yet, tomorrow, I'm going to try it again."

II:
TASK FORCE ELEVEN

"I see him, Leader. He's lying back behind the asteroid, six o'clock."

"Very well. I see him. Going to instrumentation mode. Balance of flight, on me."

The fugitive ship had been hovering just inside a deep rift valley on the dark side of the barren planet with all systems powered down to minimum. It was in fact an impressive feat of flying. The ship was half the size of a destroyer but not engineered for those kind of maneuvers; to set it into a planet so that it hovered only meters above the surface and merged in most sensors with the surrounding rough landscape was not only skillful but also far beyond what such a ship should have been able to do. Whoever modified and maintained the old hulk knew what they were doing,

23

and that in itself made them of great interest to the naval commanders supervising this operation. To take a ship designed essentially for commercial exploration and turn it into a formidable clipper was a skill worth pursuing.

"Agrippa *to leader first squadron. Shall we come in and take her with a nullifier?*" came a query from their parent destroyer lying well away from these close quarters and asteroid-filled neighborhoods for now as the smaller one-person craft ferreted out the quarry.

"Uh, negative, Agrippa. *We'll flush him out and send him to you if that's your desire.*"

There was a sigh from the larger vessel's operations commander. "Well, *we're made, so he's not gonna run for home until and unless he's positive we missed him, so we might as well take him and get the information the hard way. Go for flush.*"

The leader nodded reflexively. "Flight, spread out, and be careful. You remember the last one. We don't want this thing flipping out and gunning itself full throttle into the star. First squadron, pull around and put yourselves between quarry and inbound. Keep position and do not vary unless quarry moves clearly away. At all times keep between quarry and star. Got that, Alpha leader?"

"Got it. You'll never let me live that one down, will you? He comes my way, he gets concentrated full forward fire. His shields can't be that great after this. You flush him, we'll roadblock and you climb up his ass."

"Don't be vulgar, Alpha. Beta, on me. Let's flush the bastard."

The squadron's ships peeled off in precise order and dived on the hapless ship below as if they were somehow connected together or at least piloted by master machines with split-second timing.

The old tramp didn't wait for them to bracket him with strafing fire; he powered up and gunned it, barely missing tearing his bottom out on the tops of the mountains.

For an old commercial vessel he was surprisingly fast and agile, but no match for the military fighters. They caught up with the fleeing tramp ship before it could even fully clear the planetary gravity well and took up a formation at speeds matching their quarry so that they essentially surrounded it.

"All right, up to you," the squadron leader called on a wide frequency spread. *"Either you cut your engines and follow us or we'll shoot some holes in you. We'll try not to kill you but in space you never really know, do you? Your choice."*

"I'm thinking it over," responded a man's sour voice on one of the standard emergency frequencies. The voice was raw and raspy, an old man's voice with a lot of experience in its tone.

The squadron leader shifted to the same frequency and the tactical sounds faded into a more standard open radio back and forth. It was more like they were next to each other and speaking normally. *"What's to decide? Is refusing to pay your just taxes worth dying for?"*

"Taxes be damned! You're blackmailers and extortionists. I'd pay to be protected from the likes of you! Ah, you're just a bunch of brainwashed drones. Why the hell am I explaining it? Bottom line is I got nothin' here worth stealin' 'cept my ship, and that ain't worth all that much, even in spare parts and fuel rods. Cargo's empty. I was on my way out, not in. You take my ship I'm no better off than if I was dead, and you don't get much by takin' it. So just who or what are you protectin' me from 'cept maybe starvation?"

"We've heard all this before," the leader told him. "Just cut power and our mother ship will take you aboard. You can make your arguments there. I have nothing to do with the case, I just bring in who I'm told to bring in. Now, we know that there's more than just you aboard. Even if you wanted to commit suicide, is it fair to take others with you?"

The old man thought for a moment. "Maybe. If their choice is dyin' or joinin' the likes of you."

"We don't conscript. Don't need to."

"Then you don't know much about your own operations," the old captain responded, sounding weary and resigned. "You live in a hive like some ancient insects, but you got to renew the gene pool now and then." He paused a moment, then sighed. "Okay, pull me in. I don't like doin' it to the others, but at least I'll have the satisfaction of knowin' that at least I'm gonna be your problem for a while."

The destroyer monitoring the engagement now moved in as the old tramp ship cut power and just drifted, defenseless against all the naval might arrayed against it. Tractor beams fixed on the old ship like a spider spinning a web to ensure that the fly did not escape, and, when secure, the prey was reeled in by the tractor lines until it could be mechanically grappled by arms extending beneath the destroyer.

The old freighter held together well; whoever had fixed it up had known what they were doing, and it had clearly been expertly maintained as well. The fleet, of course, had its entire maintenance and dry-dock sections fully automated, but these people out here in the old colonies were lucky to keep anything running at all, let alone maintaining equipment to service the fruits of their scavenging.

The fighters waited until the target was safely secured and then went in for their own predetermined berths, landing automatically. The pilots sat and waited for pressurization, then their canopies slid back and they got out and jumped down to the deck below. The artificial gravity in the berths was kept low to facilitate their ingress and egress, as their trainers called it.

Each of the military figures wore what appeared to be a skintight blue-black body suit that showed them to be generally squat and muscular people, their muscles bulging as if they were about to burst through the suits. They kept the suits on, and would so long as they were officially on duty; the egg-shaped gold and black helmets were removed and placed on special holders near each fighter. On their mounts they would be recharged, benchmarked, tested and, if necessary, repaired, without ever leaving their perches. They could also be programmed with the specifics of any task the fighters might be asked to do, so that the information would be there right in front of each of them as needed. In an emergency, the crews could be at their fighters in less than a minute from anywhere they were likely to be, and in their ships and ready for takeoff with all that they required in no more than three minutes. They drilled on that constantly.

Only some of the pilots, however, were in that position or needed to drill. More than half the squadron never removed their helmets or suits at all, ever. They were machines.

A mixture of humans and machines had been found to be ideal from the earliest deep-space naval combat vessels. Nobody trusted machines alone to do the job; they could outwit and outfight everybody except a totally illogical human being who might do things they would never expect. The pilots were, however, both genetically and cybernetically enhanced. All were female, though that term had little real meaning for them except that they averaged perhaps twenty percent less mass than the men and had voices that were, on average, quite low but still a half octave removed from the men. Hairless, their breasts rock hard and their sexual organs removed and replaced with semiorganic hormonal regulators, they had no sense of sexuality at all, either to themselves or as regarded anyone else.

It was not any of the pilots who would approach and enter the captured vessel, though. That was a job for a marine squad, mostly huge muscle-bound males, also hairless, and with nothing evident in the groin to suggest sexuality, either. The naval nurseries harvested the eggs and all the sperm it needed, processed them, altered their DNA and designed what was required, far away from those who had been the donors. Like the pilots, adult marines and the other crewmen were basically asexual, and neither knew nor wondered what they were missing.

Not that they were without emotion; that was a requirement of being human. But it was the emotion of camaraderie, of friends and brothers and sisters, nothing beyond. Not that they were ignorant of sex; they simply could not imagine why it was so important or why others did such disgusting things. The marines and the pilots saw themselves not as men and women, but as specialists designed to best do their jobs. And none of them wanted to be or do anything more than what they were; only to advance in rank, authority, power, and respect.

The old captain had called them "drones," and in effect that was just what they were.

Now the marine squad went down the umbilical cylinder to the entry hatch on the old freighter.

"This is Sergeant Maslovic," their leader said using a transceiver essentially built into his thick rocklike jaw, although it was invisible to the naked eye and controlled by his own thoughts. "Open your hatch and prepare to be boarded."

There was a loud hiss and the hatch turned and then opened like the iris of a camera, allowing entry.

Although the marines were armed, they were not expecting a fight. What, after all, could these people do? The worst they could try was to blow up their ship in order to take the larger one with it, and there were energy shields all around to insure that *that* was not something that would be very profitable to do. It would kill the marines, certainly, as well as those aboard the captured vessel, but little else. The marines did worry about this, but their officers above had plenty more marines if they lost these.

The two lead men in the squad entered on either side, stun-type sidearms drawn, and flanked the sergeant as he walked confidently in, his own weapon holstered and not even unstrapped.

The marines wore suits quite like those of the fighters, but the color of dark mud, and while the squad had on light protective helmets the sergeant hadn't even bothered to put his on. Since he couldn't stop anyone from killing him nor would that thing protect him from a shot, he saw no purpose to it here, and once they'd secured the ship and prisoners and were marching their captives to Legal, the proper uniform would be no helmet anyway.

The captain of the tramp met him just inside the entranceway. He was not only old, he was perhaps the oldest man Maslovic had ever seen. Gray-haired, with a stringy, dirty gray beard, his skin had the look of ancient parchment and he stood slightly stooped in spite of a clear effort to look military himself. He wore a simple black flight jump suit that looked older and more wrinkled than he was, and some boots that had last been shined before the Great Silence.

"I'm Captain Murphy," the old man introduced himself.

"Sergeant Maslovic," the marine responded, looking around. "Sir, by authority of Combine Naval Code seventy-seven stroke six two I take command of your vessel. Where are your crew?"

The old man chuckled. "Crew? No crew. Don't need much of a crew for *this* scow, Sergeant. I have some passengers, though."

"We monitored three. Please have them come forward and then we can all go up to the Legal Officer."

"Well, now, we might need some help in transporting two of them, I think, although I'm not at all sure you'll understand why without diagrams."

"Sir?"

"This way, Sergeant."

Maslovic gestured for the guard to be posted at the airlock and the rest of the squad to fan out through the captive ship and begin to search and inventory it, then followed the old captain.

The ship stank. Body odor, oils and lubricants—it was hard to isolate the sources of the stenches, but it was not exactly a ship that would pass inspection in naval life.

The captain punched a panel and an interior hatch slid back, and Murphy gestured for the sergeant to enter.

"Sergeant, meet my passengers," the old man said with a trace of amusement in his tone.

Maslovic entered what was clearly ordinarily the captain's cabin and stopped. For a moment, he really did feel confused. Three women were inside, one in a reclining chair, one in the bed, and a third in a straight-backed utility chair bolted to the floor.

Maslovic had seen many colonial women before, but there was something odd about these. They were disproportionately fat, but not all over. Just in the . . .

He suddenly realized their condition and why Captain Murphy had been so apprehensive about them and yet amused to introduce them to him.

All three were hugely pregnant.

He suspected that *these* people would be going up to the cruiser. There was nobody here who could deal with them like *this*.

It was two kilometers long and looked like it had been assembled by a horde of drunken babies. Nonetheless, the *Thermopylae* was actually as functional as a socket wrench; in its time, its design fought wars, conquered rebellions, ran down smugglers and brought would-be dictators to heel. Its birth name was the CNC *Thermopylae*, the initials standing for "Combine Naval Cruiser." Its armament was and continued to be more than formidable; it could incinerate the average solid rock planet, vaporize a path ahead of it through the densest of asteroid belts, and its defensive shields could withstand blasts from a ship of equal or lesser capabilities.

It did not, however, have many light armaments; instead, it carried a series of externally docked fighter squadrons in what were known as "pods" and, in four equally spaced "hangars" around its midsection, it carried and could quickly launch a like number of destroyers, each with formidable weapons of their own, each with their own single abbreviated pod of defensive fighters. The destroyers could use a wormgate on their own, as could the cruiser; the fighters had no such equipment aboard and were dependent for interstellar travel on the bigger ships even as they were dependent on the smallest for the first line of defense.

For all that, they'd had relatively small human crews when the Great Silence came down and all the wormgates leading to the old Combine and Mother

Earth suddenly became inactive. Most of the systems were fully automated; the only ones aboard the large vessels were those who had to make the command decisions that it was felt no machine should be permitted to make and those who represented the human race in its projection wherever that force was required. Ultimately, it was the lowest and least of them that proved essential to remain essentially human. It was discovered, by long and rueful experience, that you could make the perfect soldiers out of robotic arts but so could the other guys. Stalemate was not the objective of a military projection; so long as machines of equal capabilities faced off, though, that's what happened most of the time.

And that was why the pilots and the grunts, supported, of course, by the best in robotics, but not governed by them, remained.

The *Thermopylae* had exactly one hundred and sixty pilots in four squadrons with three hundred base personnel supporting them when she found herself orphaned from higher command; beyond those few was one division of marines divided into four regiments of eight forty-person companies each. Six hundred and forty men and women, with twice that in support, all of whom were also rated to replace anyone in the combat division if needed. The command staff included the small complements on each destroyer, the naval commanding officer, the cruiser's captain and small support staff, and a fleet admiral. In all, far fewer than two thousand souls.

That had changed, but not as much as might be expected. More were needed in a fairly steady stream because of the time it took to evaluate and train competent personnel to replace what might be lost or what might be needed as a reserve, but wholesale expansion would have meant the end of the division as it drowned in a sea of consumers of limited resources.

Cut off from home, adrift in a sea of stars with no way home and no longer a clear mission nor view of its place in the universe, such ships as this either disintegrated or found a new purpose, new mission, and new identity. Military always had their own separate culture, their own feeling of "us" and "them" even in the best of times, and that had been reinforced after the Silence.

The *Thermopylae*, part deliberately, part without even realizing it as events and culture swept it along, became its own small world, its own society, its own unique nation and culture. Its power and isolation from higher command assured that it would be able to do so and make it stick; the rest came from the ancient human ability to justify to itself almost anything it wanted to do.

It saw itself as the law, the *only* law left in its more limited cosmos. It continued to safeguard what commerce was left, and to enforce order on the forces of chaos, anarchy and greed that always rode in to capitalize on any misfortune. Most of the other ships did the same, almost as a sense of duty, a matter of honor.

There were, of course, a few that went over to the other side and became the enemy, and those, too, ships like the *Thermopylae* sought out to battle and possibly destroy.

Nothing, particularly such a valuable commodity as security, was ever free, though, and with no taxing authority to finance it and no controlling government to set its worth and limit its reach, the ship quite naturally took a percentage of whatever was produced by those whom it protected. This was its just share for keeping the defenseless in business, and it was necessary for all the luxuries, necessities, repairs and consumables that such a military unit required. It did not make them universally loved in most places when they priced their own value and service at a rate much higher than their "clients" considered reasonable, proper, or possible, but the ships projected power that no one else could equal. There were no debates; the ships either were paid what they wanted or they took it.

To many if not most of the people on the planets throughout the old colonial sector, and the struggling commercial vessels that tried to keep them supplied and viable as working societies, it was increasingly difficult to tell the protector from the folks they were being protected from.

And now they had collected a bit more than they bargained for.

Captain Kim had always been a hardware man. He'd begun as an ensign overseeing robotic systems and repairs, gone up through the ranks, eventually commanding a destroyer and finally being selected by the destroyer captains to take over full command of the cruiser *Thermopylae* after its previous captain had reached the final stage of promotion, one of the three rotating Fleet Admirals, who were no longer bound to their bodies but were integrated with the great ship. Command at that level was always split, since the power any of them wielded was close to absolute, but the price was more than just becoming cybernetically wedded to the cruiser; demands on the human brain in that configuration were hard, particularly at the ages when they were integrated, and so Fleet Admirals, even rotating as they did, tended to wear out after only twenty or thirty years.

Captain Kim loved being the captain. He'd been the captain now for over twenty years and it was in every way the ideal job, the position to which he'd been born and bred. A man totally without personal fear, or so it seemed; the only nightmare he had other than running into something that would cost him his ship was being promoted to Fleet Admiral.

He was not, however, quite prepared for the likes of Captain Patrick Murphy.

They could not have seemed more opposite had they planned their meeting. There was Kim, a tall, muscular man with shiny pale skin and a uniform that somehow was so clean and perfectly tailored that, even on the captain, it looked as if it had never been worn; and Murphy, hairy, with cracked and burnt complexion, a uniform that looked far too worn almost to being worn out, and a kind of aura that suggested that flies should have been buzzing around the old man's head.

Kim looked at the old freebooter with some disgust, but finished reading the console in front of him before formally acknowledging the other's existence. Finally, he looked up, leaned back, and asked, "You were once a priest?"

Murphy laughed. "I hadn't expected *that* one to be first out of your mouth, Captain. Let's just say the Vatican in any incarnation and I haven't been on speakin' terms in a long, long time, and I ain't heard much from God lately. No matter what they say on Vaticanus, I am convinced that the Father, Son, and Holy Ghost are somewhere on the other side of the Great Silence. Still, it's a useful identity at times, I admit. People tend to trust a priest, dumb as they are."

"Such as handing over their daughters to your care?"

Murphy found that even more amusing. "Ah, yes. Irish and Mary Margaret and Brigit, I suppose you're talkin' about. No, they aren't with me because their families trusted me with 'em. They're with me 'cause they all paid me good to get 'em as far away from their families as fast as possible, all of 'em havin' got themselves knocked up, as it were, and unfit on pleasant little Tara Hibernius for regular lives after that. Or, that's their story, anyways. Me, I got to wonder why anybody, particularly folks what can afford even the likes of me, would get themselves accidentally knocked up when it's a simple monthly pill or potion and you don't have to worry about that unless you want to. Me, I think they got themselves knocked up so's their parents would *have* to pay their way someplace else. To avoid the disgrace, y'see."

Kim shook his head. "No, I *don't* see."

"Ah, you navy types," Murphy sighed. "You make yours in bottles after the computer mucks with 'em and you then throw away the equipment like it's an appendix or tonsils or something else disposable. Meanin' no offense, but you folks are raised almost like machines in a nice, sterile, controlled environment where there's no real questions 'cept maybe how far in rank you'll get. That's the trouble with you military types. You just got to follow orders."

"That is a problem in your eyes?"

"Sure. No lying, cheating, stealing, no con men, no deception or sin to speak of. Kind of permanent adolescents who think being bad is sneakin' off and havin' a forbidden beer or a funny joke not to let the toilet flush. The culture these girls come from is different. It was founded by folks who wanted a simpler, more primitive life, one devoted to the soil and the soul and to their misbegotten nostalgia for traditions and culture that not only are long gone, they probably never were. Lots of colonies like that out here once upon a time. That's why so many of 'em are in trouble. So they work the land in the ways their hardscrabble ancestors did back on the Auld Sod, or at least a kind of traditional working excusin' the robotics and chemistry and all, and the fact that they eat like pigs with what they grow rather than starve and never once knew the meanin' of the word 'famine.' But, never mind. It's a whole world of fifth-generation play actors who really think they're livin' the simple life and that makes 'em clean of spirit and closer to God or somethin' like that. A land where all the boys and girls are conscious virgins and all the marriages are perfect and there's no unhappiness. And they gather at the pub and they drink pints of perfect dark stout and they sing authentic fake Irish folk tunes and they play the pipes at weddings and funerals and everybody's the perfect Catholic saint." He stopped for a moment and saw Kim's blank stare. "And you don't have a bloody *clue* what I'm talkin' about, just like them legal and psychologist folks, do you?"

"Not exactly. I believe in plain speaking and being straightforward."

"Indeed? Well, it's *hypocrisy*, Captain. You know the word? One of dozens, maybe hundreds of worlds where everybody *pretends* to be what everybody else thinks they should be but nobody really is. And these girls' parents, they got fed up with it but they got noplace else to go. So they create a situation where the girls *can't* remain hypocrites and they ship 'em out to someplace where maybe they got a chance at a life."

"And you accused *us* of being thieves, I believe? What you are saying sounds both insane and quite sad. What are these young women to become with no family or friends and new young mothers without resources? It won't do, Murphy. A good story, but it just won't do. We may not burden ourselves with the old ways of reproduction, but I know enough to know that at the first evidence of pregnancy any of them could have taken a simple pill and had done with it."

Murphy sighed. "I was afraid I couldn't make you

get it," he said, trying to find an alternate way in. "There are no such pills in God's country. It's a monstrous crime to even possess them. Oh, sure, it's done, but in their own way, their culture and their parents' culture is as rigid to them as your military culture is to your people. These girls got pregnant in that culture, they were dead. The only way out for them was to give themselves and their children to the church and become nuns. 'Missionary work' is the euphemism that's used to explain where a young woman went. Oh, they have birth control, although it's illegal, but something went wrong. They shouldn't all have gotten preggers from a roll or two in the hay. So, either the families wanted them out or the church was short on nuns. Maybe both. But, given the choice of the nunnery or me, they took me. And I was takin' them to one or another place where they could have some kind of support and future. A place or places where it simply wouldn't matter. And that's when you stepped in."

Captain Kim shook his head in disbelief. "I still believe you are not telling me the truth, or at least not most of it, but I'm not here to judge you nor to save the souls of young women. But I *do* know that you've been running all sorts of elaborate contraband back and forth between these benighted worlds in this sector since I was a lieutenant, and you knew that there was a fee to be paid, and you have a very long history of not paying that fee, Captain Murphy. In fact, you've run from and successfully evaded Navy collectors for the past several years now. I don't care what you do or what you run to these poor people down there, but I *do* care that you have decided to work outside our system. We can't have that, Murphy. This fleet depends to a large degree on our fees and levies. There's no more spare parts for critical systems, and nothing to make them. Keeping things maintained and running costs an increasing amount of money. If everyone doesn't pay their share, then this fleet will simply grind to a halt, impotent, unable to do its mission."

"And what mission is that, sir, if I might be so bold as to ask?"

"Protection! Pirates raid and steal from traders both honest and dishonest like yourself all the time, and they don't care if they kill. Legitimate trade alone keeps those colonial planets running, even at more basic levels, since they have the same problems with parts, supplies, and repairs that we do. Billions of people depend on things they can't grow or make, or whatever getting to where they're needed. We're the only ones keeping it working. The only ones who *could* keep it working. You know that, Captain."

"I know you say that, probably even believe it," Murply responded. "But it's a losing battle even if you do it honestly. Piracy and political and religious fanaticism are rampant and getting worse as things grow harder for people here and supplies run down. You not only can't stop it with this little independent navy of yours, you hardly even try. You spend all your time collecting your fees even while those characters invade whole colonies, raping and looting. Since I think you have a strong code of honor, I don't think you even see it, but I don't know anybody who doesn't hate you and fear you. They can't tell the difference between you and the bad guys, Captain. That's what I mean about being machines. You have a system that's blind to reality and you still go through the motions and justify your actions even though they're entirely motivated by self-preservation urges having nothing to do with your so-called 'mission.' You just keep doing it because that's what you're programmed to do."

"I don't think we're quite as soulless as you make us out to be. I admit we can do less and less and things are going down and that we're like a small child holding up the collapsing wall and getting more and more tired as we do so and the weight of the wall comes down on us, but what is your alternative? Lose all sense of duty and honor, quit, watch it fall from a drunken amoral haze or some drugged stupor and say the hell with everybody? That's your problem, Murphy. You're so busy looking at us as machines that your total loss of faith prevents you from looking in the mirror and seeing what I see here before me now."

"Indeed? And what is that?"

"An empty suit. A dead man who doesn't have the sense to know he's already in Hell. So what am I to do with you, Murphy? You and your . . . cargo?"

The words had little effect on the old man, but he felt he had to defend his pride against this martinet. "That's *Captain* Murphy, sir!"

"Captains have ships," Kim replied. "And you don't, Citizen Murphy. Not any more. We will fumigate that scow and then take it to the nearest salvage yard and trade it for something we can use, even though its trade value isn't all that much. We can't do much to or with you, though. You're too old and too much the physical and mental corpse to have any value, and you are a deficit if we keep you around as a consumer of our resources. But since you haven't done anything to us that would warrant execution, we'll probably simply drop you penniless and stark naked on the first planet we come across and see if you can start from scratch."

"Wouldn't be the first time," Murphy responded, although inside he was seething. "And the girls?"

"We haven't decided on that yet. I have all my staff recommendations here, but I'm not about to make any decisions until I've personally interviewed each of them and made up my own mind. Why do you ask? Do you really *care* what happens to them? Or is it that you didn't get full payment until you delivered them?"

"I ain't no buyer and seller of human flesh! Them girls paid for their passages and I'm responsible for 'em until they get where they were goin'. What are you gonna do, you starched bald bloodsucker? Take their babies as your taxes?"

"I hardly think their babies would be of much use to us. It is far too late to genetically enhance them, and we begin with raw sperm and raw egg. No, Mister Murphy, I rather think I'll speak with them and then decide. They are not on our account books, but are, shall we say, left in the lurch by your actions. So unless you want to give me an account somewhere that will cover your back and present taxes and levies, I think you are out of the loop. You are dismissed and confined to quarters for now. Avail yourself of the facilities there. For God's sake, at least take a shower."

Murphy gave him a sour grin. "I don't think I can afford your water bill," he responded, turned, and started to walk out. Just before he reached the door, though, he stopped and turned back towards the captain. "Only one thing will I give you, sir. Don't put 'em together. Mix 'em up. Keep 'em separate. Otherwise you'll mightily regret it."

"What? What are you talking about, man?"

"The girls. Keep 'em apart. I'm pretty sure they're only dangerous when they're together, and I guarantee you they'll be bored to death on this antiseptic platform."

"Why in the name of heaven should we worry about those . . . ladies?"

Murphy grinned. "Well, you've been warned." He gave the captain a smirk and a half-hearted salute and turned and exited.

The captain shook his head in wonder. This was a ship that could destroy a planet. There was simply no more secure place in the known universe. He didn't appreciate the old boy trying to play mind games with him.

Another officer emerged from behind a panel near the captain's seat. Commander Sittithong looked close to the captain's age but she had aged less well than he.

Kim turned and looked over at her. "That man is hiding something."

Sittithong nodded. "Probably a lot, sir. But I doubt if we could tell truth from lie even with our best interrogation systems. I've seen his like before. Pathological. Whatever he's spinning, he believes—at least when he's spinning it. To get down to the core and learn the truth would probably destroy his mind. His sort made great spies in the old days."

"Indeed. I'd like to crack that nut, but for something like back taxes it's not something I could justify to the Admiralty and would certainly be beyond regulations. Perhaps we'll learn more from the young ladies. Perhaps *you* should question them, or at least the first one, while I duck out of sight. They might feel more comfortable."

"I doubt that, sir. Still, if you want to try, I can take the first, then if I have no luck you can take the second, and perhaps both of us will take the third if that doesn't work."

He nodded and got up. "Good idea. I confess that I am going to find dealing with them to be most uncomfortable. Compared to our ways, it is almost as if dealing with an alien species."

Sittithong shrugged. "I am not much closer to them than you in that, but let's see." The thought of actually having a man put his *thing* inside her and squirt *fluids* up into her insides, and maybe for the result to be a baby actually *growing* in there was enough to make her shudder, she who would have thought nothing of charging into a nest full of pirates with only a side-arm. It was all so . . . *ugly*. And *messy*. And to be con-trolled by hormones that overrode rationality was almost unthinkable to her, as it was to the other naval person-nel. Like most, she thought of "ordinary" humans as closer to the animals than to the purity of mind and body the military way represented.

Still, she'd dealt with a lot of them, both men and women, in her time, and even though she couldn't remember dealing with pregnant young women, she was certainly ready to give it a try.

As the captain settled in on the chair behind the partition, Commander Sittithong took the command chair and pressed a small disk on the thin, crescent-shaped desk in front of her. "Send in the first woman. No preference. Any one of them will do."

The door across from the exec slid back and a young woman entered, looking not just hesitant but down-right scared.

Murphy had stood, but there was a thin, rigid but functional chair facing the command chair. "Please have a seat if you like," the commander said as softly and as friendly sounding as she could manage.

"Uh, yeah. Thank you, Mum," the woman muttered, and sat. She looked no more comfortable sitting than standing, but apparently it was better than nothing.

The screen area of the desk lit up with the com-plete files and digest of the initial interview with this young woman. "You are Irish O'Brian? Your true name?"

"Yes, Mum. Me folks thought it sounded good, and I'm certainly Irish."

Sittithong realized that the young woman wasn't making a play on words; she meant it.

"You are . . ." *Good lord!* " . . . seventeen standard years?"

"Yes, Mum. But I'll be eighteen next March."

The commander quickly adjusted to the stock military calendar. "Then you were only sixteen when you . . . became pregnant?"

"Aye, Mum. Old enough, it seems, though the old superstitions said it was too young and couldn't be done on the first time. Guess they were wrong 'bout that."

O'Brian had a thick accent that was related to Murphy's but was much, much more pronounced. Sittithong guessed that it was the Irish dialect, whatever that meant.

The infobase picked up her mental query and gave her the details on a thin frame to the right of the personnel record. Some small island on Old Earth. A nationality, as it were. The planet the girl was from, though, was Tara Hibernius, a midway colony near the border beyond which they could no longer go. The colony had been established by a group of wealthy conservatives who wanted to found an agricultural society based on an idealized vision of an ancient state of their native land that probably never existed in the first place.

The pattern wasn't uncommon, particularly in the early days of colonization. In fact, such things had been encouraged. The irrational revolutionary nut cases with money and influence and possibly fanaticism as well could be bled off by giving them a chance to prove their ideas, and if you had a wealthy enough benefactor or group, then the Confederation hadn't even had to shell out much to set the places up. When the dissident and the dangerous actually paid to take themselves out of your society, how could you not help but ease the way?

Tara Hibernius was only two wormgate jumps from

Vaticanus, too. Strict and very conservative Catholic society. So Murphy might not have been stretching the truth about the place. They might well have imposed technological limitations on the average citizens there just to keep them isolated and their lifestyle mandated just so; this allowed for a cultlike society where people lived in ignorance of what else there was in the universe, the founders' ideal. Back to the land, back to the simple life—it was consistent.

But paying an old reprobate like Murphy to get your pregnant daughter off to some distant planet where she'd be totally unprepared to live wasn't consistent. Some of these cults killed their sinners, but this seemed neither an act of excommunication nor of loving desperation. It made no sense at all.

The computer-aided psychology report on any of the three was no more help. Except for a strong sense of deception, the physiological results were totally contradictory and so were the stories.

"Why were you on Captain Murphy's ship instead of staying back on your native planet?" the exec asked her.

Irish O'Brian shrugged. "It beat the alternative, Mum."

"Indeed? And what was that?"

"Bein' burnt up with the baby and all, Mum."

"The people of your world would have burned you alive?" The exec would have sounded more shocked if she actually believed that it would happen.

"Oh, yes, Mum. Me and me sisters."

"Sisters? I don't see any relationship here."

"Oh, it's a different kind of relation, that," O'Brian replied, sounding casual and innocent. "Sort of sisters in the soul more than in the blood. They'd already got the other ten of us, y'see, so there wasn't no doubt but what they'd do to us."

"They burned ten other young women? You saw this?"

"Yes, Mum. Didn't hav'ta, though. When any one of us goes, well, the others just sort of *know*, y'see."

"No, I *don't* see, I'm afraid. I have no idea what you're talking about."

"Well, Mum, it's like this. The Old Country, it was united by a prophet who married off a daughter of the line of Judah to King Brian. That was at the old Tara, which is why that's a part of the New Country name, y'see. They think they have the direct authority of God, and the Church is their instrument."

Were all these people totally insane? "What does all that have to do with anything, my dear?"

"Well, y'know, we don't exactly get along with God, y'know. We ain't been all that impressed with his side, y'see."

This was going nowhere. The exec did, however, notice one thing that she hadn't before. "Um, that necklace you're wearing. Is it some family thing, or a gift, or some sort of religious medal?"

The girl ran a long finger down the slender golden chain around her neck which ended in a large stone of some sort, emerald in color but looking somehow different, and certainly rough.

"Well, 'tis of our beliefs, Mum."

"May I look at it?"

The idea seemed to frighten the girl, the first real rise the exec had gotten from her. "Please, Mum. It's not good for you to touch it. It's just a stone, but it's very important to me. Please don't make me give it to you!"

Sittithong thought for a moment. What the hell, they weren't getting anywhere. "Very well, calm down." She sighed and considered where to go from here and didn't get very far. Finally she said, "That will be all for now, citizen. Please exit and wait until we've spoken to your companions. We might well want to talk to you all again after this. Unlike Captain Murphy, you haven't committed any criminal acts as far as we're concerned."

"So long as you don't send us back to our deaths, anyplace is fine, Mum. We'll get by."

Yeah, sure. Seventeen, pregnant or with an infant, little possessions, no money or credit, no education, no skills. Oh, you'll cope fine.

When O'Brian was gone, the commander called, "What do you think, Captain? You want to take the next one, or me?"

"I think these people are all lunatics," Captain Kim replied. "I've been looking over the initial examinations and interrogations of all three and that's about what we can expect from the other two, it appears. I'm not sure whether it's worth losing any more time or sleep over this." He got up and came around to the exec, who rose and yielded the chair to the captain. "Still, let's see what comes of this, if anything. I don't want to be hasty here, and we've got procedural problems."

"Indeed. Most people in their circumstance will tell us where to drop them off."

"Let's take the other two together and see if we can make any sense of this." He pressed a point on the desk signalling the marine outside. "Send in the other two together now."

"Aye, sir," was the response, and the door opened and the other two girls entered. Like O'Brian, neither seemed particularly awed by the room nor the presences within it, nor noticably concerned about their situation, either. If anything, the best either officer could sense was mild indifference to their situation.

The captain and exec looked them both over. They

looked around in a bored sort of way but did not return the stares.

To the right of the captain was a short and somewhat chubby young woman with light brown hair and bright, almost impossibly blue eyes. To her right, his left, stood a taller, more striking figure with long blonde hair that was unnaturally pure and golden yellow, a sexy stance and baby face with lips that seemed to form an impertinent but sexy pout even when at rest, and strangely unnerving hazel eyes. The fact that this one was as pregnant as the others did not in the least diminish her radiant sexuality; even the neutered officers knew what she radiated and could sense it.

The exec went over and whispered to the captain, "Sir, doesn't it strike you that these girls, all three, seem unnatural somehow? The colorations are natural according to the medical exam, yet have you ever seen eyes or hair of those colors in nature on any planetfall?"

She had a point, the captain reflected. Still, the fact that these girls were the product of some sort of genetic manipulation wasn't extraordinary, only the superficiality of the tinkering. No humans had truly natural genetic lines any more, hadn't for a couple of centuries at least.

"Ain't you cold without no hair?" the brown-haired girl asked, looking at the exec.

"Isn't it a bother to have to maintain all that hair?" the exec responded, used to the way dirtballers thought of service people.

"All you folks look kinda creepy to us," the girl came back. This would be Mary Margaret McBride. The other, the blonde and sexy Brigit Moran, said nothing.

"People and lifestyles are different all over," the captain told the girl. "You haven't been off your world before, it's clear, or you'd know that."

"You mean folks elsewhere all look like you?"

"No, just military people. But there are other differences, quite a lot of them. None of us have much choice about that part."

"Why not?" McBride asked, apparently quite sincere in the question.

The exec tried to rescue the captain. "Look, all that's beside the point. The only thing we are trying to decide here is what to do with you. You wouldn't like it here, I don't think, and you would just be in the way of what we do."

"That's easy," McBride said. "Just put us off on any world with folks who look and act more like us. We'll get by."

"You might at that," the exec admitted. "The trouble is, you are very young, you have no experience outside a very primitive culture, and your—*condition*, let us say, makes it hard for us to just do that. We must make sure that you will not suffer or die because of what we do."

"Why?"

It was such a strange question in that context that it threw the exec for a moment. Finally it was the captain who answered, "Because our ways include a code of what's right and wrong and that would be wrong. Still, if you had friends or relatives on another world we might be able to arrange for you to be with them. Do you have any family like that?"

"We got some family of sorts most everywhere," McBride assured him. "But not like you mean, I don't think. Honest. We'll be okay anyplace you drop us so long as the folks there ain't like, well, *you*, for example."

"Sounds like we should just arrange to get you back home to Tara Hibernius," Commander Sittithong said flatly. "That might solve all our problems."

Both girls seemed suddenly quite agitated. It wasn't fear in their eyes, not exactly, but it was clear that this was the one thing that bothered them. "No, you can't make us go back!"

"Never!" repeated the heretofore silent blonde in a high breathy voice.

"Perhaps a convent, then, on one of the developed colonies," the captain suggested thoughtfully. "We could live with putting you in the custody of your church."

"Convent? *Our* church?" McBride seemed to be suppressing a laugh. "No, sir. Not *them* folks. We don't fit in with *them* a'tall."

The captain noticed the necklaces the two girls wore around their necks, quite similar to the one worn by the first girl. He was going to ask about it, but then decided not to, at least for now.

"Well, those are the only two choices we've come up with. If you won't tell us your stories of why you were on Murphy's ship and why you are fleeing your native world, then we can hardly make any third decision."

McBride was having none of it. "You're just like *them*!" she responded angrily. "No, you put us back on our ship and let us go on, or you put us off on a big world with lots of folks. You *better*!"

The captain found this almost amusing. "We'd *better*? That's usually followed by some sort of threat. We'd better or what?"

"You just *better*, that's all! Can we go now?"

The captain looked over at the exec who gave a slight shrug.

"Why not?" he replied. "There's little to be gained from this. You and your companions will have adjoining cabins and you must stay in them, together if you want, or not if you like, or in the lounge that will be nearby. Marines will be posted to make sure you don't go start exploring and get into trouble. I'm going to have to take a look and see how long it'll be before we're within range of Tara Hibernius, and that's that."

"You *won't* send us back!" McBride said flatly. "You *won't!*"

"I will do what's in the best interest of all of us, and you'll have to accept it. Now, go. The sergeant outside will show you all to your quarters."

Mary Margaret McBride looked at Brigit Moran and the two locked eyes and resolute expressions for a moment. It looked quite childlike. Still, they both turned in almost military fashion and stomped out of the room.

The captain sighed. "In the old days, I was a guest for a time at a private resort where military and trade representatives gathered to discuss policy. Many brought along their families in the old style because it was such a nice holiday spot. Many of their young children would act like that on occasion. I recall one small boy who did not want to stop swimming and go inside with his mother. He threw a loud screaming fit, one so awful I thought they would have to call the medical personnel, and it was only after a while that I realized I was watching unbridled and unchecked emotion. Finally, he threatened to hold his breath until he turned blue. He tried to do so, too."

"Sir?"

"I half expected at least the talkative one to threaten the same thing just now. I hope our medical computers have full data on pregnancies. It may be necessary at some point to sedate them, and I should not like to be responsible for harming the child within."

The exec had less experience with the masses of humanity in their standard forms and found the whole thing more unnerving.

"I don't know, sir. Sedation might be quite advisable. In their mental state they are as much a threat to themselves as to anyone. I shall be happy to see them leave."

"I agree. Have them continuously monitored. Put an experienced security person on them, too. I don't want a computer deciding what is and isn't aberrant behavior."

"Aye, sir."

The captain looked down at his desktop screen. "It says here we'll be close enough to shuttle them back home in sixteen days. Let us pray that we can hold out that long!"

III:
THE WITCHES OF ERIN

The exec was decidedly not amused.

"All right, Murphy. Straight answers now. Are you all lunatics or failed experiments or just what the fucking *hell* are they *doing* in there?"

Murphy had been given a full bath, shave, and clean generic clothing and looked just as much an unmade bed as he had before in spite of that. Still, he'd been sound asleep in his "quarters" when he'd suddenly been rudely awakened by two big, burly marines and almost hauled up seventeen levels to the command and control deck.

Now he wiped sleep blearily from his eyes, and, partly resting on the side of a desk, he strained to focus on the viewing screen in front of them. It was the girls, all right, but he didn't remember there being nine of 'em. . . .

Now the figures began to come together as his eyes more or less focused, and he gaped at what the duty personnel had been watching for who knew how long.

The three Tara Hibernius girls were sitting on the deck in the middle of one of the two cabins assigned to them, stark naked except for the necklaces each of them wore around their necks, designs stained onto their bodies. They were holding hands and chanting, eyes shut, faces partially raised up as if in some kind of trance. Around them they'd drawn a design using chalk or something which they'd completed after sitting in the middle so that the drawing extended all around them.

"Kinda gettin' more'n your money's worth of what normal wimminfolks look like, ain't you?" he commented dryly.

Commander Sittithong was not amused. "If there is one single thing about those three that can be defined as 'normal' by anyone, on any world, anywhere, I have never heard of it," she responded. "Just what in heaven's name are they *doing*?"

Murphy shrugged. "Chanting, seems like," he responded.

The exec reached out and forcefully pulled the old captain around. "I've about had it with you, *Captain* Murphy! And you can stow that old folksy ethnic act, too. That may get you a few more drinks in spaceport dives, but it means nothing here! Now, just what is this all about?"

Murphy squinted at the screen. "Be damned," he muttered, more to himself than to the naval officer. "First time I ever seen 'em painted up like that. They all got hold of them damned necklaces, though. First time I seen 'em clear. Emerald, ruby, and turquoise. Strange lookin' things. I don't like this. Can you turn up the volume a bit and isolate the chant? What're they sayin'?"

The exec turned and gave a nod to one of the technicians, who pressed a few controls. The chanting grew much clearer, if no more explicable.

> *"Power of the universe, come to us!*
> *Father of darkness, heed our prayers.*
> *Send your messengers to heed the call of your brides!*
> *"Gather, darkness! Come from where nothing escapes,*
> *Hear our prayers and extend to us your power!*
> *"Give power from the darkness where no light springs!"*

It went on like that, some of it in some sort of tongue-twisting language that was unfamiliar to any of them but which fit the chanting, mostly the same words clearly said over and over again, with occasional added lines of supplication to bizarre names or creatures.

> *"Come send the goat that eats its young.*
> *"Come from the power where no light springs. . . ."*

"Those are prayers, Commander," Murphy said at last, indicating with a gesture that he didn't have to hear more. "I'm not really well schooled on it, but apparently they're praying to their lord and master and his minions to spring from the black holes of the universe and give them the ultimate power. To do what, I don't even want to think, but I kind of hope that it won't get beyond that silliness."

"Prayers! To what deity? Nothing of the faiths of ancient Earth nor the cults that sprang from the colonies, surely."

"Oh, yes. Old as any of 'em. Maybe older than all but one. That design's a kind of protection, since their deities can't even be trusted to not kill their own followers—that stuff about the goat eating her young. Some ancient symbol, and more on their bodies. But it was known on Old Earth, for sure. It's devil worship, Commander! They're summoning demons."

The exec stared at him. "You can't be serious!"

"Oh, but I am. More importantly, *they're* serious. They're witches, Commander. That's why they was bein' burned back on Tara Hibernus. Don't look so shocked. It's not that odd. The damned society there is so strict, so fundamentalist if you please, that if you don't blindly accept it, you're corrupted. It's the ultimate rebellion for the young in such a place. They only had three alternatives, you see. Blindly follow the incredibly strict and boring theocracy there or be the opposition, as it were. Mostly it does little harm and lets 'em blow off steam, since the third way is to kill yourself, which many do I'm told. I'd sure do it if I was stuck there, I'll tell you. I'm from the same ancestral stock and traditions as them people, but they're way beyond what my folks lived. Sooner or later, of course, most of the young ones pair off and wind up bein' reabsorbed into that society and that's the end of that. But these girls, their group or coven or whatever, went a bit far in the pleasures of the dark side and they got knocked up on a world where the powers that be think it's damned near impossible, almost unthinkable. Musta been a hell of an orgy, huh?"

The exec looked over at the chief tech, who was ahead of her. "Orgy, Commander. A frequent rite of ancient cults going back to the early civilizations of Old Earth involving frenzied singing, dancing, drink and drugs, and wanton and uninhibited sexual activity."

"I always wanted to attend somebody's orgy but I never could find one," Murphy sighed.

"I do not understand all that, but I do understand that it is a demonstration of disobedience and rebellion," Sittithong commented.

"Of course y'don't, you manufactured martinet! They engineered the sex right out of your society. Probably the drinking, drugs, and all the rest that make life fun now and then, too."

"We have songs," the commander responded, almost defensively. "But, never mind. So they truly were under a death sentence? And you rescued them?"

"Only in a manner of speakin'," Murphy replied. "You're dismissin' what they're doin' as just some kid's act, like throwin' a tantrum or holding their breath until they get their way. It's not like that. That's how it starts, but they're already well along. There's always somethin' to them things, I found in me long life. Maybe not what you expect, or even what *they* think is right, but usually there's reasons why things keep goin', and wherever there's a belief in somethin' supernatural, there's always the two sides. The yin and the yang. God and the devil. Angels and demons. Somehow those little darlin's sprung themselves from what must have been pretty good security. And, in that condition, they somehow made their way over forty kilometers on a world with no paved roads or mechanized vehicles to the one point of outside contact, the tiny spaceport and freight center. Security's even better there. Really good. They hire some real experts to make sure of that, since they don't want nobody on their little world to get the idea you can just pick up and leave and all. Folks like me don't even have a point of contact with the common folk there. Just a few officials, priests mostly, who do the intermediary work. Yet they got in there, easy as you please, and it was just my bad fortune to be the one in port at the time. They only can handle one ship at a time, y'see."

"But given that, tugs are generally automated or have at best one pilot. There wouldn't even be room for them, and they'd be detected by machines or pilots. How did they get aboard your ship?"

"They just—*did*, that's all. I delivered some pure breeding stock, mostly cows. I figure they used the pressurized and insulated containers to get up. But how they got in, how they kept from triggerin' all the alarms or bein' seen on the monitors, and how for that matter they got through a coded double airlock into the ship itself is beyond me. You see what I mean?"

"You asked them, I assume?"

"Oh, yes, I asked 'em. Never got an answer, though. Fact is, once they was in there, it never once entered my head to report 'em, throw 'em off, or whatever. It was like they was payin' passengers and was expected. I can't explain it, but it's kinda spooky. On the one hand, I *knew* somethin' was real wrong, but on the other, I just went along like all was normal."

The commander stared at the chanting women and considered the new information. "So these three are not the ignorant little things they'd like us to believe?"

"That's just the point! I think they *are* pretty much what you see. They're sure enough illiterate; they think the law of gravity is somethin' passed by the government, they was absolutely shocked when they discovered that their home world wasn't flat, and they didn't have the slightest idea how to turn the lights on and off in the cabin, let alone figure out how to boil water for tea. No, they think it's all bein' done by invisible demons from the depths of Hell or somethin'. But they got power that's scary as all hell. That's what I meant by you bein' sorry you ever picked us up. Looks to me like they're gettin' ready to use that power, and with all that and not a brain in their cute little heads, they're about as dangerous as a nuclear reaction."

"Why didn't you tell us this at the start?"

The old captain shrugged. "What? That them girls is three witches with supernatural powers who can do all sorts of mysterious stuff? You don't even believe my story now, Commander. But looks like you will soon. When they start them chants and trance stuff, they're up to somethin'. Just what I can't say, but you're gonna have a hard time figurin' it out or dealin' with it. *Then* you'll see."

Commander Sittithong sighed. "I sincerely doubt this, Captain. You might be so suggestible or gullible, but this is a star cruiser capable of eliminating whole planets if such a drastic action were ever needed. There's more military might, and military safeguards, on this vessel than in any of past history's entire navies, all under the ultimate command and control of cybernetic minds who themselves share power and must agree on an action. No, Captain, they're just going to sit there and chant themselves all the way home."

Murphy's head shot up, suddenly wide awake. "Home? You're takin' 'em *home*?"

"There is no other legal, moral, or ethical choice," the exec told him. "It has been approved all the way to the Admiralty. We'll be within their home sector in just a few weeks, and then we'll shuttle them back in. You, too, unless we find somewhere before that you can be put off at. Then none of you are our problem any longer."

"You're takin' 'em *home*?" Murphy repeated, barely hearing the rest. "My God, Commander! And you *told* them this?"

"We had to. Regulations require—"

"*Damn* your regulations! Any way I can be moved off to one of your destroyers? Or at least close to a disaster escape pod?"

"You're being overly dramatic, aren't you?"

"Just you wait," Murphy responded, wagging a finger at the officer. "Just you wait and see. At least you oughta break that up. Break all three up and put 'em in different areas of the ship so far apart they can't even find each other. I think they need to be together to exercise this power."

"I've indulged you this far, Murphy, but no farther. There is no reason to split them up. The very *thought* that such as they could be any danger to this ship or anyone on it is ludicrous! Now, go back to your quarters and pray to your primitive god if that makes you feel any better, but let's have no more of this nonsense!"

"You wouldn't happen to have some whiskey on this tub, would you?" Murphy asked her.

"Of course not!"

"Well, could you send one of them big marines in to my old ship and have him fetch a bottle from me secret compartment in the galley? Surely you can't deny an old man *that*."

"We found that stash of cleaning fluid you call whiskey earlier today," the exec told him. "It is marked for disposal, but I don't see why, if you want to kill yourself slowly, you shouldn't have at least one bottle of it if it keeps you calm."

"Oh, I don't want it to keep me calm," the old captain replied. "I want it to keep me nicely blotto for a while. . . ."

Lieutenant Commander Mohr, the head of ship security, was an even meaner and bigger figure of a man than most of the marines on board, yet right now he looked like a small child caught with his hand in the candy jar.

"What do you mean, 'They're missing'?" Commander Sittithong thundered. "How in hell could *anyone* be missing on this ship?"

Behind them on the viewing screen was a full view

of the "guest" cabin where the young women or whatever they were had been sitting and chanting for hours. Now it still showed the strange pentagram in which they'd been sitting, but there was no sign of them or of any life whatsoever in the place.

"I—I have no explanation, Commander. None. One moment they were there, the next they weren't. You can play back the recording yourself. The alarm went off as soon as the subjects vanished from the surveillance. We immediately did a visual of the entire cabin area and found no signs of life, and the guards were still in place outside the door. We immediately ordered the lead guard in with the other blocking the door with weapon drawn. The marine went through every centimeter of the cabin. They weren't there. We immediately initiated a shipwide comparator search. No unknowns or unauthorized persons came back. None of the three showed up in a general search, either. It's as if they vanished into some other dimension or something."

"Bullshit! Those girls couldn't *spell* 'dimension,' let alone find a new one. Has the captain been notified?"

"Not yet. We were waiting for you."

The exec nodded. "Yes, well, I'll notify him in a bit. He's sleeping at the moment and it won't do any good to wake him until we have something to tell him beyond the fact that these girls pulled a magic trick on the most secure location in what's left of the known galaxy. What about Murphy?"

"Murphy, sir?" Because the sexes were so irrelevant to this crew, all officers were "sir."

"The old freighter captain."

"Oh, *him*. He's still in his cabin, sleeping off the effects of whatever that horrible crap he swallowed so eagerly was."

"Hmmm . . . We may have underestimated his story,

or at least his fears. What about the freighter? We don't have sensors everywhere on *it*."

"We thought of that, sir, but we *do* have visuals on every pressurized area on it as well as constantly monitored seals on the entrance. All show no activity."

The exec thought frantically for a minute. Finally, she asked, "Who is your best security analyst aboard? Someone who can figure these kinds of problems out if need be?"

"I'm not sure anyone has ever had any experience with *this* sort of thing, but Sergeant Maslovic has been excellent at solving the most subtle security breaches. He's the one who found the missing neutronium, or at least accounted for it."

"An enlisted man? And a marine at that? Very well, I'll go along with you on this, but he better be good. Get him up here *now*, with every bit of data and clearances he requires to start on this right away. And bring Captain Murphy up here as well. Sober him up as best you can—check with Medical, they should have something. On the double!"

Both Captain Murphy and Sergeant Maslovic had at least one thing in common. Neither of them wanted to be there and stuck with this knotty problem, and neither of them had the slightest idea where to start. Still, Murphy, who was the most sour not only from the news that his "witches" had flown the coop, as he called it, but also that he was suddenly as sober as he'd ever felt in his adult life, was probably in the worse frame of mind.

Still, he had that deep-down sense of "told you so" satisfaction that he was more than willing to shove up these robotic martinets' noses. He looked at Maslovic with a familiar nod, recognizing him from the squadron that boarded the freighter. Clearly the man was more than just a mere guard if he was here.

"So the little girls took a powder and now the whole navy's in a panic," he said with a wry smile. "And old Murphy's been called up to help pull you out of the mess you made when you didn't listen to him in the first place!"

"And you did so much better with them, by your own account," Sittithong shot back.

"Well, you got a point there," the old man admitted. "But if it wasn't for you buttin' in like you did, they'd be where they wanted to be and I'd be rid of them by now. Even *I* had no idea that they could do *this*!"

Maslovic was less inclined to trust the old captain. "This is quite a level of sophistication for three airheaded young things who can hardly walk, isn't it?"

"'*Sophistication*' he says! 'Tis the black arts, m'boy! Nobody can teleport themselves off a ship by chantin' usin' some kind of gizmo!"

Maslovic nodded. "And there I agree with you. Not in the black magic, but in the fact that nobody can will themselves elsewhere. If these girls really could do that, why did they need you?"

"Invisible, then! Maybe they made themselves invisible!"

"Not likely. We don't just track by vision. Every living thing aboard gives off heat and makes noise and has all sorts of nonvisual emanations that we can use for detection. They show up on none of them, even though small pests in the deepest holds do. No, they didn't teleport anyplace and they didn't become invisible or any such thing. There's only one explanation that makes any sense here, and it's *highly* sophisticated. Let me see the replay again, if you please, Commander."

All eyes went to the screen, which blacked out for just a moment and then came back up with a recording of the trio sitting there inside the pentagram chanting.

"If that's not an act, then those faces show a near trancelike state," Maslovic pointed out. "But they're doing something, and more and more they're doing it in perfect synch. Look at the slight twitching in the feet, the little muscular movements in the mouths, and you'll see they get to where the slightest little thing, even breathing and heart rates, are absolutely identical, like they're one organism. It's the closest to telepathy I've ever seen. The chanting helps them in some way, combines them in some kind of shared consciousness. It's a discipline, but it's clearly deliberate."

"So they merge," Sittithong commented. "That would give them a combined IQ of our dumbest sailor."

Maslovic kept staring at the three. "No, sir. It's not intellect at work here. It's feelings, emotions, I can't tell what else." He looked at the small timer clicking off the hundredths of seconds in the lower left hand corner. "Now, finally, they've got to where they wanted to be. How they learned this I have no idea, but it will be essential that we find out. Imagine what would happen if these girls fell into the hands of someone who could direct them for the wrong ends, or if they could teach more capable people to do this. Nothing would be safe. On the other hand, if *we* can learn how it's done, nothing would be closed to us."

Even Murphy was getting interested. "What are you talkin' about, man?"

"Watch. *There!*"

One moment the trio is still sitting there, chanting, and the next moment they simply are not there. There was no transition, no fading out, nothing. They were there, and then they weren't, just like that.

"What do you see, Sergeant?" the exec prompted. "What do you see that we can't?"

"Well, sir, for one thing I can see that we need a faster clock. Still, if you go back to the precise instant that they 'vanish,' you may be able to see it. At the moment they vanish, freeze it. I mean truly at that moment, at the precise frame number."

It was done, but they could still see nothing. The girls sat, frozen, in that eerie unison that the sergeant had noticed. "Now advance one frame at a time."

Each frame was a hundredth of a second, so it was going to take a while to go through the next few moments, but there they vanished, and nothing was clearly different.

"Right there, the first very few frames, perhaps five one hundredths of a second in all. Can't you see it?"

Both Murphy and Sittithong stared as the same frames went by slowly again and again, but it wasn't clear.

Finally, Maslovic said, "Don't pay any attention to the girls vanishing. Look at the background, and in particular that crude design drawn around them. If we had thousandths of a second frames I think it would be obvious, but this isn't much. Just look at the design *behind* where the women were sitting from the point of view of the camera."

"I believe I see it. A slight distortion, a sort of blurring," the exec commented. "Is that what you mean?"

Maslovic nodded. "The information had to be interpolated for that very short period. After that, the full information could be compiled from earlier storage. You see, we don't keep every frame of every surveillance video we have. On a ship of this size the storage alone would be enormous. They'd been chanting for several hours, so the view of that part of the design was no longer in the security computer's memory. It had to interpolate. As soon as it got the full view, it back-filled the design, redrew it digitally, but for those brief first few fractions of a second it had to hold the design while reprocessing the rest of the image. Because of that, we get that distortion. It's so minor you'd only see it if you expected to see it, and then only in this frame-by-frame analysis."

Both Murphy and the exec turned and stared at the marine. "And, Sergeant, how in *hell* did you know to expect to see it?"

"It *had* to be there. And because the alarms triggered at five one hundredths of a second, it was the one small section that could not be digitally redrawn before a secure offline copy was made. The two computers are substantially the same speed, but the general security and surveillance computer had a lot to do. It *still* almost managed."

"And all this nonsense means what?" Murphy asked, genuinely confused.

"It means that your girls didn't disappear anywhere. After they did what they needed to do, they simply stopped, got up, and walked out the door."

"Impossible!" Lieutenant Commander Mohr asserted. "They'd be all over our sensors!"

"Not, sir, if the surveillance computer was told to remove them from any and all monitoring."

"*What?*"

"They are here, somewhere. They are simply being completely ignored, both by the monitoring computers and any crewmembers they might come into contact with. The background for every single security point on the ship is in memory, so only the parts that move or change need to be dealt with. Wherever they are, the computer is simply not showing or reporting them, but painting each frame and adjusting all records using prior data to have them not show up. As I say, I don't know how they do it, but the computers are self-aware and in many ways would be recognized as just other life-forms, so whatever they're doing to make them not noticed by our people is the same thing they did with the computer. I don't think *they* know how they do it. In fact, I'd rather doubt it. But they're here, as you saw them, most likely walking around the ship, and absolutely no person or computer is taking any notice of them. Is, in fact, blotting out their very existence. That's why I mentioned telepathy, although I don't think they read minds, I just do not have another term for this. They could be right here, right now, and neither we nor our highly sophisticated surveillance equipment would show it. Our brains would simply paint them out, just like the computers are doing. Since they *don't* seem very bright, sir, I think we're in very big trouble if they stop sightseeing and begin pushing buttons and interfering with other processes. This ship's run by computers that are of the same relative design as the one they've compromised."

The chief of security and the executive officer were appalled. Murphy, a queer half-lunatic look in his eyes, stroked his chin and muttered to himself, "What an idiot I've been! And me with the three most perfect burglars in the universe!"

Sittithong, however, was not convinced. "This is all well and good, Maslovic, but it's a fantasy. Never once have we ever observed such powers. We've had people working on such things for decades, probably much longer, but even if there is some sort of psychic power in some people, it's very minor and very limited and not subject to control. I'll need more than a few fuzzy frames of video to believe any of what you say."

"The Holmes Conundrum," Maslovic sighed.

"Eh? What's that, Sergeant?"

"The Holmes Conundrum, sir," Mohr jumped in. "If you eliminate all the other explanations, then what is left, no matter how unbelievable, must be the truth.

And we've had more of these kinds of powers in our histories than you suspect. It's mostly suppressed, since the results were much less than threatening to security. Still, within decades of us establishing colonies and going through wormholes, we have been getting mutations. Most are minor, of no consequence, or they simply can not be handled. Telepaths either grow up as idiots or they go rather messily insane. There's no control. Contrary to their being in *our* minds, everyone and everything around them, from the start, is in *their* heads. We simply aren't designed to cope with that. Until the Great Silence, there were squads of experts whose job it was to track down anyone with even mild paranormal talents and either recruit them into studies of our own or simply erase them if we could not. Now there are no secret laboratories and no central authority to do that. Sooner or later this sort of thing was bound to come up. It is *possible* that we have such a case here."

"I wonder if it's not more than possible, sir," Mohr responded. "Take Tara Hibernius. Isolated, out of the way, totally controlled by its governing councils. Who's to say someone there isn't trying to develop these sorts of people? And if any are discovered, well, then, there's this witchcraft thing. The planet's normal but ignorant population acts as their guardians and security force without even knowing it. Surely not all of those scientific groups and psych squads were on the other side of the Silence. . . ."

The exec was growing whiter with every sentence. Finally she asked, "Why have I never heard of these people and this operation? Why don't even our databases on a ship like this contain anything?"

Mohr looked slightly uncomfortable. "Yours don't. Ours do. You see, Commander, until now, you didn't really have a need to know."

Sittithong started to say something, but the words wouldn't come. Finally she asked, "Does the captain know?"

"Um, probably not."

"The Admiralty?"

"Um, unknown, sir. It depends on whether or not they've needed the information."

"And who decides who needs this information?"

Mohr was now more than uncomfortable, he had the look of a man with a noose around his neck. "Well, the Security Directorate, sir."

"Listen, Mohr . . . This is a small but compact independent task force. We no longer have a civil authority to answer to. You know that."

"Yes, sir?"

"And you're telling me that those who command this task force, those who make the life or death decisions on it, are having information withheld from them by junior officers and even"—she looked over at Maslovic—"*enlisted personnel?*"

"It is all available to them if they require it."

"I see. And you, and your comrades, *you* alone decide if they require it?"

"Not exactly, but in a practical sense, yes. It has to be that way, Commander. It is a part of our job, our oaths. The information we have is far more secure than anything else on this ship. If the sergeant's right, and I believe he may be, then your entire computer system, command and control and all support and subsystems, have already been compromised. Ours isn't because they don't know it isn't. Now they can't learn of it and compromise it because it remains in the Directorate and in this room."

"And if they're already here? Assuming I buy this nonsense?"

"We've taken some precautions, sir, in this area. But,

they could still be here. We do not believe it would mean anything to them if they were, though. These aren't highly intelligent secret agents. They are three units of someone's breeding stock who think they are getting their powers from demons inside black holes."

"They'da been bored to death by this point if they was here," Murphy commented dryly.

"And what about *him*?" Sittithong asked, gesturing towards Murphy. "*He* certainly knows now."

Maslovic went over to the old captain. "What about you, Murphy? Is this really a surprise or were you delivering these girls to somebody before their babies were born?"

"Eh? I don't know what yer talkin' about, sonny boy."

"You're not the science type, but you're not dumb, either. Sure, I believe these girls could make you take them along after they came aboard without you ever noticing. But if we're right, and Tara Hibernius is more than a primitive backwater, then they'd need somebody to get subjects in and out without attracting any undue attention. You and your scow are just about ideal for that, *Captain* Murphy, and while *you* might have been under their spell, I don't think they could have gotten into that small but extremely tightly guarded spaceport on their own, particularly in their condition. Don't play the fool any more, Murphy. Who was paying you to pick up ones like these girls now and then and where were they to be taken? Might as well tell us. You should know more than anybody that, in the hands of people like us, there's nobody who can't be broken."

Murphy's grizzled features broke into a slight smile, and there was still something of a twinkle in his eyes. "You're a smart laddie, aren't you? 'Course, I'm no genius meself. I had no idea what them girls was capable of and that's the Lord's truth. I mostly never know, and that suits me fine. I have—*had*—a regular route. The extra couple of folks now and then they put on at Tara Hibernius was always young, usually young girls in a family way, you might say. The pay was good, and instead of deadheading out of that hole I made a handsome profit, all below the table, as it were. I never asked no questions. That woulda been bad fer business, y'see. There was always somebody at the other end worried about gettin' 'em through the port, usually without the port knowin', if you know what I mean. And me account in the Trade Bank of Marchellus would get fatter. Hell, I never even knew if I *had* a pickup 'til I got 'em. Sometimes yes, but only maybe a third of the time if that. I *can* say that most of them what came aboard was out-and-out devil worshippers or somethin' of the sort, though. Just like *them*. All sorts of secret stuff and signs and blasphemous shit."

"Did they all seem to believe that stuff, like these girls seem to?" Maslovic asked him.

"Some did. Some didn't. You could kinda tell. But the ones that didn't seem to be into it was often the scariest of the bunch."

"In what way?"

"I can't explain it to you. Not really. But you could feel it, deep inside. But if any of *that* sort had been aboard this time, we wouldn't be standin' here now talkin' about it, 'cause they'd be runnin' this whole damned tin soldier factory. *This* lot, they're probably gettin' their jollies playin' Peepin' Tom and explorin' the place. They ain't actin', Sarge. They're really that dumb. Like little kids. I got to tell you, if I knew about what these girls could do, I'da been makin' plans to divert maybe to some worlds that got things worth stealin' before I dropped 'em off."

"And where were you to drop them off, Captain?" Mohr asked him, thinking.

"Same place as always. Didn't make sense to keep

'em around any longer than we had to, so it was my next stop. Queer little place called simply Barnum's World. You know it?"

Sittithong went over to the main console and ran a check. "Yes, here it is. Not much of a place. Apparently an old service world that bred and supplied plants and animals to newly terraformed colonies. They maintain themselves with some major grants and by replacing flora and fauna that needs it on worlds that have had problems keeping up their ecosystems. You're right, Captain. Odd place. Everything from dogs to elephants to a number of things found in exploration without Old Earth origins, as well as purebred strains of grains, grasses, trees from high altitude evergreens to jungle vines. They always pay us our fees, so I don't believe we've had cause to send anyone there in, well, at least as long as I can remember. Not much of a shore leave area. . . . Huh. Says here it's maintained by a Catholic monastic order, and its population is recruited from various colonies and isn't native."

"That's the place," Murphy agreed. "Run by an off-shoot of the original Jesuits, they are. Smart lads. Zoologists, agronomists . . ."

"Geneticists?" Maslovic asked.

Murphy looked genuinely surprised as he caught the train of thought. "Be damned! Never would have thought of that. But these are real Holy Joes. Even as a blind they'd never go for Satanism. These are more like the ones who'd still burn witches at the stake."

"Well, it would be a logical cover. And wasn't that what you said these girls faced back home? No, I'm beginning to see a very disturbing pattern here," Mohr commented. "I think maybe we've put off visiting this Barnum a bit too long. Don't you agree, Commander?"

"I believe we should notify the captain of this before

going any further," Sittithong replied. "This is suddenly turning very, very dark."

Mohr nodded. "I agree. And we've got something of a cover here with Murphy and his ship. We can simply explain our visit as taking our people where they were heading in the first place."

They all seemed to like the idea—all, that is, except Murphy. "Uh, pardon me, folks, but ain't you forgettin' somethin' here?"

"Yes?"

"I wasn't kiddin' about them girls bein' scared out of their wits at the idea of goin' back to their home world. They was all told that they would burn if they ever tried a comeback. And that's where they think we're takin' 'em now. That's why they did what they did."

"Yes, but we're not going to do that now. They're going where they want to go," Sittithong pointed out.

"Uh, yeah, well and good if you can get the word to 'em. But might I remind all of you that we ain't *got* 'em? And we got no idea where they are around here or how the hell to find 'em?"

IV:
A SUMMONS FROM THE DARK

"Okay, girls, where are you at?" Murphy's voice came, friendly and fatherly sounding with a medium brogue through the ship's general public address system. "This is yer old friend Captain Murphy here, and after ye pulled that neat disappearin' trick the folks here they decided to make a deal. You can't stay hid forever in any case. What if one of them wee ones was to decide to get born while nobody could see? No doctors, no midwives, no nothin' around to make sure the wee ones don't croak and the mother don't bleed to death. Now, you know you can trust the old captain. They're gonna let us go. Take us down where we was goin' in the first place. All of us, fast, in one of their comfy shuttles. Now, I know you can hear me. God knows everybody else can. We're in one of the ship's lounges right now and we'll stay there. All the maps on the walls will blink showin' where we are, and they all show where *you* are, so just come on down. I swear this is on the up-and-up. They just want to be rid of us."

He switched off the PA and settled back in his chair, a pint of synthetic dark ale in one hand. He took a swig, and the foam seemed to crust on his upper lip.

"You think they'll buy it? That they'll trust you?" Lieutenant Commander Mohr asked him, more than a little worried. Murphy had the feeling that the security officer wasn't nearly as confident of the inviolability of his secret computers and files as he made out he was.

"Well, they'll probably think about it for a bit," Murphy replied, "but, then, one of them baby contractions will nip 'em in the tummy and they'll get real tired out real fast and start thinkin' it over. I expect they'll eventually come here just to check it out before they show themselves, but, yes, if we're straight with them, then they'll be straight with us. I'm pretty sure of that."

Mohr nodded. "I hope you're right. And I really do want them off this ship, all three and you, as fast as is practical. In fact, the Admiralty itself pretty well ordered it. As soon as we insure that they're in good shape, I'm packing you all off with one of my best pilots and Sergeant Maslovic as company. They'll get you down to Barnum's World all right. After that, it's up to you."

"I have a feelin' you may have some problems once they're down there, at least in keepin' 'em in view, but we'll see," Murphy told him. "I'm well out of this, I think. At least their delivery will net me enough to get me to a junkyard planet like Sepuchus where I can put together another ship. Maybe a wee bit faster one."

"No wonder your ship's so banged up! You bought it at salvage?"

"Well, I bought the hulk at salvage, and the rest of the parts bit by bit. It's actually quite practical, you see. Cheap but serviceable, I can repair it with standardized parts most anywhere if need be, and nobody pays much attention to rustbuckets like that. Beats me why you even bothered to haul me in this time. Pickin's must be slim."

Mohr shrugged. "It's less that than the principle of the thing. We let you get away with it, suddenly everybody tries and we wind up in a series of mini wars just to keep operating. And I have to tell you, Murphy, that pirates and privateers are multiplying like cockroaches. Things are getting worse and worse. It's all breaking down, and one day it's going to be victims and prey and then nothing much at all. You can see it coming."

"Perhaps. I think we're better'n that," the old captain told him. "Me, I think it's about time this nasty little system fell apart so it could be replaced with something better, something that works. We got thirty, forty colonies that could be self-sufficient in food and a lot of supplies if they could kick the habit of dependin' on other worlds for things and start doin' more of it themselves. So long as they think of themselves as colonies, though, they're gonna be stuck, and eventually every pig will sink into the mud and drown. No, Commander, we got to stop this whole colonial stuff. It's time for the kids to realize they grew up."

"You're talking about anarchy."

"I'm talkin' about independence! We change or we die. That's the way it's always been."

"Then who protects these new independent worlds from the ruthless killers who'll sweep in the moment there's no navy to at least threaten them?"

"They protect themselves! They do it or they die! Faced with that, they'll protect themselves, believe you me. And it may cost a world or two. They have to see that they got no choice but to fight for their own. It's tough, but that's the way of it."

"Pretty ruthless, Murphy. You're talking about possibly millions of innocent lives."

"That may be true, but you just said it yourself. It's breakin' down, it is. It can't be held and your big ships can't defend the whole of it. They learn to do it, or they die fast and messy or slow and messier. They'll learn." He looked at the clock and changed his tone.

"I think it's time I whisper more sweet nothin's to me darlin's," he sighed, and turned towards the intercom.

"C'mon, me sweet darlin's. Can't keep the nice folk here waitin'. Besides, I don't know about you, but I'm more'n ready to blow this joint and get back to some free land. I'm gettin' kinda bored just sittin' here and waitin', and if we miss our stop, well, then, we might be stuck on this tub for a long, long time."

He paused for a moment. "Anything?"

"No," Mohr sighed. "I think—*what the hell?*"

He was looking over Murphy's shoulder at a data screen, and suddenly the screen had gone black. Now, in it, appeared shimmering almost cartoon-like outlines of the three missing girls. With just the outlines and an otherwise blank background, it was impossible to figure out where they were.

"Well, well! How are you, darlin's?" Murphy beamed.

"How do we know this ain't no trick?" came an eerie set of voices, all three speaking in perfect unison.

"Oh, c'mon. I know it's not, but think about it. You got them over a barrel, darlin's. They want you off, and me with you. What's the choice? I mean, you can stay like ye are, whatever that is, and then what? The wee ones are born and there's either messy problems or ye ain't gonna be thinkin' 'bout hidin' out nohow. They ain't gonna kill you, neither. They don't know what'd happen to their pretty ship if they tried. So come on up, get somethin' here to eat and drink, take a rest and get a shower and some clean clothes, and then we'll be off."

"In your ship?"

"Well, no, but don't let that worry you none. I ain't gonna lose as much as it seems. They'll take us on one of their small ships, nice and comfy and much faster than I could do it. And once down, do you really care about them?"

The girls seemed to be thinking it over, or, more correctly, the collective mind seemed to mull over the choices. The trouble was, Murphy reflected, even all three of them together couldn't get a deep thought and haul it out if it took three days. The problem was, were he in their position, he doubted if he would trust any of them, least of all him, to do more than dissect them to see how they did their little trick.

Finally, they seemed to come up with some sort of risky compromise, which was, after all, the best they could do in any event.

"Cap'n Murphy?"

"I'm here, darlin's."

"You tell 'em to get that little ship ready now. You tell 'em we leave *now*. You and us."

"Well, darlin's, we're more than a wee bit out of the neighborhood yet. It'd still be a long flight, and they're gonna hav'ta drive 'cause I couldn't handle a jobbie like that. Too fancy for an old trader like me. And they ain't gonna let it go unless they got some folks aboard to make sure it stays in their hands and comes back. Now, that's only reasonable."

"No! Just you and us!"

"I told you. The ship won't even listen to me, and, besides, the laws, even on Barnum's World, require somebody real to be in charge when it docks. There'll be four of us and two of them. That's not unreasonable. And I'll be makin' sure they don't do no double-crossin'."

They were silent again for a moment, but he felt better now. They weren't thinking about not going anymore, only making the safest deal. Finally they answered, "All right, but just one of them."

"They say two. That's not very many considerin' how many they got on this big bugger. They need one to pilot, one to deal with the folks on Barnum's World to make sure they allow us to come down. I been there many a time, girls. Just me, or just us, we might talk 'em into it, but with a navy shuttle we'll need somebody with permissions and such. They ain't that trustin' of the navy, you see."

He realized that this made very little sense, but if it sounded reasonable and within their control, they might go for it.

"But we go now." It wasn't a question.

"If we must, yes. It'll take longer and be less comfy, but we can go now. Let me ask the folks here." He turned and looked at Mohr, who nodded. "Twenty minutes. We'll use number twenty-four. It's got its own gate drive but is also fitted out as a lifeboat, so it has basic supplies and such. It should do. Shall I alert the crew?"

"By all means." Murphy turned back to the intercom. "Okay, darlin's, ye drive a hard bargain but they're buyin' it. The man here's callin' his folks now. The problem is, I don't know where *you* are so I don't know how to tell you to get down there."

"We can get there," the girls replied. "The spirit of the ship will guide us."

The spirit of the ship? Suddenly he realized that they meant the central computer that was running just about the whole show. To them, it was just another person, albeit a supernatural one, whose mind they were partly controlling. *All those tests and practices to get a damned pilot's license and these little girls do it by ordering the disembodied voice in the heavens. Jesus!*

Mohr came back into the room and looked over at him. "You want to come with me? I'll take you down there. I'm having a real argument with the captain and the exec over this, but short of risking the entire ship I don't see any other way but this. Maslovic's on his way as well, and I've alerted Lieutenant Chung, one of our best fighter pilots from the destroyer *Agrippa* to take her kit and proceed to the shuttle. She's been briefed and knows the situation if not the whole score. Best if as few of the crew as possible ever know the kind of power these girls showed."

Murphy nodded. "I see. Gonna be hard to keep it silent, though, I think. You better watch it with this ship's command and control computer, too, Commander. You don't know what thoughts them little darlin's put in its metaphysical head."

"I'm well aware of that," Mohr assured him. "But there shouldn't be any problem if we keep our end of the bargain, and I fully intend to do so. Good luck, Captain. And if you find out anything valuable about the people behind all this, there's a great deal of reward potential. You remember that."

"I kind of think that, havin' seen what these little girls can do, I'm best off mindin' me own business, Commander. And mindin' it as far away from Barnum's World and Tara Hibernius as well as I can. This is a kind of power I'd rather not think much on, or for long. If these girls can do *this*, imagine what the folks behind 'em, the ones with the big brains, can do! No, I think this is time to mind me own business."

The security chief shrugged. "Suit yourself. It's my duty to find out how to stop this sort of thing from happening to us again, and maybe whether or not it's a part of something nastier that we should know about.

Maybe it's not. Well and good if not, but that's what I'm supposed to do. It's why I'm here." He put out a hand and Murphy took it and shook it.

"Well, good luck, Commander. I don't know which one of us is goin' into the worst situation," Murphy replied. "But at least I'm goin' someplace."

Finding Shuttle 24 was not all that difficult, but it did take some time to get to on the vast frigate.

As Mohr said, the shuttles did double duty as emergency lifeboats, and because of that they were laid out like lifeboats along every other deck from top to bottom and from stem to stern, each with an airlock entrance and a separate small launch bay. Each was angled slightly, so that it needed only the emergency code or a pilot to shoot it out at high velocity into space, whereupon it could be either piloted by the human aboard or go on automatic if in lifeboat mode. Mohr had not been lying when he said that a pilot was needed if they were to get to Barnum's World; on automatic, it would simply head for the nearest inhabited world, and if no such world were in its range, it would head for the nearest stable wormgate and go through it and go through the procedure again. If more than half the supplies were used up, it would put everyone aboard into a cryogenic state whether they wanted to be or not and continue on, possibly forever, certainly until it found something in its programming.

With a pilot aboard it became a shuttle. The pilot generally brought a detailed flight plan from the central computer with him or her and simply inserted it, adjusting only as circumstances required. In this case, though, they hadn't trusted the computers aboard the frigate to do a solid plan, and so the pilot would have to complete it on the shuttle and make daily adjustments. From this point, Barnum's World required two jumps and would be about eighty hours subjective time at the highest speed the shuttle was capable of making. The larger ships weren't likely to follow at that rate; they would be a week or more behind at full throttle. This was going to be a long time with the three witches, subject to their powers and whims.

When Murphy finally got to the bay, the outer lock was open and lit up from within. He had no idea who had made it and who hadn't, but he was kind of hoping to be the last one inside.

He wasn't. Maslovic was there, in a new, clean uniform and looking more official, but that was it, or so it seemed. He came to near attention when Murphy entered, a marked difference from the way he'd greeted them as head of the boarding party when they'd been taken aboard not all that long ago.

"At ease, Sergeant. I'm nobody's captain here. Nobody else here yet?"

"No, sir. At least so far as I know. The pilot is on her way and should be here any minute. As for the other passengers . . . Well, I hope they'll let us know because we certainly can't leave without them!"

"Well, we could, but it would make your navy pretty unhappy, and I doubt if even me girls would like it after they finished playin' their games. They could have them babies any time now, and I don't think any of 'em wants to have 'em on board your big, antiseptic ship."

He looked around the shuttle and nodded approvingly to himself. "The bunks should be more than adequate, and there's decent toilet facilities I see." He moved from the aft compartment to the center and found a comfortable middle room, as it were, with a padded leatherette bench seat going completely around the walls and breaking only for the fore and aft doorways, all flanking a rather cleverly designed segmented table with inserts that could be raised, lowered, tilted, inverted, and moved every which way. More bunks of a more basic sort could be strung from the ceiling. Cut into the side bulkheads, one side mirroring the other, were compartments that clearly slid back.

"Serving bays," the sergeant told him. "We'll get our food there and drink through there. It's mostly made from various wastes using a separate computer-controlled device with matter to energy to matter conversion, but the food it produces is nearly identical to what we get in the galleys and is really not that bad. Drinks are from those inserts there. You simply say what you want and it will make it for you. There's a great deal of recycling here, but some loss each turn, which is why there is a limit to how long we can go. Still, we're set for weeks here if need be, and we don't need nearly that long."

Murphy nodded. "I think it best we don't mention the process and origins of the food and drink, Sergeant. Let's let it just be magic, all right?"

The marine froze for a moment, not quite understanding what the old man was saying, and then realized the context. "Oh, yes, sir. I see. Yes, we want everyone to be happy and relaxed here."

Murphy smiled. "I think we might just get along here for the duration, Sergeant. So, do you know this pilot?"

"Yes, sir. Picked her myself out of the group. *Very* skilled. When we have things we must do with some, er, *delicacy*, she's who we pick. I'm not sure *anybody's* ready for this trio of yours, but if anybody is, Lieutenant Chung would be. She's had some ground experience, mostly in finding and selecting the best things we need for repairs and replacements, but she shouldn't be thrown by a different sort of culture, no slight intended, sir."

"None taken. Your people have gone a different way than most, but I suppose it works. You're still basically extortionists, but it's an elegant sort of extortion, the kind that even you think is a public service. I suppose I can live with that. I deal mostly with ones who just pick it up by choice or as a job of opportunity."

"So our protection is extortion while your smuggling is just unrestrained business. That right?"

"That's about it, laddie. But the big difference is that to you this is the end, the purpose of things, while to me the gatherin' of money and whatever it brings is just the means to an end. You'll never even understand the sort of dreams we mortal folk have."

"Just because we're built differently and to different purposes doesn't mean we can't understand such things," the sergeant noted.

Murphy gave a low chuckle and muttered to himself, "Aye. I had a neutered dog once."

"Sir?"

"Never mind. Nothin' of importance. But where is— *ah!* Looks like our pilot has arrived."

Lieutenant Chung was smaller and thinner by far than Maslovic or any of the others Murphy had seen aboard. Not that she had a figure; she reminded Murphy less of a warrior caste than of a girl permanently frozen before reaching puberty, and, like all the others, she was hairless. But if most of the navy types were built for weight lifting and fighting, the pilot class were acrobats, built for lightning-fast action and reaction, with perfect balance and genetically heightened senses, all the better to meld with their machines almost as if one and the same. He also suspected she wasn't as helpless as her tiny form suggested. That same lightning quickness and superior senses made for ideal experts in the martial arts.

Her voice, too, was high and seemed more a child's voice, yet the tone and confidence it projected suggested a lot of experience.

The sergeant came to attention but did not salute. You didn't salute inside when on a mission. He towered over her; Murphy figured that three or four of the pilots could be made out of the protoplasm in that tough marine. Still, he was properly and professionally deferential. She was, after all, an officer.

"Stand easy, Sergeant," she said crisply, putting down her own kit. "Is everyone here?"

"No, sir. The three passengers have yet to arrive," Maslovic told her.

She nodded. "Very well. I'll get everything prepped up front. Then we'll wait. They'll either show up or they won't."

The pilot went forward to the flight deck and began going through the preflight sequence. The deck had two large chairs, either one of which could have swallowed her, and a complex set of instruments, screens, and control pads. Each chair also had a headset of light mesh that would conform itself to just about any size head. While now attached to the seat back, it actually came off and was normally worn much like a cap. Chung reached up, brought it down, examined it closely, then put it on and sat back in the chair, eyes closed, hands pressed together in a fashion that made it look as if she were praying.

She remained like this for a couple of minutes, and then, without her moving an apparent muscle, the interior lights blinked and there was a sense of low vibration. In front of her, the previously inert and rather featureless console came to life, the lights and screens now actively showing data, diagrams, lines of coded numbers, and all sorts of other information that was meaningless even to an experienced pilot like Murphy. Slowly, methodically, things went on and off throughout the shuttle, from air vents to the food server controls and doors, the lights and hatches.

Murphy understood the drill and said, "Well, she seems in good shape. All we need are passengers."

Maslovic started for a moment, then remembered that the old man, for all his looks and manners, was in fact a licensed interstellar pilot himself. "Could you fly her in a pinch?"

"Oh, probably, but I wouldn't know what half the stuff was. Probably dump fuel in the coffee dispenser and go orbital upside down and backwards after putting us all into cryogenic suspension accidentally. And, of course, it wouldn't recognize me in any event. No, I take 'em out of orbit, feed 'em the navigation data, stick 'em on autopilot and sit around until we get there. The likes of an old freighter, it ain't that hard. This, now—*this* is a speedster. I got to say I don't feel comfortable in ships that are most definitely smarter than I am."

Maslovic looked around at the food service ports. "Would you like something while we wait? Who knows how long it's going to be before the others arrive?"

"I don't think they have the recipe in there for what I need this trip," the old captain responded. "Unless that thing can dispense a good, fillin' dark ale that would feel comfy in an Irishman's gut, I guess I'll pass for now."

Maslovic shrugged. "Let's see." He turned and said to the console, "Ale, seven percent, malt brewed, very dark."

There was a tinny kind of whistling sound from the port, and then a bell sounded and the small drink compartment door slid back. Inside was a large molded cup with a bubble top on it. The sergeant took it out and handed it to Murphy, who looked at the drink suspiciously. He removed the lid, since they had gravity and no potential motion problems, sniffed it, then sipped it. There was foam on the top. Surprised at what he tasted, he gave an approving nod and quite literally downed the entire cup in one continuous series of swallows.

Maslovic was impressed, not so much by the drink as by the manner. You had to have long practice to gulp down a heavy brew like that.

"Not bad at all," the old captain said approvingly. "Where the devil did they get that recipe? I've had better, but it's pretty good."

"We have data and formulas for just about every known cuisine, food and drink both, in the big ship, and this is just a subset. We ourselves don't generally eat or drink too much exotic, but the ability is there. We have to cater to guests now and then, and we've also found that the formulas are often quite welcome on some of the colonial worlds. It breaks the ice, I think the old term is."

"Indeed it does! The only thing that it needs is to understand that you drink ale in liters, not in dainty little cups!"

"Well, I doubt if those kinds of liter-or-more vessels would fit in there, but you have a nearly unlimited supply so it's all the same, isn't it?"

"Not quite, laddie, but it'll do. Damn! Wonder where in the world them girls are. I hope they didn't get lost or decide to get into more trouble instead of gettin' outta here. They *couldn't* have been much farther away than I was!"

There was the sudden sound of girlish laughter in the air, both right there and yet as if from afar, raising the hairs on the back of Murphy's neck. As he stiffened and tried to look around, the main hatch connecting the shuttle to the frigate closed and locked with a hissing sound, and then the outer lock did the same. Murphy looked back through the aft hatch, past the bedroom area, and saw that the main door was now closed and sealed and had a red light flashing on top of it. The light steadied after a moment, and there was a second loud hissing sound, like air brakes being applied. The air quite clearly was being pumped out of the lock.

"I think our guests have arrived," Sergeant Maslovic commented dryly.

Murphy looked around. "Girls? That you? C'mon, now! Your old captain's got an old man's heart. He can't take but so much of this spooky business! Come! Give me a hug I can see and let's be off this cold place!"

He didn't get the hug, although he wasn't sure if he'd feel comfortable getting one from some unseen presence anyway. He did get more ghostly giggles, and it was Maslovic, who seemed far less nervous than the old captain, who said to thin air, "Lieutenant, our guests have arrived. I believe they want us to depart before they'll show themselves and things get back to normal."

"Buckle in or hold on," the voice of the pilot came at them over the intercom. "Five . . . four . . . three . . . two . . . one . . . *Launch*!"

Murphy and the sergeant both hoped that the girls were holding on as well, as the ship suddenly shot forward and away from the big frigate like a cannonball with too much powder, pushing them back and to the side. Murphy's thankfully empty cup of ale sped off the table and hit the wall just to the left of the aft hatch. They both could feel the thrust pinning them against the bulkhead. Then, suddenly, the acceleration cut off, and they had the rapid and uneasy feeling of weightlessness.

"Engaging gravitational field at slowly rising rate to fifty percent of norm," the pilot announced, and almost immediately they could feel weight returning to them, although not at the level that it had been before. Assuming the girls hadn't all just gone into labor at the shock of the launch, though, it would be a lot easier on them for the rest of the run to be at half weight, and might minimize some potential complications. Still, the pilot had taken a risk with that launch.

Murphy let out a deep breath and rubbed the back of his neck for a moment. The launch was surprise enough, and he hadn't been too gentle in meeting that bulkhead because of it. He was also finding it harder to get used to the sudden half gravity than he should have. Maybe it was the ale, he told himself, or maybe he was just getting old after all.

"Girls! You all right?" he called out as soon as he got his wits back. "C'mon, girls! Show yourselves! We got a long way to go here, and we don't want any mishaps!"

For a while it seemed as if nothing happened, and Murphy grew worried that perhaps they hadn't been in the room, or, if they had, that they'd been knocked about too badly by the takeoff. He hoped not. It wouldn't only be messy, it would make them madder than hell.

"Girls?" he called out, growing suddenly worried.

Maslovic gestured to the center table in the lounge with his head and eyes, and Murphy looked and saw what the sergeant had noticed.

Slowly, deliberately, somebody was using some kind of paint or marker to draw a crude design on that shiny clean tabletop.

At first it was more or less a closed circle, and then inside of it a five-pointed star with some odd symbols that looked mostly like swashes inside the outer portion between each star point.

Murphy and Maslovic both stared hard now, not at the design but inside it, and above it, and, to their mutual surprise, they could actually see the three witches, sort of. They seemed to flicker in and out, and parts of them flashed here and there. Finally, though, they attained a more permanent solidity, and the two men could hear them chanting in some unknown tongue.

They looked bedraggled and downright filthy, their hair in tangles, their bodies stained with not only whatever they'd used to paint themselves a day or so earlier but also grease and all sorts of other stuff. There were some fresh scrapes, too, and the red-haired one had a cut on her leg that was still bleeding slightly. Others had small cuts and scratches all over that had healed, and were in a few cases already beginning to bruise.

They also stank of piss and shit and body odors and more. Clearly they hadn't cleaned themselves up in any way since they'd gone missing, and it was going to make them tough company unless they decided to do so on their own here.

Now all three were standing within the ancient symbol, eyes closed, as the chant came to a rhythmic but definite end.

It was as if they were suddenly out of a trance and back to normal. They let go holding hands, opened their eyes, and looked around. *"Ew!* Something *stinks!"* said the red-headed Irish O'Brian, her nose up and contorting her face.

"You said it," Mary Margaret, the brown-haired one, agreed. Brigit, the blonde, simply said, *"Bleah!"* in a tone that left no doubt as to her meaning.

"Ah, girls! So happy to see you again!" Murphy said effusively. "But I'm afraid that the stench you're smellin' is your own ordinarily sweet selves."

Mary Margaret looked at each of her companions and then at as much of herself as she could see. "Oh my *gawd!"* she exclaimed.

"Jeez!" Irish chimed in. "We need *baths,* and *bad!"*

"No baths here, darlin's," Murphy told them, "but there's a shower here and a place to clean up and make yourselves presentable again. If you wanted more you shoulda come in while we was still on the big ship, but this is what you asked."

"Shit! How was *we* to know?" Irish O'Brian responded. "Well, look, if you two can help us down off this thing, at least we can *try* and clean up!"

The sergeant got to his feet. "Allow me," he said pleasantly. In turn, each of the trio came towards him and he picked them up like they weighed nothing at all and put them down on the deck.

"Wow! Feels like I don't weigh nothin a-tall," Mary Margaret commented, sort of stomping up and down with her bare feet on the deck. "Neat!"

"It'll be more comfortable this way," Murphy assured them. "Now, look, I'll show you where the toilet is, and you go back there and get clean and nice, and then we'll all sit here and have somethin' to eat and talk a bit. We got a long while to go to get to Barnum's World yet. Three days most likely. No rush."

For him, though, they couldn't get there fast enough.

It did not bother either of the military people aboard that the three girls wore just about nothing on the trip, but it made Murphy uncomfortable and he couldn't even say why. Certainly he wasn't sexually attracted to them; even if they weren't so hugely pregnant, he found himself more frightened of them than anything else, something he hadn't even thought about before being intercepted by the navy. Possibly it was that demonstration of power they'd done; but, he reflected, it was more like being uncomfortable because he felt helpless and surrounded by three idiots with loaded weapons.

Interestingly, though, they barely remembered the experience, and could not explain how they'd done what they'd done. It did not, however, bother them much.

Ignorance was true bliss sometimes, even when you didn't know that what you did was so remarkable.

At least with all that time to Barnum's World they didn't have much to do but eat, sleep, and talk. It was tough to get them to stay on that or any subject for long, but slowly Maslovic began getting some information from them that seemed useful, and Murphy got more than he thought was healthy for him. There was, for example, the eerie feeling in his gut that, even in this small shuttle, what everyone was saying and doing was somehow being monitored and recorded and analyzed. Not by the navy—he expected that, and did not fear it one bit. No, by someone or something else, the ones behind this strangeness.

It's them damned medals, he decided. *I don't care if they're worth a fortune or what, there's something unnatural about 'em.*

They had allowed the trio to eat, and they'd had really massive appetites, although for some combinations that not even Murphy could tolerate thinking hard about, and then they'd slept for ten solid hours each. They seemed to sleep a lot, which Murphy put down to their condition. He was most frightened that one or more of the young women would decide to have her kid then and there. He knew the two military people weren't prepared for such a thing, and he was damned sure *he* wasn't.

It was easiest when one or another of them would come to the lounge leaving the other two still asleep. This happened quite a lot after that initial sleep-off, although if it was the blonde-haired Moran, you couldn't get a full sentence out of her if you tried. O'Brian never stopped talking, which was quite typical of people who had little to say, and McBride seemed the most normal of the bunch although no brighter, willing to engage in small talk or not as needed. She also seemed the most curious about the navy pair, which allowed for a give-and-take exchange of information. Over a few sessions, Maslovic in particular was able to get pretty direct with the brown-haired self-described witch.

"Where'd you learn to do that magic spell that caused the vanishing trick?" he asked her casually as she ate. Murphy sat away from them, curious but not exactly motivated to join in.

"Tip told us how," McBride responded with that slightly off-kilter view of conversation they all shared and which had nearly driven the senior officers of the *Thermopylae* nuts.

"Tip? Who's Tip? A kind of spirit?"

She nodded, munching on a potato pancake and sipping very dark tea mixed half and half with cream and sugar. "Tip can't do things in our plane without us, we can't do nothin' neat here without him and his friends givin' us the power and all."

"Tip talks only to you, then? Not to Moran or O'Brian?"

"See? There y'go again! Why do you and the driver up there always use only the family names? Don't you have another name?"

"What? You mean like you?"

She nodded. "Yeah, I mean, I got *three* names, and only one isn't just me. And there's Brigit Maureen and then there's Colleen Megan, and *she* even has a name all her own that everybody uses instead of them."

"Irish, you mean? Why do you need all those names?"

She shrugged. "'Cause I guess there's only so many names and we don't want to have nobody else's, that's why. Don't always work even then. I mean, I can't *count* the number of Mary Margarets back home. I always thought I wanted me own name, like Irish done, only I never come up with none I really liked."

"We have ranks and we have numbers," the sergeant explained. "The numbers are never the same so we can always be ourselves. The rank changes if we do a good job, but the number is unique. The number's all we really need, but it's just too much of a mouthful to say, particularly when you're in a hurry. Easier to say 'Sarge,' or, if there's more than one of my rank, 'Maslovic,' instead of, oh, 'Hurry up, M2174-34K77-41CK!' See what I mean?"

She laughed. "That's funny. But we gets our family names from our das. When we was goin' 'round your big ship, we saw lots of you folks with none of them fancy if borin' clothes on, and you don't have no das or mums. How could you?" She sighed. "I'll be glad when the wee one comes out and I can wear pretty clothes again."

She was starting to drift away from the thread, so he brought it back.

"Oh, we have parents, if that's what you mean. We just don't know who they are. But the family name of my parents is Maslovic, which is why the name's there. Some of my looks, and I guess more, come from them. I've met other Maslovics aboard and we kind of look similar."

"But how *can* you have close family when you ain't got no dicks or wombs? Don't make no sense."

"It's done by doctors and machines," he told her. "It's less dangerous and completely controlled, so there's little chance of us not coming out right."

"And a damn sight less fun, seems t'me," she muttered, finishing her food.

Murphy had always thought that as well, like the military types were more machines than humans, unable to feel the same emotions as "normal" people. Now he still wasn't sure what their lives were like internally, but he was beginning to wonder if others like the girls weren't just as much manufactured to somebody's order and requirements.

Hell, it almost made you paranoid thinking that maybe somebody actually made *you*, too, and he wasn't thinking about God when that awful idea crept into his mind.

Maslovic had no such worries. He and Chung not only knew that they were designed, they felt great comfort in that. It was who or what was perverting the same technology that had them worried here.

"You were telling us about Tip," the sergeant said, as breezy and conversational as if he were just killing time.

"Yeah, well, what's to tell?" she responded. "I mean, like, Tip is just *Tip*, that's all."

The security officer looked around. "Well, now, let's see. Is he some sort of invisible entity? Some kind of creature who speaks only to you?"

She giggled. "Of course not, silly! Little kids got make-believe little friends. Tip's different. We're kinda like, married, in a way. Y'know, like Irish's got Tad and Brigit's got Tod."

"So there are three of them? And where are they if not in the air like spirits of old? Inside your body?"

"This is gettin' borin', it is. I don't wanta talk about this no more right now. I'm just so *tired*. I think maybe I should sleep some more. How much longer to this world you're takin' us to?"

"We're better than halfway there," Maslovic assured her. "Not much longer now."

But by this time Mary Margaret McBride had forgotten even the question, and she was on her feet and making her way back aft to the bunks.

When she'd gone, Maslovic looked over at Murphy. "You're the expert on these people," he said. "Is she crazy?"

"Most probably, although who's to say if it's them

or us?" the old captain retorted. "Still and all, I think there's somethin' to it. I been goin' nuts starin' at them jewels the girls got round their necks. They're not just good-lookin' gems cut right, they're more than that. I seen their like before. Not for real, I don't think, but in pictures and such. Some museums and real rich folk got 'em. Them's Magi stones. The livin' gems said to come from the legendary Three Kings."

That got the sergeant's interest. "Indeed? Exotic stones from—where?"

"The Three Kings, man! Everybody's heard of the Three Kings. They may not be real, or if they are they're almost certainly not what folks think they are, but they're the stuff of legend, just like the three originals. Of course, you probably ain't heard of them, either."

"Not particularly. I wish I had my complete reference databases handy, though. I hate being the last to know when somebody throws in a curve."

"Well, I can only tell you what everybody seems to know. Three planets around some gigantic ringed star, supposedly discovered during the Age of Exploration a couple hundred years ago by one of the missionary monks who was half man and half scouting ship. Sent back the news of great treasure and miraculous living and all that stuff, and he said there was lots of evidence of advanced alien life. Named 'em after the three kings who brought gifts to the baby Jesus. Said anybody who could get there and keep clear of the snake would find riches beyond compare."

"Pardon? The what?"

"The snake, man! Serpent. The incarnation of the Beast who got humanity to sin and heaped that sin upon all its descendants. The devil, if you will. The sort these three girls claim to be their god or whatever."

"Interesting. There are so many mythic religions

I admit I know little of any. Doesn't seem relevant unless it's a key to solving something practical. Still, it sounds like I could do with some information on this sect."

"'Sect' he calls it!" Murphy muttered, genuinely appalled at the dismissal. "Faith of me fathers it is, boy. You navy boys know Vaticanus and its influence and orders, I think."

"Ah! *That* one! I know a little. Enough, I think. Sorry, no offense meant. It's just not in our nature to take seriously old men in the sky and stuff like that. Okay, so this missionary and scout reported riches on three worlds, lots of powerful aliens, and so forth. Why didn't somebody follow up and see if anything was really there instead of making it some kind of fairy tale?"

"Aye, that's the rub. The coordinates for stabilizing wormgates were jumbled. Made no sense. And only part of the detailed information came through. Enough to make it a riddle, not enough for even the best minds and computers and all to solve. And the old boy was never heard from again."

"So now we have cults like this one the girls belong to because of some lost colonial coordinates? Amazing!"

Murphy shook his head from side to side. "No, it ain't that simple, y'see. Somebody a long time ago thought they solved the riddle and went off in one of them big scientific and speculative expeditions. Fancy ship, fancy equipment, well heeled. Nobody heard from it until after the Great Silence. Then, one day, it suddenly reappeared from someplace in the Draco Sector. The Dragon, another of the devil's disguises. The whole ship was in perfect shape, but there wasn't anybody aboard and all the data records had been wiped clean."

"You mean erased?"

"Or maybe just fried. Who knows? But it had pictures of some pretty worlds, a bunch of really oddball little mechanical thingies, some sort of artifacts of alien design and unknown purpose and origin, and it had a stash of them gems. The very gems like the ones around these three girls' pretty necks."

Maslovic gave a soft, low whistle. "And did they later find more of them?"

"Oh, 'twas said that somebody did, and that a few more fell into the hands of a big-time evangelist—a *protestant* one at that! And he went off chasin' 'em a few decades ago and they never heard from *him* no more, neither. Which leaves us with just the hundred or so from that original mystery ship, unless there's ones nobody knows about. Rare, beautiful, and among the most expensive gems in the known universe. And three of 'em seem to have wound up around our darlin's pretty necks."

"You're sure they're real and not fakes? Imitations? I imagine there's a lot of *those* considering the legends and the rarity."

Murphy nodded. "Oh, tons I'm sure. But 'tis said you always can tell a fake one from a real one. Not just the quality, but the effect."

"The what?"

"The effect. 'Tis said that when you look into 'em you get visions and weird feelin's and all. Nothin' specific, mind. And eventually you get an overload and somethin' scares you. Somethin' that lives inside the gems or somethin' like that. In any case, no fake has *that*!"

Maslovic leaned back and thought a moment. "Tad, Tod, and Tip. Three demons in three gems. If they *are* real, then if you or I stare into one, we should meet someone, eh?"

"*You* meet 'em. I'm perfectly content to be ignorant this time," said Murphy.

✦   ✦   ✦

Irish O'Brian never seemed any smarter than the other two, just far more suspicious of everything and everybody. She also wasn't all that happy to hear how much Mary Margaret had told them just sitting around, although she seemed more disgusted than surprised.

"Why does it bother you that we talk to the others?" Maslovic asked her in that same friendly conversational tone he'd used so successfully on the other.

"It just *does*, that's all," O'Brian responded. "We're a team. A sisterhood. It's not good that we blab about to strangers without the rest of us bein' there, so to speak."

"What're we gonna do, lass? Trick ye into the secrets of the universe or somethin'?" Murphy put in. "We're just as bored as everybody else. You always was friendly to me, so why not to them, too? It's all goin' your way."

She looked over at the sergeant with a look of distrust. "I dunno, Cap. I just don't trust 'em no farther than I can throw 'em, that's all. They ain't like us, y'know. They'd probably get along just fine with the folks back home. If them stuffed brains could figure out a way to have kids without sex they'd jump on it. But to *really* do it . . . You ain't real human if you don't got no sex."

"I can't know how different we are, really," Maslovic admitted. "I've never been somebody like you or the captain, so how can I? But I *feel* human."

"Well, you ain't. Got to be cold inside with your balls chopped off and all. And that weird one up front. Don't she never *move*?"

"Lieutenant Chung's the pilot. She monitors everything on the ship and gets us safely where we're going," the sergeant explained. "To do that best, she actually plugs in and becomes part of the ship. In a way, we're kind of riding inside her now."

O'Brien made an ugly face. "*Ugh!* That's what I mean. You don't know what's human and what's machine. It's all the same to you 'cause you don't feel inside. Not like people. I mean, the captain here, he never was connected up like that to his ship."

"That's true enough," Murphy responded. "But that's 'cause I never got the implants in me head to make it all work. If I had one big, fancy ship with all the modern stuff I might'a done it, but them old junkers . . . Who'd want to become one o' *them*?"

O'Brian looked around the lounge from eye level to ceiling. "So can your pilot see us now? And hear us?"

"Absolutely," Maslovic told her.

"And in the back, too?"

"She's the ship, like I told you. She and the ship are one. You wouldn't want the gravity to go funny when you flush the toilet in the head, would you? Or have the air go bad, or any one of a million things that she can keep in her head and do something about because she's part of the ship? Space will never be anywhere that's really safe, you know. You're always one tiny thing wrong from death."

O'Brian shivered. "I don'na wan'ta think on it."

"Well, that's why she's doing what she's doing. So *we* don't have to think about it or worry about it. And, unlike some people who actually become permanently part of their ships, she can disconnect when we're in port and become a real person again."

"There are folks who make themselves into the machines?" Irish O'Brian was appalled at the thought. "They do it by *choice*?"

He nodded. "Many do. Particularly the ones who are scouts searching beyond anywhere we know for new worlds and new life. Not just navy people, although the big ship you were on, the one we came from, has *three* minds permanently a part of their system."

"Oh, my god! And you wonder why we don't like the way things are goin' here?"

The sergeant shrugged. "Who's 'we'? Your sisterhood? The religion you're serving? Just curious."

Irish O'Brian gave a sly smile. "Ah, but you'll not be gettin' me to speak more of *that*. None of your tricks there, if you please! We got our secrets, y'know."

"Okay, then, let's talk about something else." Maslovic seemed to be thinking a moment, as if deciding what to talk about. His eyes came to her neck after a bit, and he brightened and asked, "What's that gem around your neck? Or is that some kind of religious secret, too?"

O'Brian's hand went to the large gem and seemed to cover it from his gaze for a moment, then she relented. "It's a relic, y'might say. A kind of way of sayin' who and what we are, like them Holy Joes back home what think they got the direct word of God straight from Heaven to their holy book. They wear their crosses and their medals. We got ours."

"It's an excellent imitation of a Magi stone," the sergeant remarked, as if he'd heard of them before an hour or so previous and knew all about them.

"*Imitation!* I'll have you know this is the real thing! 'Twouldn't do to have no fake around *our* necks!"

Maslovic chuckled. "Now, come on. I don't doubt that you believe it's real, but everybody knows that there are only a few hundred of those in the whole known galaxy, and most of them are in the hands of museums, governments, and the very rich. How could you have a real one, let alone three, coming from a primitive world like Tara Hibernius?"

Her left hand went to the gem and held it up defiantly to him, still on the neck chain. "You see? It's *real*."

"Even *I* know that those things give off some kind of rays that affect people deep inside," the sergeant pressed. Murphy kept silent but decided to watch his back from now on around the military man; he was pretty damned good!

"You want to see if it's real? C'mon over here. I know you ain't got no feelin' for me tits, so come close and look straight into it! You don't hav'ta hold it, just get close and look inside! You'll see!"

"Maybe he won't," Murphy put in. "Even if it *is* a real one, how can a machine feel what them things are said to give off? Or is that nothin' but the blarney?"

Maslovic slid over very close to her and let her angle the gem towards him. It was quite impressive, more elaborate than any gemstone, real or artificial, that he'd ever seen or studied about. It was as large as a hen's egg, colored as if a translucent emerald with a center of some darker material substance that, when viewed from different angles, seemed to form, well . . .

"Can I hold it?" he asked her. "You can keep it on the necklace around your neck. I just want to feel it."

"Gettin' to ya, huh? All right, but mind your manners!"

He reached out and turned the sparkling emerald-colored gem so that its slightly flattened face was towards him and stared into the darker area.

The deep green exterior sparkled with each capture of the light and seemed to flash and move with every breath the girl took, or every slight movement his hand caused.

The darker area inside was also green, but a green so dense and deep it seemed like some sort of liquid, swirling and going down much farther than the gem itself was deep.

And in that dark area, pictures began to form.

Maslovic couldn't decide if those pictures were in fact real and emanating from the stone or somehow in his mind, caused by some sort of radiation from the stone, but they nonetheless seemed very real if also very surreal, as if actual shapes and places were being viewed through some dense liquid lens.

The images were strange, bizarre. Human figures twisted into grotesque shapes, creatures very nonhuman twisting and writhing and swarming, all superimposed against alien landscapes, distorted scenes of people and unknown animals in lush but unknown tropical bush; a swirling hell of intense storms and volcanic fire; and, finally, a barren, dark landscape with structures, structures clearly not in current use but rather the remnants of ancient cataclysm.

The sets of impressions never came fully into solid focus for all their sense of three dimensions and movement, nor did the various parts ever blend with one another, but rather continued changing in a constant series of superimpositions. It was endlessly fascinating, yet totally mystifying. Was he seeing something real in there, or perhaps many realities, or was this being dragged from his subconscious or, just as possible, from the nightmares of Irish O'Brian and perhaps even Patrick Murphy? He couldn't tell, but if they were from anyone's subconscious, then they were disturbing indeed, and if they showed some twisted realities, then it was more disturbing still.

Slowly he became aware that one of the images was not changing radically, but rather in distance and perspective only. It was the dark world of wreckage and the sense of death and gloom, and slowly, ever so slowly, the image was coming to the foreground as the point of view resolved on some sort of eerie cavern.

He felt himself pulled down towards the cavern, and then, just inside in the darkness, there was . . . *another*.

He let out a sharp, short cry and dropped the gem, which settled back against Irish O'Brian's cleavage, and he backed away. It took him several seconds to compose himself again, breathe normally, and regain complete control of himself. Captain Murphy was looking at him, curious and puzzled at one and the same time, but Irish O'Brian had a smirk on her face that was almost unbearable.

"So you met dear Tad, didn't you?" she asked with a sense of total satisfaction.

V:
OF MEN AND WOMEN AND MACHINES

"All right, lad, so just what did you see in there?" Murphy asked Maslovic when both were again alone in the lounge. "You looked like you saw your own death in that devil's thing."

Maslovic shook his head. "No, no. Not that. Something infinitely more disturbing, I think. The trouble is, I don't really know just *what* I saw. I can't explain it. *You* take a look in one next time and we can compare notes."

"No, I think not," the old captain responded. "Maybe I might have just for curiosity's sake, but after watchin' you, I ain't got no yen for that sort of thing. Makes me wonder why in hell them rich bastards pay so damn much for them things. Pay a fortune to be shocked and scared to death? I guess the rich are really different than you and me."

The sergeant nodded. "I can see the appeal, oddly enough. You just have to know where to look and sense when to look away. I don't know. Maybe even *that's* somebody's thrill. The pet demon in the gemstone. Nobody *else* would have one."

"Could be. But was it real?"

Maslovic thought a moment. "I've been trying to decide that. It's certainly real to the looker, as an experience, and I think it's possible that *part* of the experience, if you can call it that, is real. I'm going to have to get my datalink and see if it says anything about these Three Kings. Descriptions, maybe."

"Oh, I can tell you that. One's supposedly a kind of paradise, a Garden of Eden place, and one's a land of fire and water and mineral riches, and the third's a cold, dark place of mountains and caverns. That's all part of the legend and, I suspect, it's from the original scouting report."

"That's certainly close to where I was looking. But how is that possible? I mean, how could I *see* real worlds so remote we've never rediscovered them? And what of all the stuff superimposed on them? I'd love to get one of those things in the lab. Then at least I'd know if what I was looking at was a real, natural kind of gemstone or some kind of alien device that merely looked that way."

"Well, they say that nobody who looks into 'em sees the same thing, but they all see the Three Kings. Beyond that, the other images, them's personal. Sooner or later, though, everybody backs away with the absolute conviction that even as they're watchin' the show, somehow the show's watchin' *them*. I saw how you jumped. So did she. The difference is that she's the first one I ever heard of who wasn't scared of whoever or whatever was lookin' back. You get any idea of what the devil the thing looked like?"

"Not a bit. It was only a shadow. It was more like a meeting of minds that caused the reaction. I could sense that whatever was in that shadow could not only see me, it could look straight through me and into the deepest part of my mind. It was a sense of . . . oh, I don't know. Violation? Being unable to stop anybody from going where only you can go and maybe into parts of yourself you don't want to look at, which is why you put them there. Does that make any sense?"

"Kinda. Look up the term 'rape' sometime and you'll see a lot of the same feelin's and terms used. That's sexual, but there's a lot more to the act than just sex. Congratulations, Sergeant. I think you've just proved you're human after all."

"Perhaps. If nightmares are what make you human, then I guess that counts. But, the point is, we've proven two things. First, those gems are the genuine articles, and that raises as many new questions as it answers. Second, that, natural or artificial, they are some sort of communications medium. A two-way medium at that."

"Are you sure? That would make them machines of some kind in my book. Interesting."

"Not necessarily. You can create a primitive radio using quartz crystals. You can generate a mild current that is still sufficient to run some very small devices using the stored energy in a potato. No, they could still be either, and it really doesn't matter which. I now think that your legendary scout's signals were intercepted and interfered with by someone or something that did not want all the details of their existence known. They probably didn't know enough about us and our technology at that point, considering the sample they had, to react in time to keep all the knowledge from us, but it was enough. Later on, when the second expedition solved where it was

somehow and made it there, it was a different story.
By that point, whoever is out there had a fair cross
section of humans along with their data, both in their
minds and in their ship and computers, to learn quite
a lot. The second contact, that exploration ship, was
sent back. Sent back by whoever it is, with just
enough of those gems. They knew what would happen to them, where they would go, how they would
be used. Their captives or whatever could tell them
that."

"You mean they were spies. Remote control windows
to look at us."

Maslovic nodded. "And if they can also *transmit*
using those things, then they could learn an awful lot
fast and have unwitting agents tell them all that they
needed."

"*Witting* agents, more like, considerin' not only them
girls but also whoever is sendin' 'em to Barnum's
World."

"*Now*, yes. But how long ago did this legend start?
Centuries, you said."

"Seems like. I dunno for sure, but it's been around
longer than I have, and that's a fair amount of time.
Sounds like our aliens are pretty patient buggers,
though. Surely with that mind control stuff, they had
enough information on us ages ago to conquer us if
they wanted to."

"I don't know. Conquer might not be the right word.
Maybe they're just curious. Maybe they're toying with
us. The devil worship business indicates that they've
achieved a pretty sophisticated sense of humor as well
as a sense of how to utilize humans. Maybe there aren't
very many of them. Or maybe they don't know anything more about the Great Silence than we do and
think that whatever happened to our ancestors will be
coming for us and then for them. It would be useful

to keep us as a permanently monitored buffer race. We're only guessing, though, and those girls can't tell us. Whoever's behind them, though, is closer to us than to the alien masters, you're right about that much. Whether they're partners or surrogates for the watchers doesn't make much difference. The trouble is, if they're on Barnum's World, they're going to be a lot better positioned than we are, and they'll know us because now one of their remote masters knows *me*."

"I dunno where you're gettin' that 'us' business, if you include me in that," Murphy said. "I, for one, am willin' to let 'em play their silly games if their money's still good, and I think I'll be long dead before they start doin' whatever it is they're plannin' to do. Still and all, you got to figure that it ain't just you and your pilot that they know. Not now."

"Huh?"

"I wonder if they ever had the chance to poke into the innards of the most powerful military battle group left in this whole region? Maybe in all this side of the Great Silence? Three rovin' eyes plus access to that whole blasted ship's master computer of yours. Your nabbin' me with them three had to be a godsend for 'em, don't you think?"

The master of logic seemed suddenly dumbstruck by the enormity of Murphy's words and the implication of it all. "Of course! I was just too close to it to see it! Damn! They really *do* have it all, don't they?"

"Don't feel too bad," the old captain consoled. "You're a pretty bright lad who brung it this far. You just were born and raised in that navy factory. It's your mother, father, sister, brother, womb and probable grave. It's the most secure place you can think of in the whole damned galaxy. It takes an old scoundrel like me to pull you that last little bit, that's all."

"Yes, but they know *everything! Everything!* And

we—we know exactly nothing at all. Militarily, the only thing left for us is to take out ceremonial swords like the ancient warriors of Old Earth and rip our guts out."

Murphy shook his head slowly from side to side. "Nope, I don't think so, Sergeant. I don't think they're gonna let you or any of us off that easy. . . ."

She lay there in an almost fully reclined position, strapped in and padded so that she was unlikely to shift and fall out, with small motors exercising and massaging various parts of her body while other probes monitored all her vital signs down to the most minute detail to insure that she was not in any way suffering injury or long-term impairment. Small tubes fed her and others took away her waste, so that her mind did not have to have any part of itself occupied with such things nor distracted from them.

The mind, in a sense, wasn't even there.

Many who had never experienced at least this level of bonding, mind and machine, could not imagine why so many in the past had elected to simply discard their human bodies and mate brain and ship into one permanent organism. In the Meld, as it was generally referred to by those who did it often, it was easy to think how wonderful it would be to be like this permanently, to become one with the machine and live with this enhanced power, trading a fragile human body for one that could withstand the cold vacuum of space and the heat of a reentry, who could see and control all parts of themselves at once, with senses enhanced beyond any ordinary human's imagination.

The navy, however, reserved that entirely for the Admiralty, insisting that you remain with your body and exist when not on station or on a mission in that body and not in the permanency of the Meld. It limited you in ways that you could never explain to others, and it meant that you would have to constantly readjust to the situation, but the navy wanted no Meld that it could not control, no cybernetic bond that it could not break. Humans had almost been wiped out when they'd allowed their self-aware machines free rein and will, and they were not about to trust even partly human cybernauts with it, either.

Lieutenant Chung preferred the Meld with a fast, sleek fighter, leading a limitless team with maximum power and abilities at their command, but this was fine compared to the alternative. Even if they some-how entered lifeboat mode, she could exist like this while having only the most tenuous connection to a cryogenically frozen body. But she still needed that connection, that body; it was part of the ship, and the ship was a part of her, but if it died, her thoughts, her personality also died. She was well aware of that.

For three days now she'd flown the ship and expe-rienced the joys of the Meld, but that was about to come to an end, at least temporarily. This was a mis-sion, and she, not just her flying, was a vital part of its completion.

She had watched the three young witches with her enhanced powers, and sensed the enormous energy within those jewels they wore and just how they cloaked their wearers, much as the force field protect-ing the outer skin of the shuttle protected her. The field would strengthen sometimes, and then weaken, but it was always there, always in at least a minimal way both protecting and controlling the wearer.

Chung did not get close enough to pull that energy towards her own sensors. She was well aware that the mysterious energy was not limited to the wearer but could extend itself, perhaps sufficiently to have taken control of a great star frigate. This shuttle and her own single Meld consciousness and databanks would be child's play for the energy, and she'd have no defense. So she studied it, and watched it, but from a distance.

The energy wasn't a visible thing; it was something tangible and living but beyond the abilities of a mortal human to see and feel. Only in the Meld was it clear, a writhing mass of almost protoplasmic pulsing and oozing, pure energy that acted like organic matter. She had never seen or encountered anything quite like it before, but it was clearly real and it was clearly not emanating from the three girls nor their developing fetuses nor from some sort of parasite or some other sort of life that might live cooperatively inside the girls. The source was external, from their gemstones or, more likely, *through* the stones. There was no evidence of a Meld of any sort with or within the stones; whatever was guiding it was using some sort of remote control. From where, and how, was by no means obvious.

It *was* clear that it could not stray too far from the stones on its own. It needed the girls to wear the gems around their necks to extend its own limited reach, but if they were in contact with something then *it* was in contact as well.

Still, mere contact with electronic channels aboard the *Thermopylae* had been sufficient for it to have penetrated the ship's primary computer core, at least enough to give it a program to erase the witches from the sensors. And while all three combined didn't seem to be powerful enough to have actually taken control of the huge ship, they *had* been able to sustain their modifications, undetectably access the database whenever required, and also essentially operate the three girls' bodies as remote extensions. That was impressive, and meant that, if those entities wanted to, they could certainly do what they willed with Chung's own Meld.

The fact that they hadn't apparently done so meant that either she had nothing to offer but the ride and that's what they were getting anyway or, possibly, that she *had* been fully compromised and reprogrammed not to know it. She put that out of her mind for now, though, not so much from paranoia as from pragmatism. If that were true, then it really didn't matter insofar as there was nothing she might be able to do to discover or counter it.

Chung had watched with fascination as O'Brian's operator—there was just no other way to think of it right now—had flowed rather nicely into Maslovic's hand and then through him, until he had sensed it and let go, cutting the contact. That had yielded some very interesting and possibly useful facts. First, that the more it extended into and over Maslovic, the thinner the energy field around both he and the girl had become, so there was a real limit to how much that gemstone device could put out after all. That was probably why all three were needed to do what they did aboard the *Thermopylae*; the power had to be combined.

Still, all three together had also been sufficient to have somehow reprogrammed the living sentry's memory of them leaving, and the memory of anyone who came close to them. The three of them together, in perfect symmetry, had been necessary to create a field that could fog the mind of anyone coming into its proximity. Nobody could create a condition where someone would be invisible to everyone and everything across the whole catalog of senses and monitors, but apparently together, the three could create a thin field that would make no one and no thing notice that they were there. Fascinating.

It also implied limits to that power, however vast. They could put in their clever little program to the ship's computer, but they couldn't stay there and keep the girls supplied and protected or, worse, controlled. They could use the girls' bodies and sensors to explore, almost like robotic probes or ferrets, but the requirement that the field, however thin, be stretched as far as possible vastly limited what they could actually *do* during those explorations.

She had never experienced this sort of energy, did not know its full properties or potential, so there really wasn't a lot she could do to tell more about it without attracting unwanted attention from it, but it *did* allow her to see the energy in its ebbs and flows and something of where it went and what it could do.

It always had at least a slender thread directly into each girl's cerebral cortex, and it also had a similar hairlike thread into the same region of the nearly fully developed fetuses. It certainly wasn't using those connections for control, at least not now, but it did occasionally send quantities of energy in short, coded bursts along those connections, sometimes to the mothers but more often to the almost children within.

What would a newborn be programmed to do? What *could* it do? It wouldn't even have full vision or control of its muscles for some time. Latent programming, probably, or lots of data and routines to be activated once the child was old enough for it to matter.

Were these, then, a class of invading soldiers being created by an enemy almost from the moment they had a developing brain? Or the perfect agents, or spies? What were the operators on the other side of those stones doing, and why?

As much anxiety as she felt, Chung also felt a great deal of excitement. No more pushing around little toads like Murphy or doing shows of force to get taxes from poor worlds growing poorer; this was what a military was for.

Now there was an enemy, a bit out of the shadows where those like her could see them at work, if obliquely. And if the operators were friendly, why had they spent so much time and trouble keeping in those deepest shadows?

How she'd like to follow that energy back to its source! And not in this little shuttle, either, but with her fighter, perhaps the whole fighter squadron, and on their own, without potential corruption from the mother ship's master computers!

As it stood right now, though, this ship had four weapons, all personal weapons of no real use in space, and none of them was assembled and charged.

And with the last of the gates looming ahead, they were only a few hours out from those who sent those images that so troubled Maslovic, someone who, like herself, was without the fear of death and whose entire self was devoted to the mission, and not to some intermediaries in this obviously vast interstellar plot.

She saw the wormgate ahead, quite suddenly, but it was no surprise. Directly on the flight path, just where and when it should be, here it was, out then, with only a slight adjustment, back in for one last, very short ride.

It had been decided from the start that she would not communicate with those inside if she could help it, only observe, but they were now at the point where there was no more purpose to the silent treatment, meant to simply not remind the girls and whoever was behind them that someone else was aboard and watching. Now it was moot; they were almost there.

"Please awaken our passengers, Sergeant," her voice came from the lounge public address speaker, sounding crisp and professional. "There are clean, loose whites in the locker aft, and whatever else they might wish to wear on exit. They certainly can not exit looking like *that*, nor, I suspect, would they want to."

Maslovic sat up straight, almost at attention, and nodded at the speaker. It was conditioning; in this circumstance and until they actually landed, the lieutenant was the captain.

Murphy simply looked startled. It had been long enough since he'd seen the pilot that he'd forgotten that the whole thing wasn't automated.

"You can clean up and get some fresh clothing as well, Captain Murphy," Maslovic told him. "We have time yet." He glanced at his watch, which now read 2:44:06. Murphy did the same, and chuckled.

"Three pregnant lassies, one toilet, one shower, and under maybe four, five hours tops from right now and some of that time strapped in. You're dreamin', man!" He paused for a moment, then added, "I'll skip the prettifyin', if you don't mind. Bad for me reputation anyway. In fact, I think I'll spend this last comfy time enjoyin' what I can of that pretty good stout, and maybe a couple of scones or sweet rolls to settle me stomach. Tonight it's a celebration! I'm free of them and all of you starched machines, and it's payday to boot!"

"Suit yourself," Maslovic responded, getting up and making his way aft to the beds. Somehow he suspected that the old captain wasn't nearly as free and clear of this business as he might have hoped.

Murphy was a bit worried about that, too, but he was equally certain that he felt neither kinship with nor obligation to the military folks, now or at any foreseeable time in his future. If this was any sort of menace, they were probably the least equipped to handle it with their rigid codes and genetic specializations. Pirates, con artists, and maybe a physicist or two, *they* might at least make a go of it. He'd grown to like

Maslovic, at least a little, and respect his mind and almost con artist-like manner, but, deep down, Murphy knew that the marine was essentially an act, a performance, trained and programmed and superimposed on a hard and cold body and mind. All that surface charm and friendly company could shut down in a moment and the same fellow would shoot him and never think a moment on it beyond that, and blow away his mother, too, if he had one. Of course, his mother had been a machine, so in that sense he and the rest of his kind were the spitting images of their parents.

Not that Murphy didn't have the con man's personable manner and coldness of heart as well, but at least, he told himself, he'd *earned* that in the school of hard knocks.

The sergeant came back in and nodded. "Well, you were right. They can't even wash their long *hair* in three hours. *Each!*"

"Aye. Told you so. Of course, it would help if they had some hair dryers. Guess that wouldn't be likely in a ship built for a bunch of baldies, though. Well, they'll make do. This is, after all, where they, or them what's behind them, want 'em to be, so there's not likely to be a lot of patience with the folks on the ground if they decide to take a few hours before clearin' the authorities."

"You're probably right there," the sergeant agreed. "I wonder who the hell is picking them up?"

"Well, they was to be dropped off to members of the Knights of Saint Phineas on Barnum's World. That's all I was told. The others I delivered now and then, they was all a bit different, or at least seemed a wee bit more normal, so they just went off while I did me paperwork and that was that."

"You trusted them?"

Murphy shrugged. "What could I do? Besides, I

didn't do much except transport 'em, and all but these girls I had to bring in kinda on the quiet, if you know what I mean, so there wasn't much I *could* do but trust the others. The money was always there, though, in the accounts, ready to spend, and the notation of credit equivalent to the amount was posted with the bank down there. Why not? If they stiffed me, I didn't exactly have to come back the next time, you know. It's not like there's a hundred ships dock regular at Tara Hibernius."

"I see what you mean. Well, there's no sneaking these young women in, I don't think. Not now. And that means either somebody meets them or they have to use their voodoo on the authorities down there. Either way, I figure they aren't going back on this shuttle!"

"No papers. Be interestin' to see if they *are* expected, won't it? Uh, that is, interestin' for *you*."

Maslovic smiled. "Yes, for us, I guess." Like Murphy wasn't dying to know who or what was behind this, particularly now that he'd seen the power in back of it and the possible real money and valuables they had at their beck and call. "The Knights of Saint Phineas, you said. Know anything more about them?"

"Nope. It's been eons since I been anywhere near a church, let alone catechism school, and I'll be blamed if I ever heard of a Saint Phineas, although, I admit, that blamed church's got ten saints for every day that is, was, or ever will be."

"Fascinating. Not one of the major ones, then."

"Definitely not. I dunno. Maybe they ain't so well known down there, if you know what I mean. I don't know if I should ask about 'em, strictly out of concern for the lasses, you understand, or keep me trap shut. Sounds like some old crusader stuff, or order of soldiers for God, like the Knights of Malta back in ancient times, but I don't think these folks would be them kinda soldiers, and not for God, neither."

"Well, not *your* old god, anyway," the sergeant said. *Maybe for some dark gods lurking in the shadows of a cave upon some bleak and distant world, though*, he added to himself.

The full ship's intercom came alive, and Lieutenant Chung's voice announced, "Five minutes to gate emergence. Depending on traffic control, no more than twenty or thirty minutes insystem until at least orbit."

"Put the traffic control low on the speaker when you emerge, Lieutenant," Maslovic requested. "And if we can get a visual of the planet and resolution to ground as applicable, I'd appreciate it."

"I will do it if I can, Sergeant," the pilot told him.

Murphy shrugged. "It's generally an easy in and out. Mostly freight modules in orbit, a few tugs but mostly storage containers, and service bays for two freighters. Port Bainbridge is the single ground spaceport, but it's pretty decent size for the fairly low traffic it does. When they export, though, it's usually very large and often fragile consignments, so they need the equivalent of a much larger planet. There's towns with specialists all over the world, including a large number of underwater domes, but the only one that can be called a 'city' is Port Bainbridge, population under half a million, and that's where we'll come down. Almost entirely import-export and inland supply. That's all they do. A lot of the world is self-sufficient, or so they say. I never been more than a few kilometers beyond the spaceport meself. Why bother? Go out into the bush and wind up gettin' eaten or worse, or spend time in a station feelin' like you're infested with creepy crawlies. Nope. Not me cup of tea."

"It doesn't sound like a particularly good place to send

three girls, even *these* girls, pregnant and without much knowledge of the outside."

"Oh, I don't think that's a problem for 'em here. They're from a far more rural place than even this, 'cause it's not so high tech and managed as Barnum's World. They'll have good facilities for birthin', and, let's face it, *somebody* is expectin' 'em. Be hell tryin' to track 'em if they go off into the bush, though. Never thought of it before, either, but Barnum's World's actually a pretty fair place if you want to keep secrets and be out of the public view. Wilderness, mostly, lots of ways to hide and lots of places where even if you were found you couldn't be snuck up on, high tech as you need it, low population for less questions, and yet a fair amount of in and out interstellar traffic. If it wasn't for them creepy crawlies, I'd say it'd be a good place to run anything not legal, come to think of it. Me, though, I got this thing about them creepy crawlies."

"What do you mean by that?" Maslovic asked the old captain.

"You'll see. Think of the whole world as a zoo, an animal preserve, and a botanical gardens to boot. Just about everything that was still livin' when the place was set up, a century or more before the Great Silence, goin' back to Old Earth species and through any of the stuff we found out here. Animals, plants, you name it. So if some nasty booger comes along and all Tara Hibernius's sheep get sick and die, here's where they come to get more, genetically perfect and maybe immune as well. New Siam short on their kind of elephants? Got some. And if you're terraforming a place to specific design, here's the plants and bugs and bacteria and crap you'll need, and they can be specially produced to adapt perfect to what you can't terraform. Hell of a business, even now on some worlds. And now that nobody can go back and pick up any species not already extinct, and there's tons of those, the folks down there think they got a kind of sacred trust. Me, I just think most of 'em prefer animals to people."

"I scanned the database on it. Fascinating sounding. But I've never been on a world with a full eco-system including everything down to the microbe level. This could be quite interesting."

"The first time you get stung by a bloodsucker insect and then you come face-to-face with a jumpin' spider bigger'n your head, you'll think different, Sergeant. I promise that."

The intercom came on again. "Out of jump. All nominal," Chung reported. "I'm now in the system control region of Barnum's World. Too far out for a really good picture but I'll give you what I got."

The wall area between the two food service ports flickered and came to life, and there was a realistic three-dimensional view of the new solar system they'd just entered, looking inward. The sun was a bright yellow-white but too far to require any optical filters or adjustments, and towards it they could see several planets, mostly gas types. It looked quite normal, just the kind of solar system that produced terraformable worlds which were used for colonies.

One of the girls popped her head out the hatch and looked around. She was wearing a white pullover and had her long hair wrapped in a towel, turban-style. She saw the display and said, "Oh, *wow*! Neat! Which one is *ours*?"

"I don't think it's quite in view yet," Murphy replied. "It'll be comin' into sight on the right-hand side in a few minutes, maybe less. Don't look too hard, though. Compared to even those planets ye can see there, it'll look like nothin' much more'n a dot at this range."

"*Shuttle THP stroke two four Navy, you have flight path two three niner,*" said a reedy male voice over the intercom. *"You are cleared to proceed in system. Coordinates coming your way. Acknowledge receipt."*

"Received, Outer System Control," Chung responded. "Am on the beam. Do you wish control?"

"Negative. Passing directives to your navigational computer. Estimated inbound ninety-two minutes standard. Recommend force field be maintained at this speed. Orbital Control will take you at insertion point."

"Who's *that*?" Mary Margaret's voice came to them. She came in, dressed pretty much like the other one who'd first looked in.

"That's Barnum's World," Murphy told her. "Or, rather, it's the controller computers bringin' us in. This is one time when we're better off aboard here than on our old ship. For one thing, on the old tub we wouldn't be here yet, maybe not fer another week or so. And, second, we could never come in at this speed and we'd be all strapped in."

"So we'll be landing in an hour and a half?" she asked.

"No, longer than that, but it won't be comfortable then, so you'll have to be up here and strapped in. They'll bring us into orbit around the planet, scan us, ask us who we are and what we're doin' here and all that, and if they like the answers they'll let us land."

"Who needs *them*?" she responded. "Why don't we just, like, *land*?"

"Well, we could try'n do that," Captain Murphy admitted. "But then they'd just atomize us and we'd be all dead and gone without a trace. No, you do it their way when you come in like this. Don't worry. This is where you wanted to be."

McBride nodded, looking suddenly a bit bewildered, almost like a child who suddenly wasn't sure if this really was where Mamma said to head for if lost.

"Yeah, that's right," she said, more to herself than

to them. "This is where we all want to be. Only, like, I wish I knew why. . . ."

Customs and Immigration at Barnum's World was not initially pleased to hear that the primary purpose for their visit was to drop off unwelcome guests, but the navy still had considerable clout in the older colonial sectors in particular because of its firepower and its ability to set its own protection rates.

"Why isn't Captain Murphy with his ship and cargo as scheduled?" the controller wanted to know.

"We have confiscated his ship for transporting contraband and for longstanding refusal to pay his tax bill," Chung answered.

"Yes, well, put him on. We need to know if he has a way off."

"Aye, you miserable dung beetles! Of *course* I have a way off," the old captain fumed. "Just check my credit. My letters of credit should be sufficient to get me off your colony for creepy crawlies as soon as I can, and I should have more in there within days, which is why I still have to come here at all!"

There was a pause. "Very well, then. But the three young Hibernians are also your responsibility, Captain," Control warned him. "If you bring them in, it is under your own authority and responsibility, and if no one else gives them finances or takes over that responsibility, then you will also leave with them. Is that understood?"

"Of *course* I understand, you officious reptile! Hell, I'm stuck with 'em now! I've *been* stuck with 'em for far too long! I might as well be on me own with 'em down there as stuck here as a guest of the damned navy!"

Again there was a pause. "Very well. Naval shuttle, relinquish control to Port Bainbridge Interstellar Spaceport. We will bring you in to a merchant tug pier.

There you will be allowed to discharge your passengers. Do you wish a berth?"

"Affirmative, Port Bainbridge Control," Chung responded. "Two naval personnel, ID and genetic information now downloading. We will require a routine service for turnaround and a berth for seven stellar mean days until our ship passes close enough to here to pick us up. Our standard credit will be covered when the *Thermopylae* comes in system. We will wish to discuss some security matters with the Port Captain's office, but no other naval business is pending with you at this time."

"Understood. Are you permanent pilot or Meld?"

"Meld."

"Then please disengage now. We can not dock you unless we have full navigational controls."

"I know the routine. Disengaging and standing down." Chung felt the sense of regret and loss as she initiated the disengagement procedure. It always was hard to let go; it was like a god suddenly becoming mortal and puny, and the mind fought it even as training did what was required.

She punched the intercom. "All passengers please strap in. You have three minutes to get ready and show ready on my board. You can not land until it is done. They will not land you. Is this understood?"

Maslovic and Murphy had no problems, but the girls were fidgety and didn't like the idea of wearing the basic weblike restraints even though they were hardly uncomfortable. They didn't like being confined.

Still, it *was* necessary. Even though Chung had brought up the gravity slowly over the past few hours to equal that of Barnum's World and had also begun the slow adjustment to a Barnum's World atmospheric mixture, it still was bumpy and often uncomfortable coming in for a real planetfall.

Once free of the Meld, Chung went through a series of breathing exercises to adjust her mind and body back to being merely human again and proceeded with some isometrics to insure that her muscles and reactions remained in good shape.

Then, even as the spaceport took control of the shuttle's systems to bring it in, the pilot checked to see that the system was acting as programmed. Then she turned in her chair, still webbed in, and began a series of manual instructions in a code only she currently knew and of which she would be wiped clean once it was fully executed so that even she would have no further knowledge of it nor lingering subconscious memories of her actions that might be picked up by suspicious types below, insured that all was going nicely according to plan, and settled back for the landing.

The authorities on Barnum's World would not have approved, but she didn't care. They were a bunch of biologists and tree huggers; this was military business.

It took under half an hour to bring them down in their own lane and put the shuttle gently into an enclosed horizontal ground bay. The angle of entry and speed made sightseeing not really possible, but everyone on board did get a glimpse for a fraction of a minute of the city below and the deep green world, distant mountains, and swirling clouds.

The sensation was similar to a flight simulator used in training; a bit on the queasy side for those not used to it, barely noticeable for those like Chung or Murphy who had done it more times than they could count. There were also some bumps in the lower atmosphere and some really violent sways as the shuttle actually entered the parking bay and settled in on standardized rails.

There was a sudden cessation of all movement and

all external sounds. They were now parked on Barnum's World.

The webbing automatically retracted and they were all free to move again. Chung leaned forward, stretched in place, and then hesitantly got up, holding on to the chair with her left hand. It was odd to be walking again, feeling all those moving parts of the body, and trying to regain a comfort level. Still, training was everything, and within a minute or two she felt much like her old self again. She went over and removed the programming module from the bridge controls and put it in a small compartment inside her flight suit, and then she picked up her small case and walked back towards the lounge.

The others were already up and about, and the girls were more than ready to go. Still, Mary Margaret at least seemed surprised to see the pilot come aft, as if she'd forgotten that somebody real was actually up there. It wasn't, after all, like they'd just had a long time in transit with Chung as company.

"Gee, I thought they was all big brutes," she whispered to Irish O'Brian. "Most of the women we saw looked more like the men back there. She's *tiny*."

"Aye, but still bald, muscled, and with the expression of a stone carvin'," O'Brian whispered back. "I guess they built her for speed or somethin'."

"Naw. They're gonna build her into the ship sooner or later, you wait and see!"

Murphy couldn't help but notice that the girls already seemed to have put aside their fears and uncertainties and gone back to the banal. In a way, he envied them that. His stomach was already turning and he could use a good slug right about now, and he *knew* Barnum's World and where he was headed. At least he hoped he did. These girls seemed to have the damndest knack of destroying his plans.

Lieutenant Chung went back to the airlock and

pressed her palm on the identiplate. The lock hissed but turned, almost lenslike, then moved aside. The second did much the same, and when it, too, moved out of their way, the strong smells and hot heavy air of Barnum's World came in, enveloping them like an invisible blanket.

"Jeez! The whole place smells like cow poop!" the normally quiet Brigit Moran commented in that high, breathless voice of hers.

"Yeah, smells like home," Irish responded.

Murphy chuckled. "Ah, that magnificent scent of this here world isn't just mere cows, girls, although there's sure some of 'em about, nor horses, neither. You'll see once we get out into the open and past these formalities."

Some illuminated arrows on the wall of the docking bay indicated direction, and they turned, Chung as pilot leading the way, and headed for the customs symbol. Murphy went behind, then the three passengers, with Maslovic bringing up the rear. The sergeant wanted to make good and sure that he had the whole party in sight the whole time, even though he knew that any modern freight terminal like this one had to have full monitoring. He had seen these girls disappear from the state of the art in monitors before.

You could certainly tell that they had landed in the industrial part of the spaceport, if indeed there was any other part. The place was dirty, stained with who knew what on the floors and walls, and it looked like you could take your fingernail and run it across any point and come up with a large glob of unknown composition.

Once out of the bay and into the loading dock area, they had to go slowly and carefully to keep out of the way of robotic vehicles moving containers full of goods or running empty ones back to the various ships. There were also some really nasty-looking creatures about, most quite small and trying to feed on the dropped matter without getting squashed. These included millipedelike insects so large that a few were the size of human arms, with ugly pincers at their heads and giving off threatening looks; huge hairy spiders; lots of flies and roaches; and quite a number of scuttling things that looked not even close to anything any of them had seen before. The one thing that struck them all, though, was that the seamier side of wildlife on Barnum's World seemed to be oversized.

"*Yuk!*" Mary Margaret McBride said over the din of port business. "I suddenly feel like things are crawlin' all over me!"

"Just don't step on anything livin' or the remains of somethin' live in them bare feet," Murphy warned. "Some of these got poison. Otherwise, just ignore 'em and they'll ignore you for the most part. They got their business here and we got ours!"

The arrows ended mercifully at a large set of double doors that slid open as they got to them and remained open long enough for them all to get inside.

"*Ow!*" Irish O'Brian exclaimed as her foot hit the point where the door met the floor. "What the hell was *that?*"

"Critter barrier," the old captain told her. "Just don't step right on that place where the door's kinda rubbed from openin' and closin' so much and you'll be fine. It's just a mild shock to keep them things from comin' in with us."

There was a second doorway forming a flimsy airlock of sorts just ahead, and from the ceiling a blue energy field, very thin and quite transparent, formed a kind of curtain they would have to pass through. It didn't take a genius to figure out what it was doing; the carcasses of incredible numbers of flying things not only had piled up just in front of it but there was a constant crackling and buzzing as more things that made it past the ground barrier were stopped in midair.

"This one'll tickle you all over," the old captain warned. "But if ye think ye picked up anything, it'll nail that, too. No hitchhikers!"

He was right. It *did* just tickle. Still, both Moran and McBride stopped ahead of it and seemed unwilling to go through, while Irish O'Brian hardly gave it a thought.

Maslovic smiled. "Come on, girls! It won't hurt you, your babies, or anything else! Promise! But no more creepy crawlies," he promised, adding to himself, *until we get back outside, anyway*.

Eventually, first McBride, then Moran, got up the nerve to step through, particularly when some of the large flying insects started making for them and their hair, and it was done.

The terminal wasn't really a passenger terminal, either, although it had a small section for that. Mostly it was for captains of orbiting freighters to check in, get their records and orders and bills of lading straight, and to arrange to have whatever part of their cargo was destined for here off-loaded by tugs and delivered to the right docks or for the cargo to be picked up to be put aboard. Only small vessels like port tugs and the occasional shuttle came through this area; there was a commercial passenger shuttle bay on the other side for the use of such passengers when a liner or fully equipped passenger module on a freighter was available.

A woman with short hair and dark skin and eyes wearing a lime green uniform approached them, nodded crisply, and said, "Military shuttle passengers follow me, please!"

Maslovic couldn't help noticing that the woman,

clearly Customs and Immigration, had given a more than cursory glance at the three pregnant young women and there was a fleeting look of surprise, perhaps disdain, when she'd done that.

If anyone was here to meet the passengers, clearly they weren't going to be wearing a uniform.

The young woman punched in a code and a sliding door opened on the far wall to reveal a moving walkway. "Does anyone need to sit down?" she asked. "You can pull down seats if you like from the far wall, but please do not touch the area outside of the walkway."

The three young women all looked more than relieved and, when they followed the leaders onto the belt, immediately pulled down the hinged seats and sat.

As they went, they were scanned as thoroughly as they ever had been in their lives. By the time they reached the end point of the walkway, perhaps a kilometer or so, the master Customs and Immigration computers could tell them how many hairs they had on their heads (if they had any), where their scars were, what they'd had for breakfast, and almost everything else. At the end, each of them had to stand and place their right index fingers in a small fitted slot before moving on. Although none felt a thing, their genetic histories were now added to the files.

It ended at an unstaffed set of kiosks. A green light would go on, and you had to enter, one at a time. Lieutenant Chung was first, depositing the credit and authorization cube from the shuttle. It would allow the navy pair to charge throughout the city region and order whatever maintenance was necessary on the shuttle. The others were simply asked by a disembodied voice to state their full names, their planet of origin, and how long they would be on Barnum's World. The girls were told to say "We don't know at this time," to that, which resulted in a warning that they had a week to find out and notify authorities or they would be located and deported.

There was nothing else required of them. No matter where they went on Barnum's World from this point, their own DNA matched to the database just compiled would be known, and their every move tracked within the city. Outside of the city, the transport would be known, so that authorities generally could find them as needed.

The one thing the girls couldn't do was buy anything. That made them totally dependent on Murphy for now, or on whoever might meet them. Murphy wasn't all that worried about that part of it. Even on their own, he bet himself that the girls and their funny gemstones would allow them to buy almost anything they wanted without the transaction ever even registering. When you took over a naval frigate, what was a government tracking system?

For all the precautions taken, and this was typical of modern, well-run colonies now, even Murphy knew how to bypass almost every system they had, and he didn't even have to.

Finally, they reached another double door setup quite like the last part but this time much cleaner and better maintained. When they went through the second of them, though, they were back into the hot, humid, and smelly air of Barnum's World and now facing transport into the city. It ranged from robotic taxis and a basic mass transit train to the more exotic. There were carts about, and carriages, and all sorts of other conveyances, which were in many cases pulled by great beasts the likes of which none but Murphy had ever seen before. Elephants, both Indian and African type, and camels, among others.

"There's some of the smell, ladies," he told them, pointing. "The local cheap and scenic route."

They just gaped at it all, the taxis and trains as exotic as the bizarre animals, unable to take it in.

"Welcome to Barnum's World," said Captain Murphy.

VI:
THE ORDER OF SAINT PHINEAS

The maglev train, with no sound to speak of and no obvious driver, pulled into the station and came to an equally silent stop and opened its sliding doors.

"Is it alive?" Mary Margaret wanted to know.

"Of course not!" Sergeant Maslovic responded, sounding amused. "You've never seen a train before?"

"We've never seen *nothin'* before," Irish O'Brian responded, looking as nervous as the others at the prospect of actually getting inside the thing. "Just pony carts and horses and the occasional spaceship. Stuff like that."

"C'mon, girls, just step aboard and take a seat!" Murphy urged. "This won't wait forever, and I want to get into town."

Chung was already on, and Maslovic and Murphy

helped each of the young women to come aboard even though there was no step and no gap. It was just now striking even the old captain just how fish-out-of-water these girls were. He'd been going back and forth in his mind, calling them "girls" but knowing that they were older and more experienced in one way than the name implied, but it worked here more than anywhere else as a truthful term. They *were* mere children in most experiences.

Even though they'd pulled an amazing fast one on the navy and actually partly taken control of a sophisticated craft, they really didn't know what they were doing or even what they were seeing. They were being fed, led, or controlled when they did that. In actual fact, none of the trio had ever been off Tara Hibernius before, and the world in which they'd been born and raised had been kept deliberately backward and primitive, more nineteenth century than twenty-third. It was one thing not to have seen an elephant before; few had who hadn't been on one of the very few worlds where they were a part of the culture. It was quite another to consider that none of the three had ever seen a train, a taxi, even a paved road or sidewalk. Now here, everything was new and scary and mysterious. No matter what powers they had, without the mind behind those necklace gems or the minds here they were pretty much helpless, not to mention clueless.

The trains were extremely fast as well as being isolated from just about all bumps and grinds, and if there hadn't been several stations between the spaceport and the city, they would have been there in just a few minutes. As it was, they reached the downtown section of Port Bainbridge in about twenty minutes.

"We might as well get off at this stop," Maslovic told them. "This is the center of the main commercial district. I don't know where else would be better."

They all exited at the stop, and as the train closed its doors and floated silently away down its maglev track, Murphy turned to Chung and Maslovic and asked, "So, now what?"

"What do you mean?" the lieutenant responded.

"I mean exactly that," the old captain explained. "We're in the middle of town in what looks like the middle of the day and these three sweet things can't even get a cup of tea on their own. They stand here basically clad in the navy's bathrobes helpless as babes. I know where *I* have to go, but what of them?"

"What about them?" Chung asked him. "We're free of responsibility to you and to them at this point. We've landed you successfully at the nearest inhabited and interconnected colonial world. We have naval business here, and then we are on leave until our ship comes insystem. Our responsibility to you is done."

Murphy looked like he was about to have a stroke. "But—but—you can't *do* this to me! I got me own business here and then I want off! I can't be saddled with the three of 'em indefinitely! I mean, I ain't even been *paid* yet!"

"I'm afraid they *are* your problem, Captain," Maslovic put in. "I mean, when we intercepted you, you were in the process of smuggling these three here, or at least bringing them here. Three very young, underage in fact, pregnant teens without the permission of any of their family or even that family's knowledge. That can result in some pretty serious stuff if it were to come to that!"

"Oh, c'mon! You know they was runnin' fer their lives!"

"So *you* say. Well, you also said you were being paid to bring them here. They're here. We didn't stop that. Now they're your problem. You're lucky we don't turn you in, or at least charge you for the robes."

Murphy's face was beet red and he began to sputter.

"But we ain't even due here for another week! What do I do with 'em until then?"

"If we didn't have other things to do, we'd be quite curious to find out the answer to that," Lieutenant Chung said to them, trying to keep a totally blank expression on her face and not quite making it. "Farewell, Captain. Farewell, young ladies. Sergeant?"

"Yes, sir?"

"Let's get on with our business," she said, and the two of them walked crisply away from the other four and were quickly gone down the escalator at the far end of the station.

Although there were some informally dressed commuters around waiting for the next train, they were otherwise alone on the platform.

Irish O'Brian asked innocently, "Where do we go now, Captain?"

Murphy sighed. "I've half a mind to just leave you here on the platform meself," he muttered in reply, "but then I might not *ever* get paid and you'll pull some of that blasted witchcraft and the locals'll all be comin' lookin' for *me* to blame and pay damages." He sighed in resignation, and the color began to go back to *almost* normal. "All right, ladies. Follow me."

The fact was, while he knew he had *some* credit left on Barnum's World, which was, after all, one of his regular stops, he nonetheless wasn't certain that he had enough to cover four people, three of whom would need practically everything, for a full week each. They were not too charitable here when it came to folks who ran out of money, and the last way he wanted to wind up was out on the street begging or stealing with these three in tow. He wished right now that he could access their power, whatever it was, as easily as whoever was on the other side of those damned gemstones did.

Well, there's a thought, he considered as he led them

to street level and then down the walk towards the hotel area. *Either whoever that is on the other side of them things better damned well pony up or we'll hock one of 'em little sons of bitches. Should bring a tidy sum, particularly on the black market here. Real Magi stones. Not bad.*

He stopped at an information kiosk on the street and checked his credit. It was better than he thought, but no retirement stipend. If it was more than a week here, or anything unexpected came up, he might well be in some trouble getting started again without going on the grift. Not that he hadn't done that many times, but he was getting too old for that shit, and it would have to play out here, on a world he'd just love to get off of as quickly as possible.

The fancier the place, the more real humans you dealt with. Not that they were much better than machines, but at least they made you *feel* like it mattered.

"Your—*daughters*, sir?" The clerk tried mightily not to sound dubious.

"Aye, can't you tell by the accents?" he asked the man. "What do you take me for? A dirty old man? Hell's bells, man! You can *see* that they already *been* knocked up, all three of 'em!"

The clerk looked embarrassed and tried clearing his throat. "Oh, yes, sir. Please don't think I was suggesting something untoward here. I apologize." Money was money and, in fact, the clerk probably didn't give a damn if Murphy *was* a dirty old man and the father of all three forthcoming children. Barnum's World was used to the unconventional; indeed, it had been settled by and, outside the more structured city environment, still was inhabited by some of the least conventional people humanity had left. So unconventional that if the old man had introduced them as his wives or companions there would have been less of a surprise. There was always a kind of reaction to robbing the cradle, though.

"Luggage, sir?"

Murphy chuckled. "We was just dropped here cold by them damned navy tax police. They even charged us for the clean clothes! It's only good luck that I have credit accounts here that them bums can't touch! No, no luggage. But I hope to heaven we'll have some goin' *out*! Me, I'll be here only a few days, until me daughters' families come pick them up."

"They are local here, sir?"

"No, but they're here now. Nosy sort for a spaceport concierge, ain't you? Are ye a hotel man or a cop?"

The hotel rep was looking nervous and uncomfortable. "Oh, I work for the *hotel*, sir! Just making idle conversation while the room is checked." He looked down at a panel in front of him and seemed visibly relieved. "Ah, yes! It's ready now, sir. Just a moment and I'll take you up to your room and show you the features."

"No, I know the features. Just tell me which room and we'll go up and let you know if it ain't suitable," the captain told him. The fellow probably was just hotel personnel, but he wouldn't blink twice at feeding some tidbit of information to the local cops or maybe even the local crooks if it was worth his while. Murphy knew the type. All the fancy clothes in the world couldn't disguise a grifter. In some ways he preferred this type. More his kind of people, and sure a lot better than the ones who were part of some damned religious group. Those types made him nervous.

They went up to the room, which was also keyed to his right index finger and right eyeball patterns, and it was a *very* nice room. Almost too nice, Murphy thought, looking around. With a bedroom and spacious furnished parlor, he felt that a level of privacy might be maintained here while not interfering much with comfort. Even the couch seemed luxurious when compared to those shuttle hammocks.

The women, too, seemed to like the look of the suite, and investigated every square millimeter of the place and all the buttons and voice command gadgetry available. Most popular was the huge bathroom, with its whirlpool-style tub and huge well-stocked vanity. He let them have their fun; he suspected that soon they'd find things more drudgery and sleepless nights, and they might as well enjoy this while they could.

For some reason, he felt tired, almost drained of energy, in spite of having spent so many days doing nothing at all. Some might have suggested that it was the copious amount of whiskey he'd consumed during that period that might have been catching up with him, but his old Irish soul rejected that as somehow unmanly. Still, this pretty room was costing a fortune and it seemed criminal not to use it, particularly since he was stuck until he could unload the girls. In the meantime, they seemed so taken with the bath and such, and so lively and awake, he thought he could take the opportunity to simply crash on top of that big bed with the satiny spread while they played their games. Kicking off his shoes, he went into the bedroom and plopped down on top of it. The sensation was so wonderful he was asleep in less than a minute.

He didn't know how long he slept, but he awoke suddenly, sitting up on the bed wide awake as if cold water had been splashed on his face. He was surprised to find that he was actually *in* the bed, and that the covers had been pulled up over him, but he was much more startled to see that it was almost dark.

And silent.

Pushing off the covers, he got up and walked out

into the parlor, suddenly worried about what those girls were up to while he'd slept. The lights came on as he walked through, and what was most disturbing of all was the fact that nothing seemed to be out of kilter. Everything was as fresh and undisturbed as when they'd entered, and although the sumptuous bath had been clearly used, there was no sign of the ones who'd used it.

"Jesus, Mary, and Joseph!" he swore aloud. "Them girls is out in this town in nothin' more'n bathrobes and sandals and no experience with the denizens of civilization at all!"

He immediately left the room and took the lift down to the reception area. No sign of them there, either, nor of the concierge who'd checked them in, but hotel reception people were there. None could remember seeing three young women of those descriptions or any other descriptions pass through the area since they'd been on duty, and some had been there all afternoon.

Damn them! They pulled another one of them witch vanishing acts again!

He started to go out into the shopping district, which was just coming to life with its lights and glitzy signs and exotic smells, when he suddenly stopped and just stood there in the hotel entrance, staring.

What the hell could he do? He had no more chance of finding them than anyone else, and if they were in that invisible mode or whatever it was they could pull, then nobody else would have noticed them, either. At least that situation would help defend against the nasty people and things around the city, and they were unlikely candidates for much in the sex side of things right now, so he couldn't do much except sweat a bit and wait them out and hope that they came back.

He turned, went back up to the room, cleared off the parlor table, and called room service for a good dinner. While waiting, he decided to see if anyone of interest might be in the city directory.

Computers were very good at figuring out what you wanted and finding it for you, but he hated having a dialog with a machine. He called up a holographic screen with a print listing and sought some information.

Phineas . . . Phineas . . . Nope. Wait! Not Phineas! Saint Phineas, wasn't it? Yes, let's see . . .

There was nothing in the commercial or institutional directories that seemed to fit what he was looking for, but the plain contact listings, without the three-dimensional super ads and special effects, did show an *Order* of Saint Phineas. Not much of a description, but it was in the southwestern suburbs, a residential area mostly, but easily reached by mass transit.

"Research," he said to the screen floating in front of him. "Expand on any cross-references on directory entry highlighted."

"St. Phineas, Order of, rel., frat., priv. Chapel, grounds, residences. Members only. No visitors unless invited. Strictly enforced. Security A five."

That was interesting. A security level like that might be expected at banks and dealers in art and precious gems or the like, and higher-level government offices. Rather unusual for a religious order, which is what the thing also said. Of course, if the girls really meant it when they said they were Satanists, then any such order might well have that kind of security and more.

He sat up, frowning. "Information, can you find me anything on Saint Phineas?"

"No information on Saint Phineas is in my records," responded a pleasant and human-sounding female voice. "However, there is an Order of Saint Phineas listed in the communications directory."

"Never mind." That was going in circles.

He probably was one of those obscure Catholic saints, of course. There was one for just about every name or combination of syllables in the known universe, or so it had seemed when the religious calendars came out when he was growing up. Not likely to bother having all of those on a secular world's directory like this one. Not much of Vaticanus here, that was for sure. More likely here would be Buddhists, Hindus, Moslems, Baptists, that sort of thing.

And all of a sudden it hit him like a bolt of lightning from the heavens themselves. Where was he sitting, anyway? Those *rascals*! Those damned *scoundrels*! People after his own heart, most likely.

"Information," he called again. "Phineas Barnum, please."

"No listing for a Phineas Barnum."

"Not a listing. Who was he?"

"Barnum, Phineas Taylor, lived eighteen ten to eighteen ninety-one, Old Earth calendar system. Established museum of curiosities, later created a traveling circus called the Greatest Show on Earth. Descendants of the circus, merged many times and split among many units, perform to this day on established appearance circuits, with some periods of interruption. Credited with the saying, 'There is a sucker born every minute.' Barnum was also a politician and mayor of a major city at one time in his career. He—"

"That's enough!" As the signal bell sounded indicating that dinner had arrived, he sat back and laughed heartily to himself. Phineas Taylor Barnum. A sucker born every minute!

It made perfect sense. Nobody paid anything to see robots battle or holographic shows that did the same things time after time, and even if you could walk right into a virtual reality game and battle gladiators in ancient Rome, there was some prurient interest and even some artistic appreciation for those folks of the old school who could still perform the old acts, live, in the ways you couldn't.

There's one born every minute.... He almost choked on the steak, good as it was, because of his inability to suppress chuckling spasms.

This was a scientific reserve, but it was more than that. Lots of genetics work was done to order here, and lots of preservation and even resuscitation of extinct plants and animals from preserved DNA and stored encoding sequences were done here as well. It was also one of the few places where, for some substantial fees, you could do some special-order genetics on humans as well. Not well publicized, and in the old days before the Great Silence it was never advertised, but it was done here. What better place for breeding controlled mutations if that's what you wanted to do? Lots of museum and performer types here as well, because of the laid-back attitudes. And even universally condemned activities might be done here, no questions asked.

And *that* was what he'd been doing for them all this time. They had their performers who might even get around now and then to out-of-the-way worlds like Tara Hibernius. Who would look twice at them? Such a backward nontechnological society would be a natural for live performances.

So you dropped by and you already carried the seeds of the project, whatever it might be, and thanks to the strict claustrophobic society there would be a lot of teen rebellion, perhaps against both church and society, so you had a seemingly unthreatening underground organization that attracted some of the young. The best prospects might be impregnated with the project seed, and then good old Murphy comes along delivering atmospheric purifiers and super fertilizers and he picks up the impregnated ones who also have been chosen as ones who really wanted out or else and deposits them here. Who would notice? Even if something in the chain blew, it wouldn't look like any kind of illegal genetics work, it would just look like what it seemed, with the Satanic stuff thrown in for an even smellier bundle of red herrings.

Still, somebody had gone to a lot of trouble and expense for what seemed easy to do right here in a compound out in the bush. Why go to all that trouble, and for so little result? Three engineered babies you could grow in test tubes?

No, he had some of it, but not all of it, not yet. He was certain of that.

It was well into the night before the girls returned, much to his relief. Not that he was so terrified for their welfare, of course, but *he* had to get paid, after all.

His relief was short-lived, though, when he saw that they were under no apparent spells but dressed quite differently, and followed by a robot cart carrying a ton of packages. They themselves had on loose but rather colorful one-piece dresses, wide, floppy brim hats, fancy designer sunglasses, and nice-looking sandals. They also appeared to have discovered the application of makeup, were wearing earrings and finger rings, wearing painted lips and painted nails.

"Good god! How'd you get all *that*?" he asked nervously. "You didn't spend every single bit of credit I got, did you?"

"Oh, of *course* not!" Irish laughed, sounding tired but happy. "We didn't spend nothin' at all for these!"

Murphy frowned. "Then how . . . ? I mean, they got print and retinal checks and you need the money or else here! Or did you just walk out with it while makin' nobody see you or somethin' like that?"

"Oh, nothing like that," Mary Margaret laughed. "We

just did like everybody else. We picked what we wanted, we gave 'em our finger and looked through their eyepiece or whatever it is, and it said we was okay. Worked every place we went."

He sat back down, a bit dumbfounded. "Heh! Best damn security system for payment and credit I know, and you girls just breeze right past it 'cause the machines all think they know you and want to make you happy! Sweet Jesus! As hard as I had to work to steal things over me many years!"

"We didn't steal," Irish O'Brian insisted. "We just did what everybody else did for payment and it was good. So who loses? The shops got paid, right? So if there's no money there, it's the government's own fault for giving it to us!"

"I wanta try on that stuff but I'm beat," Mary Margaret McBride put in.

"Me, too," chipped in Brigit Moran.

Irish came over to the old captain and kissed him on the forehead. "So can you be a dear man and put them things someplace here for us? I think it's bedtime."

You didn't argue with these gals, that was clear. He let them go in, get their showers, and stake out their bed places and get settled, then he quietly made certain that the connecting door was completely shut and went back to the comm console.

"Manual mode. Keyboard, please," he said quietly.

In front of him a holographic keyboard appeared. Few could read and write these days, or needed to do either, but there were times when that was a real advantage for someone who could.

With his index finger he tapped out, "Order of Saint Phineas, Dir." The same listing came up as before. This time, however, he input, "Call. Low volume."

A weak electronic signal buzzed on and off several

times. Then a woman's voice answered, "This is the main number of the Order of Saint Phineas. Leave your message and contact information and someone will get back to you."

He waited for the tone, then said softly, "Captain Patrick Murphy, Hotel Aden, suite five five four. I am in early with cargo for you. Please contact me and arrange delivery or pickup. Message ends."

He suspected that they already knew he was here, and probably just about all that had happened, via those stones or whatever they were, but it never hurt to go through the motions. Now there was nothing left to do but to wait for contact.

Truth be told, he almost would miss the girls. If he could get them to trust him with that power of theirs, there was no limit to what they could do, and the fantasy of a man his age with three very pretty companions wasn't at all unpleasant to him. Still, they'd probably get him in more trouble than he'd ever been in in his whole life just by being their own sweet ditzy selves and, besides, it was beginning to look more and more like the very last folk you'd want to cross would be these Phineas people.

Still, all the previous deliveries had been a bit older, a bit smarter, and generally just one or two at a time. He really wondered what the future held for these girls, or if they had one once he delivered them. Clearly it wasn't the trio that this Order was interested in, it was what they carried in their bellies. This was a huge, mostly wild, and very unpopulated world where folks could disappear forever and never be missed, in spite of all those state-of-the-art police controls. Once relieved of their babies and their fancy gem gadgets, they were just three pretty, helpless, far-too-young girls, fit for cleaning up the place or making bushmen a bit less lonely or, if all else failed, providing a nice dinner for some of them creepy crawly types out in the wild.

He began to feel depressed. Not so much at their fate, but at the very clear evidence that, after all those years and all that shady living, he was somehow developing at least an embryonic conscience.

The communicator rang softly. He jumped, startled at the sound, then said simply, "Murphy."

"Ten hundred tomorrow morning," said a woman's voice, not the same one as in the message. "Tanzania Park. North entrance, then to the Great Apes pavilion. Bring your delivery."

"How will I know your person?" he asked.

"They'll know. And we know you."

There was no use in going any further; the line was definitely dead. He sighed. Well, it was more cloak-and-dagger on his part than he was used to in these things, but at least it would be over.

He wished he had some way to work out with the girls some kind of signal so that, if they got into trouble or didn't like where they wound up, they could contact him or someone else for help, but it didn't seem likely he could do it without also giving the same information to these clients of his. The girls weren't about to take off those Magi stones, and not being able to read, there just was no other way to get private.

In a way, that made him feel a bit better. If he *couldn't* do anything, then he could hardly be guilty of any serious breaches, right? Nobody, not even he, could blame him if it all went wrong for them. Not so long as they had that power and also wanted to go.

He decided to let them be for this last night and go down to the hotel pub and relax with the best it had, at least until he really believed that himself.

❖   ❖   ❖

Tanzania Park looked and even operated very much like a metropolitan zoo. It charged an admission, had the usual amenities, and allowed people to see ancient animals, mostly Old Earth species, some long extinct from that planet even before the Great Silence, in a kind of natural habitat recreation, but that wasn't its primary purpose.

Like its aquatic, arctic, and other planetary biome zoos, it was a place where the old species were born and bred until strong enough to be released into the wild, and trained as much as possible to be self-sufficient out there. It was also where injured animals came for treatment, was used for research on animal biology and behavior, and as a transit point for outgoing orders as well.

The three young women loved it.

Murphy had done his best to brief them that this was it, that they'd be meeting the people they were supposed to meet and going away with them from the park, but that seemed to be the farthest thing from their minds this nice morning. The only thing they'd asked, when he told them earlier at the hotel what was going to be going down and where, was how they were going to get the bulk of their brand-new purchases to wherever they were headed next. Murphy assured them that he'd have all that sent over, and that seemed to be the end of that.

The cab didn't look any different from the others waiting outside the hotel and probably wasn't; if he was bringing the "merchandise" to them, why bother?

The north entrance was imposing, consisting of giant prefab stonelike columns carved with ancient tribal symbols, colors, and designs that matched the original long-ago land of these creatures. His finger paid their admission, but he had to work hard to keep the trio from immediately heading for the souvenir shop. It was already almost ten, and the map said they had about two kilometers to walk to get to the Great Apes area.

Murphy realized that whoever they'd be meeting probably had them in sight the whole way now and he didn't want to be perceived as deliberately dawdling to miss the appointment.

There weren't a whole lot of people in the park, or so it seemed, but there were small hordes of children running about here and there, often being chased by nearly exhausted teachers or nannies, and now and again there were groups of twos and threes looking like business people killing time or people there on zoological business. A few families, yes, as well, and the occasional, but rare, individual.

It was already hot and growing hotter and about as humid as air could be without suddenly turning to rain, and the walk in full gravity was hard even on him. He couldn't understand how the three girls were handling it so well considering their condition; most women he knew that far advanced had backaches and could barely waddle a hundred meters without getting winded or, even more likely, seeking a bathroom. Not them. They looked well enough along, but acted almost as if their condition had little or no effect on their energy, aches and pains, or general mobility. How anyone could seem that energetic carrying a watermelon between their legs was beyond him; it wasn't at all natural.

It was further proof that, in spite of their primitive and humble native world, these ones had been designed by someone specifically for this purpose. No wonder they'd all gotten knocked up so young and so easily; their entire design was towards pregnancy as a natural condition. These were baby-making machines, designed not to simply continue evolution but to control it.

Walking slowly but effortlessly down the path, the trio entered ape country long before their titular guardian got there.

It was almost as if they were expected. As they came

around a corner through the dense jungle on the artificial track carved out for visitors, they suddenly found themselves quite close to a whole colony of large hairy apelike creatures sitting on a pile of rocks above and around a small pool of water.

The apes seemed nonthreatening and quite pleased for the company. It didn't take more than a minute for anyone to get the impression that, from their point of view, they were sitting there waiting for the attractions to come and parade by the waiting colony. To the apes, the people were the animals.

"Jeez! They're like little hairy *people*!" Mary Margaret exclaimed.

"Some of 'em ain't so little," Irish responded, gesturing to an area behind and to the right of the ape colony. Up in the trees some really huge apes with bright orange fur and really dumb-looking expressions watched the whole world go by. They seemed very slow and almost to flow rather than merely move between positions, when they moved at all, but there was no question that they were aware of everyone and everything around them.

"Look! That one's preggers!" said the blond Brigit Moran, pointing to one of the nearer apes in the group.

"Yeah! Wow! I think a couple of 'em are," Irish said, looking at each in turn. "I wonder if they talk?"

"That's *dumb*!" Mary Margaret shot back. "They're, like, *animals*. Animals don't talk!"

"I had a hog once could grunt 'Danny Boy'," Irish insisted. "They ain't all so dumb."

"Yeah, well, maybe. I mean, *we're* the ones had to pay to see *them*, right? And then *we* got to walk all this way to parade past *them*. Maybe you're right at that," Mary Margaret said thoughtfully.

Murphy by this time had caught up, although he was a bit winded and his calves were already threatening revolution. He spotted a comfortable-looking bench under the jungle canopy and made for it, sinking down onto the seat and feeling blessed relief. This *was* where they were instructed to be, and by his watch they were within a couple of minutes of being on time, so he was satisfied at that.

"Can we go over and *pet* them or somethin'?" Mary Margaret wondered.

Irish shook her head. "Don't think so. I bet there's some kinda wall we can't see around. Remember, just 'cause they kinda look like us don't mean that they wouldn't like to beat the livin' shit out of us. We all know more human animals that'd do *that*, don't we?"

The other two nodded seriously and made no attempt to get closer to the pool and its colony of large chimpanzees.

Murphy looked at the apes, both the chimps on the ground and the orangutans in the trees, and wondered if they weren't a lot smarter than they were supposed to be.

You're gettin' paranoid, Murphy, he chided himself. But who wouldn't be after a week or two like he'd just had with *those* three?

Truth was, he wondered if they could possibly be as airheaded as they let on. Could they really match wits against those apes over there? And which group would win the intellectual battle?

He also wondered why anybody bothered to keep great apes around and preserved in their natural habitats like this. What good were they? Kind of like keeping a prehistoric virus around because it was the ancestor of pneumonia. Just because people and apes shared a family tree didn't seem to him sufficient reason for some folks, some civilizations, to actually *pay* not only for their preservation but also for real live pairs or colonies of them for some distant colonial worlds who would find better use for those resources making sure that they came through the upcoming economic and social train wreck everybody knew had to be coming.

He thought he heard someone come up in back of him. Turning while not getting up, he found himself staring down an enormous black-pelted gorilla not three meters from the back of his head.

That made him move faster than he dreamed he was still capable of moving.

The gorilla didn't try and lunge, and seemed almost amused by his reaction, like it had deliberately crept up behind him just to spook him and see what he would do.

"So, you big muscle-bound beast," Murphy called to him, "think you could catch Murphy in a panic, eh? Well, here I am!"

The gorilla, on all fours but seeming more massive for all that, looked up at him, seemed almost to smile, snorted loudly in the captain's direction, then turned and vanished back into the forest.

"Jesus, Mary, and Joseph!" Murphy swore aloud. "Why the hell would *anyone* want to make sure a brute like that survived and prospered is beyond me!"

He turned to see how the girls were taking his sneak attack and suddenly realized that he was alone in the glen. Alone as far as humans went, anyway. The chimps and orangs were still watching and *they* seemed *highly* amused.

"Girls! Where are you?" he shouted out as loud as he could, causing the chimps at least to start jumping up and down and screeching at him in obvious mockery of his genuine concern.

He walked slowly towards them, almost ready to grab one and make it tell him where the girls were hiding, but just beyond the edge of the track he felt the solidity and crackle of an energy barrier.

He tested it out, and it seemed to go the length of the track as far as he could see in either direction. Okay, so they didn't go that way, at least not unless they were using that infernal power stuff again.

He walked back to the bench, then around it, and immediately hit the same sort of barrier on the bench side as well.

Thinking that they might have gone towards the exit, he walked back up the track for a hundred meters or so, all exhaustion forgotten, until he could actually see almost to the north gate. People, yes, in increasing numbers, but no sign of the girls.

He quickly whirled and walked back down past the chimps and around the curve where, he found, he had almost as good practical visibility to the next area. A young couple seemed to be walking slowly and close together, hand in hand, enjoying the day, and there was a maintenance robot moving towards him to his right, apparently collecting trash and checking the status of the energy barrier as well.

He doubted that the girls were trying that invisibility or not notice trick; that seemed to require a long period of time chanting together to get themselves in synch. And while they did have some level of hypnotic abilities, they weren't all that clever and no good at all at preplanning, so he doubted if they were biding their time and then controlling his mind so that he wouldn't notice them going. Not that they'd have to. He'd been having enough concerns with that gorilla.

He went back over to the bench and sank back down onto it. Most likely simple diversion. They *might* have put the gorilla up to it somehow, but he doubted it. Easier to just wait until his attention was fully somewhere else and then move. If it hadn't been the gorilla, it would have been something or, eventually, somebody.

After a half hour he was convinced that it wasn't any trick of the girls that had caused it, either. They would have come back and lorded it over him by now.

He felt kind of empty, almost, and it surprised him. As much as he wanted to be rid of them, they'd been the closest thing to family he'd had in fifty years.

Slowly, suddenly feeling the weight of his years, he walked back up to the nearest entrance to the park and looked for a taxi, settling instead for the maglev about two blocks farther down. It was cheaper, and he wasn't in any hurry any more.

When he got back to the room he half expected them to be there, but when the door opened, it revealed a suite so immaculate it seemed as if nobody had ever stayed in it. Everything had been made up, and it seemed sterile, empty. It was another minute or so before he realized that the packages the three had brought in last night were also nowhere to be seen, nor was the mess in cosmetics, bath oils, and the like they'd littered the bathroom with even that morning.

He looked over and saw that the holographic plate was pulsing, indicating that there was some sort of message for him. He went over, sat down, and said, "Communications, replay message for Murphy, Patrick."

"Message is nonverbal," the comm reported.

"Really? Well, put it up on the screen."

It was from his local bank. It showed a massive infusion of real cash into that account. Convertible cash, useful for transfer as well as just sitting there.

More than enough for passage first class almost anywhere he wanted to go, for buying another junker of a freighter, plus sufficient funds for several weeks of one damned huge and wondrous bender.

It was more than enough, and it wasn't nearly anything he particularly wanted right now. It was more than a credit statement, it was a message from the Order of Saint Phineas and those behind it.

Payment due on acceptance of the delivery of the ordered merchandise.

Damn their dark souls!

VII:
THE DISLOYAL OPPOSITION

The street might have been out of some idealized old history film or photo save for some of the exotic trees and flowers that could be seen both in front of the stately line of cleaner-than-nature brick brownstones and in the small flower boxes set outside oversized upper-floor windows. The places were larger than they looked at first glance, but still might have been dismissed as middle-class housing but for the gilding around the windows, doors, and immaculate edgework, and the fact that few middle-class townhouses sported upper-story gargoyles and such intricate wrought-iron works placed almost purely for decoration. More Embassy Row than Accountant's Row, although there was no sign of any more formal function on any of the houses than as homes. The exception was a single city block stuck almost incongruously in the middle of the double rows of brownstones, a block that contained not houses but something more like a compound.

High wrought-iron gates, or gates of some material that seemed like it, blocked vehicle-sized entrances at both ends of the block, and between was a long and quite tall brick wall of the same complexion as the facing houses. Looking in through either gate's lattice work revealed a semicircular driveway around a formal garden leading to a single large brick structure two stories high but fully a third of the block in area. It might have been an old-style mansion house or the headquarters of the local historical society.

Murphy thought it looked like a funeral home.

In the dwindling light of dusk it appeared as a remote chunk of near pitch darkness, out of place here or most anywhere in spite of the attempts to blend in using the brick and iron facade. It barely looked inhabited, but the light from two upper-floor windows was bleeding through drawn curtains, and the indirect lighting illuminated the walkway up to the rather imposing pale yellow front door. He had no doubt, though, that there were cameras galore embedded in or perhaps peering over that wall, and all sorts of security monitors covering every square millimeter of the grounds. The mere fact that it wasn't already victim to hordes of robbers attested to that.

Murphy really didn't know why he was there, not exactly. Concern for the girls, certainly, even though they might well be far from the city by now and nowhere near this mausoleum, and possibly curiosity as well. These people had used him many times; now he thought it was about time to stop just counting the money and taking the rest for granted.

Most of all, he didn't like the way things had been handled. After all this time, he deserved a bit more than going down to the local monkey house and having his charges snatched right in front of him. There was simply no call to do it, particularly since they knew he knew who the client was and even where in the city they dwelled.

If they were aware of him at all at this point, then they certainly would recognize him. He didn't mind that so much, except that they might think he was double-crossing them and now represented some sort of threat. There was always that angle, he reflected. To them, he was a shady agent employed on a need-to-know basis and not needing to know very much, working strictly for money. They had always dealt with him at arm's length, by electronic messenger and security level calls, never in person, and that alone said to him that they had a very low opinion of his character.

He took a flask from his back pocket and drank a slug, letting it burn as it went down. How *dare* they impugn his honor and his motives! Never in his entire life had he ever betrayed his word, nor failed to protect the interest of his paying clients.

He reached the end of the long block, turned, and began walking down the side street along the now unbroken wall. Definitely sensors all along it. He didn't dare bring any really good surveillance tools with him, since he assumed that strangers on foot would be observed, but he did have a few things in his clothing that could give him silent readings. The electrical fields were quite clear. The wall was literally riddled with top-of-the line security monitoring systems, that was for sure. Anybody trying to climb over that wall would be known in nothing flat. Anyone using any kind of cloaking to prevent that monitoring would still fail, since the continuous energy field their stuff set up would create a moving silhouette of any intruder that would be just as obvious as someone tripping the alarms. Even the best cloaking would reveal sufficient distortion to draw much attention to the one who was cloaked.

One thing was certain: the Order of Saint Phineas had money to burn and used it to buy only the best.

Hell, they'd used it to hire *him*, hadn't they?

There were two small service entrances in the back wall off an urban alley, but neither afforded any view at all of the inside, not even what could be seen through the front gates. The big house was set back, so it was much closer to the alley than the main street, but there was still a fair amount of space to cover if you went in here, and those sensors were *everywhere* and quite directional.

So, okay, Murphy. You're an old fart way past your prime who gets winded going downhill. How the hell would the likes of you get into a place the likes of this one?

He didn't have an answer for that. In fact, the only answers for the really tough ones were twofold: local, preferably inside information, which he didn't have, and whatever money it took to finance what was needed to pull it off once you had that information.

He had the money, but it would take far too much to pull something like this off, and to what end? To see the inside? To say goodbye to the Three Ditzy Colleens? Hardly.

Nope. You'd have to go in by air somehow, and silently at that, then land quiet as a mouse on one of them attic dormers, then find one that you could neutralize the alarms for and then open and squeeze in undetected. You'd need night vision, a couple of good ferrets to scout ahead, and personal shielding just in case you stepped on the wrong floorboard and they came looking just to check.

Magnetic field levitators would be out, they'd surely be detected by this setup. Parachute, then, from someplace a few blocks away and at night. The good old ways. In fact, except for the night vision and the ferrets, the best way to do it at all would be with as little technology as possible. Folks who could afford this kind of super protection paid to guard against every damned piece of potential burglary in all creation, but often forgot that folks often could do things without all those machines. A bit of diversion—say, a runaway elephant or somesuch charging at the gate—and it wouldn't be that impossible to get in.

Getting out would be a different and more complex matter.

What are you thinking about this for, you old fool? he scolded himself. *You said yourself that there's no rhyme or reason to doin' it, no profit, only the gravest danger.* And he was certainly in poor physical shape for such an operation.

Damn it! That's what made the damned challenge so appealing!

And when you're caught, Murphy, what do you tell 'em then? They'd put your brain through a wringer with one of them stones of theirs, find out what an old idiot you were, then scrub your brain clean as a whistle and you'd wake up in a trash dumpster someplace not even rememberin' that you ever done it.

Idly he wondered just how many of those gems they had, and whether or not all of them were in use or stuck in boxes someplace. Just a few dozen of them wouldn't depress the collector's market but would set him up nice for life.

He couldn't forget the effect on that young sergeant, though, looking into just that one. But it showed that you had to basically touch one, or be very close to it, *and* look into it in order for it to work its voodoo. No getting around touching, but you sure as hell didn't need to look into the damn thing's cursed eyes.

It seemed so strange, standing here in the middle of genteel civilization, thinking of those girls and such things as those gem necklaces. It wasn't the idea of losing his soul to the devil—if he had one, the devil long ago owned it outright. But he preferred not to meet the old bastard until he had to.

So what the hell are you doin' here, you blasted idiot?

At just that moment he sensed that he was not alone in the alleylike back lane. It wasn't anything he could see or hear or smell, but there was some old survival sense that told him that he was being observed, and not through some remote camera or sensor. Someone, *something*, was right here with him, watching, waiting, and, somehow too, he felt that it knew him.

He tried to seem natural, looking eventually up one direction and then back the other. Nothing. Nothing but some of the inevitable big bugs and other creepy crawlies that were too much a part of this world to even be banished from these sorts of neighborhoods.

He knew, though, that he wasn't imagining it. Life and death more than once had depended on him accepting these feelings, and more than one promising young scoundrel he'd known had died by dismissing them.

The back doors and windows? Maybe, but the feeling didn't seem that remote, nor did the stone walls lining both sides of the alley lane make for good, consistent angles from which to observe an intruder. Robotic systems would be used for security by folks with this kind of money and status; maybe some suspicious, noisy pet with big teeth as well. This wasn't that. It was more like the sense you got in a jungle when you knew that the snake was just two meters from your neck and ready to pounce. And since nothing that large and intelligent and dangerous would be allowed outside private grounds and certainly would never get this far into the city without tripping all sorts of animal control sensors, that meant a mind.

But where? The brickwork seemed unbroken, the tops of the walls and fences were high but not high enough to conceal somebody like that, and certainly there was nobody in the middle of the road.

Suddenly a male voice whispered to him, so close that he jumped.

"Captain, go down the street to the end, make a left. Someone will meet you at the end of the block."

He went from jumping to freezing solid, and then he turned and slowly, warily, looked closely again. Nobody. Nothing.

He started walking down to the end of the block, casually, but rather obviously in a hurry, taking out his hip flask as he did so and going a wee bit faster with each step. He got to the end, took a hard swallow, looked around, saw nobody yet, took another, and then began walking down the street as directed. At this point, he was too committed to run, and too curious and involved to want to.

Near the end of the block was a lamppost and an ornamental tropical tree. As he approached the tree, a figure seemed to ooze right out of it.

"Captain Murphy, what in the world are you doing here?"

He stared at the small figure for a moment. "Why, it's Lieutenant Chung, isn't it? I could ask the same of you."

"I can't believe you'd miss them or worry about them at this point," she said, shaking her head. "Not *you.*"

He looked a bit sheepish and shrugged. "I know, I know. But there was just somethin' about them, somethin' that was *wrong*, if you know what I mean. Volunteers is one thing, even young girls, but them devil jewels—they was runnin' the show. I don't like that sort of thing. Never held with it. Besides, somethin' in the whole stinkin' mess just got me Irish up. Hundreds of years the damned Limeys run our old land, worked us on our own home soil like slaves, treated us like no better than animals. We threw 'em out finally. Got fed up with it. I'll be damned if I see some other group doin' the same damned thing again."

His answer surprised her. She hadn't thought him even that deep. "My people had a similar experience with the Japanese so I can sympathize. Still, what were you going to do?" she asked him. "Be a new hero of your people? Rush in, blow open the iron gates, find them and steal them back?"

He seemed to sag a bit, and sighed. "Somethin' like that, I guess. Or maybe not. I dunno, really, *what* I was thinkin' of doin', or what I might be *able* to do. But I had to see if there weren't *somethin'*, y'see. And," he added, needling a bit, "it didn't look like there was anybody else that cared."

"We've been here ever since they were brought in," the lieutenant told him. "That's why we couldn't stay with you. That way, we were an obvious and public danger to whoever went to so much trouble to get them."

"You saw who took 'em, then?"

She nodded. "We know a fair amount at this point, although not nearly enough. We didn't have to put a one-on-one tail on them, you see. There was enough chemical tracer in the bath wash in the courier ship that I could probably eventually trace them down within a couple of parsecs of this planet if need be."

Murphy glanced back up the street towards the compound. "So what do they look like, these devil folks?"

"Ordinary. I don't think they're behind this at all. Just

tools, like the girls and many others. Rich folks playing
at being naughty. Their kind's always been with us. Some
can be quite dangerous, fanatics who have become lost
in their own fantasy world, but they can be dealt with.
Oddly, they are usually intellectuals with good contacts
and influence. We would rather not have to harm them
if we can avoid it, but they must be dealt with."

"You're sure the girls are still in there?"

She nodded. "As of now, yes. But people and vehicles
come and go around here, and we sincerely doubt if this
is their final destination. They're going to want those
babies born outside the city, outside of authorities and
monitors and records. We're scouting the place now as
minutely as possible to see if there is a good, easy way
in. The problem is, the girls are only a part of our problem. We need to know who is behind all this. We need
to know just precisely what this is really all about."

"Hmph! Well, I wish I was, but I ain't much of a
burglar. Not at *my* age," the old captain told her.

"That's all right," she responded almost instantly.
"We are."

The next big shock Murphy got was the discovery
that there were eight commandos in the team, not just
the two. The other six apparently spent the trip in a
lower compartment of the courier in some sort of
quick-acting suspended animation. The girls, and the
powers they had thanks to the gems, apparently never
sensed their presence for just that reason. When the
enemy's got hold of your computer, it seems, don't tell
your computer anything you don't want everyone to
know.

Of the group—four men, four women—only a five-
person team were the kind of commandos, all marines,
who went in and engaged in the action; the other three
were naval technicians who backed them up and

oversaw an arsenal of high-tech spy devices and systems. Although Chung was the nominal officer in charge, she was Navy; the man in operational charge was Maslovic, or, as the others chuckled, whatever he was calling himself that mission. They generally referred to him as "Sarge" or sometimes "Chief," but he clearly outranked the only identified commissioned officer in the group. Murphy suspected that not even these men and women who trained and worked with him regularly knew who he really was or what true rank he might hold, but he took his orders from Intelligence and possibly reported directly to the cybernetic Admiralty. To Maslovic, it didn't matter, either. Only missions mattered.

They were set up in an upstairs apartment a block down and on the opposite side of the street from the Order of Saint Phineas. It was as close as they could get and have a back entrance that couldn't be observed from the street and which therefore allowed for unhindered comings and goings by the team. The owners of the place were away on business; they were not expected back for more than a month, which was weeks longer than the Navy would need the place. All wore stock nondescript clothing and hairpieces when going in or out and drew no particular attention from the other neighbors. People in the neighborhood tended not to socialize with one another and to keep their lives pretty much to themselves.

Maslovic stood in back of a small bank of monitors the techs had set up in the back room. He nodded at Murphy and pointed.

"Well, can't say I'm glad to see you on this, since you're not part of the team, but since you're here you might as well get comfortable and watch the show."

Murphy pretended to be hurt. "And here I thought you was just pinin' for me company."

"I had enough of that on the courier. Seriously, Captain, everybody here has worked and trained with everybody else so long that we almost know what the other is thinking. That's why things generally go right when they send us in and why we don't suffer many losses. I'd feel the same way if you were Lieutenant Commander Mohr or even higher up. We need you to keep out of the way no matter what happens. You can watch, but it's not your show. Understand?"

Murphy nodded.

"We've hesitated up to now to send some ferrets in there because we don't know what their alarm systems are like. It's entirely possible we could tip the whole show by doing it, but I don't see any other way. We're going to send two in late tonight and see what we can see anyway, but we'll have a small team ready to go in if things go bad. You've already had a run-in with our Sunday suits, as we call them. Turns you into the spirit in a hurry. If I don't move, that thing'll make me look just like whatever I'm against. We've got the same kind of AI camouflage on the ferrets, small as they are. They're quiet, fast, and efficient, but the fact is that ferrets still make noise and they still put out electrical fields. There's no such thing as a perfect ferret any more than there's a perfect disguise for anybody, but we are damned close. Morrie? You got them tuned up?"

A small tech with a round face and hawk nose looked up from his data screens and nodded. "Any time you need 'em, Chief."

"Well, then, as soon as we're sure they've settled down, we'll go. I don't like the fact that there's a landing pad out front of the grounds there. They could go any time." He looked eager for action. "Now we'll give them a little taste of their saint right back at 'em."

Murphy grinned. "And it's sure that you know who that patron of this world and that society really is?"

"Not particularly. Nobody in the small databank we have with us, anyway."

Murphy's grin widened. "Phineas T. Barnum. 'There's a sucker born every minute,' he once is said to have proclaimed. The trick is to know which is the sucker and which is the Barnum."

"But this whole *world's* named Barnum!"

"Exactly. He also ran the biggest and greatest circus in the world. And when he quit being a showman and a con man, he became a politician. Got elected, too. Con men and circus men and politicians. All one and the same."

"And you're sure that's the Barnum of this world? And the saint this society says?" Maslovic wasn't convinced.

"Oh, yes. It's even in the bloody information line in the phone directory. I think the old boy would have loved this place, and the idea that it was named for him. He'd like these ferrets, too. All the more because they're such clever machines."

"Chief, I think we got a problem," the tech at the control screens said without taking any eyes off the displays.

Maslovic turned quickly. "What?"

"Company coming over there. I think maybe we waited too long."

On the full scanner they could see the identification symbol and blip for a private transport headed down towards them, and a corresponding ID line from it to the Order's front lawn that it was following like a glide path to the landing pod there.

"Might not be for the girls," the tech said hopefully.

"You know it is!" the intelligence agent snapped. His hand went to his chin and his eyes fixed on a spot on the wall as he tried to decide what to do next.

"You gonna follow 'em out, Sarge?" Murphy asked.

The other man shook his head. "No, no, not necessary. They're going to be traceable over the whole damned world for several more days yet. We don't have everything here until the ship arrives, and I wouldn't want to bring them down blind in that jungle. No, if they're going, let them go. Broz, get a ferret over there on the double. At least we should see who the hell is on the thing."

"Rolling now," another tech said in back of them.

Murphy turned and saw a chunky woman remove a small cylindrical object from a specialized case, then go out to the back door area. In half a minute she was back and said, "It's off. Pick it up on Control One."

Although various ferrets were common throughout the colonies for a vast number of jobs, ones of this sophistication were rare. The military model was damned fast, and smart enough to think a bit for itself, at least insofar as carrying out its primary directives. Added control by cybernetic link or by simple voice or typed commands was possible from the control panel.

Several local flying things seemed interested in the speedy little unknown as it raced across the street, up the wall and over it, and down into the garden area inside the compound, but the ferret was too smart for them. When one predatory insect the size of a large bird swooped down on it, the little robotic probe simply stopped, then used the millions of control pixels that made it look covered in fur to match the purplish grass it was on. Without motion, scent, or distinguishing color, the ferret went instantly invisible to the predator, who seemed a bit confused but broke off and flew away into the distance.

On the control screen, they had a very nice three-dimensional "window" seeing just what the ferret was seeing. Smaller, two-dimensional windows across the top and bottom showed views of what was in back of it and what was above it.

"Observe from above, position and freeze," Broz told it, and the ferret scampered most of the way up the front of the large house or lodge or whatever it was and then stuck there, looking back at the landing pad. It was nicely positioned before the aerobus landed and settled with just a deep whine.

A door slid back from the center of the small craft and two women got out, both wearing medical blue uniforms.

"Doctors? Nurses?" Maslovic wondered.

"Midwives, like as not," Murphy responded. "I'd put 'em as nurses overall. Neither of 'em have that command swagger you'd get from a doctor in this kind of position."

"No matter. It's pretty certain now that they're gonna take them out of there," Maslovic commented.

"Door's opening," Broz noted.

Out of the doorway came two people, a man and a woman, both dressed in rather too clean and clichéd tropical clothing, from khaki shorts to pith helmets and wearing heavy-duty boots. The angle didn't give too good a look at the faces, but they both seemed middle-aged and plump, perhaps a bit dowdy or dumpy, and they moved almost like they were playing a game. Some sort of adventure, perhaps.

"Georgi Macouri and his companion Magda Schwartz," Maslovic said, filling Murphy in. "He's the spoiled rich idiot playing at devil worship and she's even more into the play than he is. Don't underestimate them, though. The local police files suspect him of being behind some disappearances, mostly young women, and she's formerly employed by Crossline Shipping as their security director and knows all the gimmicks and tricks."

"Disappearances? You mean he . . . ?" The captain's voice trailed off as he thought of the unpleasant possibilities.

"He could indeed. Human sacrifice wouldn't be beyond him if it was part of the ritual and gave him a thrill. He's spent most of his life being incredibly bored and now he isn't bored any more."

"But—the *girls*! You don't think he'd . . . ?"

"He might, but I doubt it. They're not innocent in this and they're not for sacrificing, at least not right now. Too much was invested in getting them here to just do to them what he's probably done to poor locals. It looks like we may be in a *little* luck here, though. The way they're dressed and taking charge, it sure looks like they intend to go on the bus."

"Right at sunset," Broz noted. "Good timing."

"Earlier than I'd expected, though. It complicates getting the girls, but it does allow us the opportunity to see just what the hell's inside that place. Ah! Here come the girls!"

Their angle, again, was overhead and offset, but there was no mistaking the three of them. Each had been cleaned up, their hair was nicely fluffed and brushed, and each wore a robe whose color roughly matched the colors of the three Magi stones they had. None seemed to be very comfortable walking even the short distance, and it seemed to Murphy at least that they hesitated as they reached the aerobus's open doorway, but each in turn ducked down a bit and entered. The medics or midwifes, whatever they were, then got back in and, finally, the two from the house started to enter the vehicle as well. Then Macouri stopped, turned, and asked Schwartz in a voice that sounded sinister and gravelly, "You have secured the place, my dear?

"Absolutely, darling," she responded in a deep,

businesslike tone. "If you're that worried, call and leave someone."

"No, we'll be gone too long to make that practical. I just have that feeling we're being watched, that's all. I shouldn't like unwanted visitors in there while we were away for so long."

"Oh, relax. It would scare the living daylights out of any silly policeman who tried. Come! I'm anxious to be off!"

Macouri nodded and sighed. "Very well, my dear. I suppose you're right." He turned and entered, followed by his companion, and the door slid silently closed.

Within a minute or two, Murphy could hear the low whine of the engine and feel the vibration even a block and a half down, and the aerobus lifted up and quickly moved off and away into the darkness.

"Darch?" Maslovic asked.

The man at the main panels shrugged. "No problem. They're showing up just fine. Going to be a long trip for them, though. They're heading out over the ocean. We're going to need our own wings to catch them, Chief."

"We'll manage. Broz, you heard Schwartz on that house. Sounds like it's pretty well rigged."

"We'll send the other ferret over now. Our best bet is to go in right away and remotely, even if the systems are all on. The odds are that anything serious that might require their attention or draw their alarms would be better triggered when they're making their trip than after they get where they're going, get settled in, and can call their security computer and maybe friends and associates."

"Fine with me," the sergeant replied. "Let's get moving. I *really* am curious about that place, and this suits me fine. Captain, grab a chair from the other room and bring it in. This may take a while."

"I got nowhere else to be right now," Murphy replied. "And 'tis curious I am as well about all this business."

"Second ferret's away," Broz called from the back.

Maslovic nodded. "Okay, then. Here we go."

It usually wasn't as easy to get a ferret into an allegedly unoccupied house as this was, but in spite of the junglelike animal life that was all over the city and much of the world for that matter, most of the houses that were tightly built still had weak points to be exploited, from slight warping and settling causing small gaps in the foundation to exhaust ports around the upper stories that were blocked mostly by heavy mesh screens and used by the automated systems to exchange air in otherwise climate controlled environments. It was one of these that proved the way in.

The military ferrets could have cut the screen, but in earlier scouting the operators had discovered two small duct ports where the mesh had come loose and could be easily pushed in to allow entry by something the size and plasticity of the ferrets. While there were some dangers following them down into the house, most notably lasers guided by sensors whose sole purpose was to zap any wildlife that might find similar openings inside, they tended to be of a standard sort for which electronic countermeasures were already in the ferrets along with routines to deploy them. The sensors were easily fooled by the simplest of mechanisms—making them see and focus on some suspicious small moving object away from the ferret and then targeting the lasers there while the ferrets darted by on the opposite side.

"Too easy," Murphy muttered.

Broz, the self-styled Commander of the Ferrets, shrugged. "Not easy at all. Probably cost a bloody fortune. What good's a ferret if it can't get by the simple systems designed to swat cockroaches?"

"Maybe. Still and all, didn't you say the lady was some kind of security expert?"

"Efficiency," Maslovic put in. "You don't set bombs and dogs to kill flies. You put your security where it will best secure what you need to secure. If we'd come in over the walls ourselves or through the doors, I think we'd have quite a mess right now, but the ferrets are not us. They'll have something that can detect them, I suspect, but not yet. Ferrets, after all, can only report, they can't carry out the family jewels."

Ferret One was already pushing through the vents built into a top-floor room and now looked down upon it. A quick scan showed it to be on the right side of the house, third floor, and most likely a bedroom.

An old-fashioned-looking ceiling fan turned just below the ferret, keeping the air moving so that it would not get stuffy or build up smells even if the room were left unoccupied for weeks. The ferret could see the air and sense the movement and feed the information back to the computer a block and a half away for analysis. It betrayed no traps, no hidden passages, nothing like that. It was as it should have been.

Below and against the wall was an enormous four-poster bed, its linens still thrown randomly back, indicating that it had been recently used and not yet serviced by a robotic or human housekeeper. Overall, the place looked pleasant and lived in but contained nothing odd or suspicious even if it did seem to be out of another time and place. The ferret stuck to the wall but registered no serious concern. Whatever traps and sensors there were weren't here.

"You'd think they'd at least have somethin' on the windows," Murphy noted.

"Pastine," Broz explained. "The kind of material used in making transparent windows for spacecraft and camera and sensor covers for space work. Not unbreakable, but what it would take to punch a hole in them would not only alert the household but probably the neighbors a kilometer away. Vacuum welded. You aren't going to go in and out of *those*."

"And remember, this is the third floor," Maslovic pointed out. "Second floor's more of the same, and the first floor adds a vacuum layer through which pass some of the most accurate sensors made. And if you were really observant, you'd see that the roof overhang and gutter system covered the grounds around the house to a distance of three meters. Anything heavier than two kilos would trip it, so you're not likely to walk up or use a ladder, and if you're on some kind of floating platform, you'll break the sensor webbing for more than five seconds and that will set off the alarm. Anything more sensitive and you'd have alarms going off every time a bug flew by or a heavy rain rolled down too much for the guttering. The ferrets are less than one kilo and were on the building's siding in under five seconds in any event."

"You make me feel like a rank amateur here," the old captain said respectfully.

Maslovic smiled. "Now you know why you should always pay your defense taxes."

With both ferrets now inside, they fanned out, mapping the entire third floor before going down one level. Some nice bedrooms, sumptuous baths, a full spa in the east wing, but nothing threatening nor of interest to them.

A center atrium framed a circular staircase which the ferrets declined to take. There was a small but detectable electrical current in the stair that indicated some connection to the master maintenance and alarm systems. As usual, the walls were much nicer.

"Interesting paintings hung on the atrium walls there," Murphy noted.

"Yes, I agree," Maslovic responded. "Broz, let's see them in turn."

They were huge and ornately framed, yet there was something about them that didn't seem quite right.

"Separated, but a triptych," the old captain said. "Odd. Go in on the one on the left, if you please."

Broz framed it perfectly in the monitor. Although it didn't come through properly on their screen, it was clearly some kind of holographic photo, a scene that in person would seem almost suspended in the framing. It was a violent scene, a landscape of stark barren landscape, volcanic activity along a rift in the back, and with storm-tossed clouds seeming to close in as if ready to engulf the whole scene.

"Is that a creation of someone's imagination or a photograph of a real place?" the Irishman wondered, the question rhetorical.

"Impossible to say. Let's see the middle."

A dark, cold, threatening landscape it was, with little sense of life of any sort. In the background, rolling hills seemed to fold like dough or plastic in and out of the undulating landscape below a sky of bright, numerous stars.

"And the right," Maslovic requested.

What was dangerous in the first and bleak and cold in the second was absent from the third, a veritable garden of trees, flowers, sparkling pools and even a small waterfall. It was as bright and cheery as the others were threatening and desolate.

"Pull back a bit."

On the wall, between the first and second and again between the second and third picture were ornately carved symbols, three each, overlapping and with one above the other two creating a small pyramid of frozen, mechanical facelike designs.

"Those are like the girls' stones," Maslovic noted, trying to figure out the grand scheme.

"More than that," Murphy responded. "The one up top's quite dark and shiny, the two below are lighter yet have duller finishes. Not the Magi stones but the Magi, Sergeant. Wise men, magicians, astrologers. Balshazzar, Melchior, and Kaspar, the Three Kings of Christian lore. One carried gold to the Christ child, one frankincense, an exotic scent, and the third a rare spice, myrrh."

"I thought you weren't religious."

"I'm not, but by God them catechism classes finally come in handy. 'Twas a Catholic monk that found 'em, so there's a common source, if you please. Me sainted mother always hoped I'd become a priest, but there wasn't no money in it."

"And what's all that have to do with these pictures?" Broz interjected, impatient to go on.

"You don't get it, do you? You never heard of the Three Kings on that shiny sterile factory ship of yours? The three lost worlds of treasure and ease, where all your wishes can come true. That's them, you see. That's what they look like. Shows how much ugliness gets lost in the legend, don't it? That's where the stones come from. That's where whatever this is all about is centered. *That's* where your mysterious enemy is."

"So why don't we just pack up here and go there and face them down?" the tech asked, both bored and confused.

"Aye, see, that's the rub. Nobody knows where they are or how to get there, and them few what did never got back. Devil worship my ass! They found some rich suckers to do their dirty work for 'em, that's all."

"Who?"

Maslovic frowned and turned back to the screen. "Let's see if we can find out. What's that down at the base of the atrium, Broz? I thought I saw it as we were descending until we got sidetracked on the pictures."

The ferret's cameras turned back and then down. "Looks like the top of some kind of statue," she said. "Pretty big, too. Comes up not quite to the second floor itself. Must be real impressive when you come through the door."

"Get around and down a bit. I want to see as much of it as we can without actually touching anything on the ground floor for now."

"Can do. Now zoom out and—*what the . . . ?*"

The position of the ferret allowed them to see the head and a bit of the neck of the statue, and it was not exactly as expected.

It was the devil, all right, complete with horns, pointed ears, and goatee, but it was one *happy* devil, with a grin from ear to ear and the happiest overall expression ever seen on a human or humanoid face. And on top of his head, balanced on one of the horns, was an outrageous top hat tilted to one side.

"He looks rather chipper," Captain Murphy commented. "I wonder if he'll break into 'Melancholy Baby'?"

As Ferret One made its way back up to the second floor and began, along with its companion, a survey of that level, Broz said, "They're not serious, are they?"

"*Very* serious," Maslovic shot back. "That statue's a thumb in the eye to all the religious types who might get in for some reason or another. These aren't people who are comedians, Corporal, they're people who are supremely confident."

"So far, all they look like are a study in the rich and lazy," Broz responded.

"Well, now that we've met Saint Phineas of Barnum himself, maybe we'll be able to see a bit of what they're up to," Murphy said hopefully. "But the greatest show off Earth won't be here, it's gonna be on them three worlds in the pictures. Too bad we ain't yet found a map to the places."

Maslovic thought about that. "We'd run the legend on the Three Kings when we went to identify and quantify those stones," he told the captain. "Now it seems that we have a more basic link. Not that those places looked like paradises. In fact, they don't look all that different than other worlds in these areas. Interesting, though, if they're true pictures of the real thing."

"That garden one looked pretty good," Murphy noted. "I could see meself lyin' there while voluptuous nymphs peeled me grapes."

Maslovic nodded. "And if I had to pick the one I'd least trust, it would be that one. Compared to the other two it's like sweets to a baby. It's the one we're *supposed* to look at. The hot, stormy, volcanic one, though, looks too unstable for any kind of base for any sort of advanced civilization. It must have a function, because if those three are real, then they were either built or terraformed, designed that way, but staying alive and staying healthy would be a full-time challenge there. No, if I were hiding out and running things, I'd go where nobody was likely to pick. I'd go to the smaller, dark, barren one. Not on the surface—that's the blanket you hide under. Underneath. Under the ground." He looked over at Murphy. "Those aren't mystical or nostalgic pictures, they're guides. And if I knew where they were, I'd use them to take me right to the enemy."

"You seem pretty sure they're an enemy."

"They aren't acting like anything else. We're cut off from our mother world and more than half of all that's human, and if you aim at the area where they were that we can no longer reach, you find the place boiling, almost a hell of gamma ray eruptions strong enough to sterilize the whole sector. They don't tell you that because if they did the combination of panic and despair would be incalculable. We've seen such things happen before, but never this close, never even in this galaxy. Until now, there was no reason to think that it wasn't natural, some kind of thing that just happens in the physics of the cosmos. Now, though, we have a question. So far, all the major emissions have been away from us; it's barely been a ripple here. But if they were to go off in this direction, or almost anywhere in this sector, all of us, and everything we've ever known, everything that is left of the human race, would be gone forever. All life gone, a sterilized museum."

"You really want to fill a man with cheer," the captain commented. "And you think all this is a part of that?"

"We don't know. It doesn't seem likely that we encounter this kind of nasty business wielding this kind of power and have it not connect." The sergeant turned back to the controls. "Full second-floor sweep done?"

"Yes, sir," Broz responded. "Large formal dining room, a number of meeting rooms, library, formal study, that sort of thing, as well as one heavily sealed security zone right in the center behind the atrium stair. House maintenance has started, so we'll have to watch it. Lots of robotic cleaning and polishing, but if they happen to detect the ferrets, then they'll bring security on full."

He nodded. "All right, then, we'll ease down to the ground floor. Watch the floors and lower halves of the walls, though. Keep to the inside walls. This will be where maximum security would be deployed."

"I'm well aware of that, sir," Broz responded. "I know

my job." Even as the ferrets descended on either side of the giant statue, though, the controller looked at the monitors and the instruments and suddenly had a sharp intake of breath, freezing both ferrets.

"Corridors in back of the security column aft of the statue," Broz noted. "Both sides are protected with pretty strong force fields powered from within the security unit and separate from the house power. These are full fields, backed up with lasers and ray sweepers. They sure don't want anybody or anything going back there."

"Think we can get in there?"

"I'm running the checks now. The security room's out of the question. Sealed right, best I've ever seen, and in a vacuum as well. That woman and her company know the business. No way to tell if it runs over all the way to the back of the house through the ceiling. Not without ripping up the ceiling from the top, which is more than these ferrets can do. Under is even less likely. Under that fake polished-wood veneer is an energized plasma running through layers of weapons-grade material."

"How does the air get in and out?" Maslovic asked.

"It appears common air molecules pass without hindrance in and out and through the force field. Interesting effect, too. Note that thin line of material on the floor there? That's dust and pollen, possibly a few insects. The air that gets through is purified as it goes."

"Messy. How do they clean it, I wonder?" the captain mused.

"Eh?" All three of the military team there turned and looked at him in puzzlement for a moment.

"Fancy pants like these, they sure as hell won't let some nice, thin lines of dirt show up so clearly just beyond the entrance. What would Lord and Lady

Triplefarts think when they came for tea? You see what I mean?"

"No," they all answered at once.

"You just don't have no experience with these kinds of folk. That floor, and that line of crud, has just got to be the most cleaned up and maintained little place in the whole damned house. And if it even cleans the dust and pollen in the air, then it's got to happen just about all the time, not just when the house is bein' treated, y'see. I'll bet you that the two lines are vacuumed and polished every couple of hours. No longer, surely."

"So it's blown and vacuumed. So what?"

"No, no. Can't be. That just winds up with a lot of it goin' back and forth into the air. We'd have dust all over, and we can't have that. It'd show on the white gloves. And there's no border or seam, so the thing has to be close vacuumed or washed and then repolished, and I mean repolished directly under the beam. Are you gettin' it now?"

Maslovic gave a low whistle. "You've saying that something, some gadget, is immune to the force field. Either that, or the force field's off for a few seconds, maybe longer, while that happens."

"Got to be."

"Let's see. Broz, keep one ferret on that force field where it meets the floor. If the captain's right, it shouldn't be too long considering the size of that dust ring right now. The other we can use to carefully survey the rest of the place."

"Fair enough."

The sergeant turned and looked at Murphy with unusual appreciation. "How'd you figure this? You a better thief than I took you for or what?"

"That, perhaps," the old man admitted. "At least in me own day. That and the fact that I come from a family with a pretty long line of charwomen . . ."

It wasn't quite as quick as Murphy guessed, but, eventually, they saw it: a tiny round robotic cleaner with a fanlike action that came out of an eight-centimeter-high compartment on one side of the opening and seemed to glide along picking up the accumulation right along the force field, half in and half out. It was lightning fast and the field above it ceased only so long as it was traveling its small route along the floor, a width of no more than fifteen or sixteen centimeters, but for that very brief time and in effectively constant motion, there was a gap.

"Sloppy," Broz commented. "Lots of small remotes could get through."

"Yeah? Then how come *you* didn't think of it?" Murphy asked.

Broz ignored the insult. "The only question is, is there a second line of defense inside that would make this meaningless? If so, then we're still stuck and we might as well just blow the thing. If not, though, it's a lapse in either logic or cost that can get us in. That is, if you want to risk one of the ferrets."

"Why not?" Maslovic responded. "I have a feeling we'll have to blow our way in there anyway, but at least we can see what we're up against. If it's destroyed, we've got a dangerous problem. If it gets through, then the security's basic and for show."

"Not like *your* security, of course, which thought of everything 'cept maybe three wee girls compromisin' your whole security system," Murphy said with a half smile.

Again, his comment was neither acknowledged nor returned.

They almost missed their next opportunity, even though it was something they should have expected. The next time, the cleaner came from the opposite side back towards where they'd first seen it. Fortunately, the ferret was smart enough to refigure the angle and keep to the basic instruction, which was to breach the force field. At the precise moment, it leaped and passed over the cleaner at an angle, giving it just enough time to clear the field.

"We're in," Broz said needlessly.

"Better than in," the sergeant responded. "There are the basic controls at that wall panel. Doesn't even look like a code pad or biometric pass. Don't go for it yet—it still might set off an alarm. Let's see what's back there."

The ferret had no choice but to be on the floor at this point, but got back on the side wall as soon as it could do so.

The two sides of the hallway around the sealed security master console joined again on the other side and, in the area beyond, descended into a large semisunken chamber that could be seen only using the ferret's high-capability, low-light system.

The room itself was out of another age, but not like the house. Instead, it seemed from some ancient time, a burial vault in ancient Egypt, perhaps, or some long forgotten prehistoric civilization. If it hadn't been so antiseptically clean, it might have been taken for something original rather than some kind of show business set.

"I'm half surprised he doesn't have robotic rats and cockroaches and such scurryin' about," Murphy noted. "Kind of loses some of its atmosphere without 'em."

"But it gets it back with that central altar," the security man replied.

And, in fact, that was the dominant part of the room: a raised rectangular object made to look as if carved out of solid stone, and on top was space enough for a human of average build to lie in a concave area designed for that purpose. From the sacrificial area came careful channels running off and down to the sides, and then down to a depression that went completely around the altar stone.

"Spectroanalysis on the stains along the channels and sides, please," Maslovic ordered.

Broz adjusted some controls, focused on a particularly promising spot, and almost immediately began getting data.

"We don't have to go very far in the analysis to figure this one out," Broz commented. "It's blood."

"What kind of blood?"

"Human. Beyond that we'd need a sample for DNA analysis."

"Hardly worth it. We probably wouldn't know them anyway," Maslovic replied. "So, he's loonier than even we thought. I bet the ceremonies here are right out of ancient thrillers. I'm not sure we need to see much more. We can feed this to the local cops here and they'll have a field day, but I'm beginning to think now our best interest is in assembling the team and going into the bush."

"If Macouri has this much guts in town, in this surveillance paradise, to do *this*, imagine what he does out there, where there's nobody to catch him," Broz said.

"I doubt if he's any more, or less, dangerous out there, but I don't think he uses the bush for that kind of cover. No, he gets off by doing this under the noses of everybody. The risk is part of it for those types. The idea that he's doing this sort of thing right here, in a rich section of the city, under the noses of the best human and automated policing systems around. That said, I want to nail this bastard out of the city if possible."

"With this sort of evidence? Why not make it the locals' problem?" Broz asked him.

"Because he might beat it, or it's possible he has a very efficient trap under there or in that sealed security module that might eliminate not only the evidence but several square blocks around including here. No, as much as I'd love a crack at that house and particularly the records inside, all this has convinced me that we have to move on him *now*, where he is, while he's away."

"And me?" the old captain asked him. "I was thinkin' of the girls, y'see. I *did* bring 'em, after all. And others, too, before 'em."

Maslovic turned and looked at him. "Were all your previous passengers women?"

"Well, no, come to think of it. And not all the women were preggers, neither. But these are, and it don't mean that some folks I was responsible for didn't wind up on that slab in there."

Maslovic shook his head. "No, Captain. We train for this. We practically know how one another thinks, and we have all our own gadgets as well. You can follow with the techs, but you have to stay with them until we finish what we have to do out there and signal that you can come in."

"I figured as much on that. But the girls . . . You're not gonna git 'em in the middle of a firefight, are you?"

"We'll do the best we can. Just remember that they aren't captives, they're a part of it."

"But them devil's gems—"

"Those things give them power and direction, but I didn't have any sense that they hadn't knowingly put them on, nor that they had any intention of fighting the power and influence. No, Captain, this isn't the rescue of the innocents. What happens to them will be partly their own choice. We're after not only the bastards like Georgi Macouri, we're much more after the ones he's serving and the ones behind those devices. If we're all lucky, the girls will have a choice, but only a choice. They can help us, or the others." He turned to the two techs. "Recall the ferrets as soon as possible. I'll get Lieutenant Chung and we'll start prepping the team. Let's move!"

VIII:
A DEVILISHLY FOUL FELLOW

They were named Sanchez, Ndulu, Rosen, and Nasser
and they all looked like they liked bending barbells with
their bare hands as warm-up exercises.

Sanchez and Ndulu were female, but you could
hardly tell that until you were pretty close, and in the
case of the strike team seemed irrelevant anyway. These
were not in any way the kind of folks Captain Murphy
thought of as normal.

He met them only briefly, as Chung and her tech
team set up in an aerovan they had rented and then definitely violated the lease renovating. He would remain
with them, and watch and hear the action secondhand.
Chung would coordinate wearing the same sort of virtual command helmet she'd used to fly the shuttle; it
would augment her senses and abilities sufficiently to

effectively monitor all of the automated backups for the team at once, and to effectively watch the combat personnel's back. Darch would insure that all of those things, including Chung's apparatus, were deployed and working properly and he would manually back her up; Broz would oversee the equipment they'd assembled in the van as well as the shuttle's own protective systems just in case they were spotted, even though they would be several kilometers away and in the middle of nowhere when it all went down.

Murphy was surprised they didn't use robotic soldiers for all this, maybe controlling them like Chung ran the show, but then, he thought, these people were the closest thing to combat robots that he knew and probably both biologically designed and cybernetically augmented for just the jobs they had. He felt helpless, though, just sitting there in the van watching and listening as others determined everything, even though he had no desire to be one of these people.

Maslovic had hoped to put this sort of thing off until he had the full navy task force at his disposal, with any personnel, supplies, gimmicks, and whatnot backing him up, but he felt now as if events were overtaking them. The fact that Macouri hadn't destroyed the Order's headquarters when he'd left pretty well said that he expected to return to it, but the manner of his leaving and the totality of the lockup said that he had no plans to return soon.

That left the question of where the rest of the members of the Order were, for there were surely quite a number of them, and also what the hell three pregnant girls from a rural backwater world had to do with all this.

It was his call and he'd made it. They were going in.

The objectives were basic. Incapacitate and capture for interrogation anyone who might be likely to yield information on this business. Seize as much in the way of records and other intelligence as might be available. And, if possible, get those damned jewels, any and all of them, but insure that they were *not* in the position of being used by wearers against the team. It was that last that worried them all, but at least now they knew the power of the things and they respected it. The order was clear: anyone, and that included the girls, who tried to use the power of those things against the team or any of its members or in aid of anyone in the Saint Phineas group would be simply eliminated. They could not afford to take a chance.

Each of the team members wore a combat suit made for them and for no other person. The suits were almost like living exoskeletons, usable only by their matched wearer and, in fact, were grown in tanks and wedded to individuals through a kind of symbiotic connection that only those who oversaw the process knew.

They had several means of propulsion, but in cases like Barnum's World, where there was a very strong magnetic field, they were able to literally float above the forest floor and, using magnetic pulses, propel themselves with no more than a low whining sound just about anywhere their wearers wanted to go.

The suits were also thin and plastic, like a thick second skin, and they covered the whole marine save for the face itself. Cybernetic implants throughout the body allowed not only for full control of the suit's range of functions but also allowed for near silent communication between team members as well as between themselves and the tech coordinator, in this case Chung.

They followed the basic rules of those who created and deployed these teams, a cardinal one of which was to never do anything in the daytime if you could avoid it. The marines' eyes, from a biodesigner and included in their very DNA, allowed them an amazing visual acuity in dark areas, taking in light at such an efficient rate that they were often nicknamed for big cats. In this case they were Tiger One through Tiger Five, with One being Maslovic himself. With augmentation from the suit electronics, they could if need be also see in spectrums ranging from the infrared to the ultraviolet.

The ferrets had done a nice preliminary recon of Macouri's lodge and camp, but they could only go so far here. Unlike the house, which had to contend with everything from city power and broadcasts to air conditioning and such, defenses out here could concentrate on the abnormal, which would be anything of any significant size and mobility approaching the compound. Even the ferrets would have been noticed, as they would have shown up as small but potentially threatening animals yet without biological signs. They simply weren't designed to fend off the kind of probing rays that fed any signs of danger, natural or human generated, to the security people there.

The ferrets could, however, tell the military team what kind of probes and guards were there, and the away team could compensate pretty well for them. They would probably be noticed when they breached the perimeter, but they'd be pretty damned hard to find once they did.

The same went for the team. Once they found a way in, they could make themselves next to invisible to people and virtually all known electronic monitors. That was how they'd surprised the captain back in the alley. The suits could so attune themselves to backgrounds that they were virtually invisible, and because they also masked body heat and emissions if the faceplate was in, they simply didn't show up as life-forms.

Several kilometers away, completely suited up,

Maslovic floated near the compound and observed it through all the filters he had available.

The place itself was as luxurious as he and the others might expect. Built out of a combination of synthetics and real jungle hardwood, it was almost half the size of the big house in town, although far more rustic and exotic looking. It was also round and anchored in the swampy soil on sturdy stilts of the best building support materials, probably anchored to bedrock far down in the earth. The panoramic windows looked out on a jungle lake so unspoiled that it might have been out of some ancient naturalist's book, and light was not only artificial and direct inside but also outside, again for atmosphere, given by external blazing torches on long poles. These also marked and illuminated well-manicured trails down to places like the boat dock, supply sheds, stables, and whatever else was there.

There was a strong electronic fence around the main compound as well, but it was basically designed to keep things out that might wander in with feet or tentacles or whatever on the ground. This was an area where ancient animals of Old Earth had been released after being brought back from extinction, so there were hippos and crocodiles and a lot more about that might well wander into camp. Those the fence would discourage.

More imposing was the aerial protection. Using the full capabilities of their viewers, the marines could see a vast spiderweb of crisscrossing lines covering the place like a dome, all in the spectrums invisible to the human eye.

"We're not gonna squeeze in *there* without being noticed," Sanchez commented, merely voicing what the others already thought.

"Yeah, anybody bring anything for tunneling?" Rosen asked, only half joking.

"Knock it off, team," Maslovic responded. "Nothing we haven't seen before there."

"Maybe, but when you look at the amplitudes they're using, they could short out these suits breaking through," Ndulu put in. "To get through we're going to have to break the web ahead of time."

Maslovic concentrated on the main lodge. "A number of people in there. I wish we could tell how many. Broz, what about the ferrets?"

"See if you can drop one between the fence and the shield," the tech responded from the command center. "They might be plastic enough to breach that web at some point. No place to climb, though, so we're talking going straight through on the ground."

"No good, then," Maslovic replied. "There's a base band that ties the webbing together. No way a ferret's getting through at the base. Whoever did this knew their stuff."

"Schwartz," Darch put in from the command center. "That sort of thing is what she's good at. It should also absorb a pretty good series of energy bolts, I'd say, and the moment they know they're under attack, webs like that automatically go to lethal strength."

"Maybe. But why have the perimeter fence if you have *that*?" Maslovic wondered.

"Maybe the thing's a series of waves going to that central cap," Nasser suggested. "That would mean that right at that base would be the weakest point. Your lethal pulses would come from that ring up until they met that cap and were dissipated. I think the distribution's uneven in any event. You can almost see it."

"Not much room between outer and inner, though," Ndulu pointed out. "Which of you wants to volunteer to try it?"

It was an interesting point, and a potentially lethal one. If you blew the outer fence, the alarm would go off all over and then, even if the inner web was as weak as the theory went, there would be time for it to concentrate lethal energy on that small area.

"I think maybe we're going at this wrong," Maslovic said after thinking a moment. "One missile and this place is history. This isn't designed to repel an army, or anything like one. It's a defense against spies, thieves, and large animals. Too bad we don't have some large animals around. We might be able to panic them into all that and short it out."

Back in the command center, Captain Murphy moved forward. "Darch? You got a high-up view of the animal life in the area?"

The tech frowned at the interruption but switched one of the screens to a broader view. "Yeah. So?"

"Hmmm . . . Forget them big suckers in the shallows there. They're hippos. They'd do the job but they don't exactly herd. But there's some grasslands off to the east of the lake. They wouldn't generally come into the jungle, but they could probably be convinced. See 'em?"

"No, I—oh, yeah! Look mostly asleep, though."

"Indeed they would be. They're daytimers mostly. Still and all, I don't think we're gonna sneak into that pretty place out there. That means we either just watch it or we take it down. What do you say, Sergeant? Take it down?"

Maslovic heard the exchange and examined the options. "I think he's right, troops. But it's going to take a while to set up, and in the meantime maybe we ought to sit it out for several hours. See who appears tomorrow morning. By then, maybe, we'll be in position to take this damned place and all that's in it."

They both looked like something out of another world and a far earlier age. Georgi Macouri wore a

lightweight but semiformal coat and tie and matching
dark Bermuda shorts; Magda Schwartz was in a long
flower print dress. Both wore substantial chukka boots
that provided substantial if incongruous protection.

"What a *gorgeous* morning, darling!" Schwartz
gushed, looking at the sunrise over the lake beyond.

"Indeed. Shall we have some breakfast, my dear?"
Macouri asked her.

"Oh, yes. Out here, of course."

Marcouri turned towards the front door and called,
"Joshua! We will take our morning repast on the
porch!"

Within a minute, a huge bearded man, easily two
meters tall and dressed in white jacket and black pants,
emerged from the house carrying a silver tray with two
pitchers and twin cups and saucers on it. Only his
gunbelt and holstered pistol seemed unusual. He
approached the duo now seated at a small table on the
porch and professionally put the cups and saucers on
the table and then poured for both of them.

Magda Schwartz turned and looked out to her right,
frowning. "Frightful noises over that way, darling! I
wonder what in the world that can *be*?"

Marcouri nodded and turned in the same direction,
cocking his ear, as he sipped his morning coffee. "Can't
say, but it's not quite anything I've heard before from
here."

"Goodness! You can feel the ground shaking a bit!
If I didn't know better, I'd swear that was a herd of
elephants approaching at full gallop! I hope the vibra-
tions don't set off all the alarm systems!"

"Elephants! Yes, that's *exactly* what it sounds like!"
Marcouri was on his feet. "*Joshua!*" he shouted. "Come
at once! Everyone else to their places! I don't like the
sound or feel of this!"

Schwartz looked confused and concerned. "A herd

of wild elephants? Why would they be coming this way? My god, there's swamp and dense forest between their area and here! They must be frightened as hell of something!"

"Or being driven! *Joshua!* Bring me the shotgun!" He turned to his companion. "You wish anything, my dear?"

Magda Schwartz pulled up her flowered print dress along her left leg and withdrew a nasty looking energy rifle from a leg holster. "Not exactly in period, but sometimes one must do what one must do."

Joshua emerged, handing a double-barrelled shotgun of the type approved by the Barnum's World gamekeepers to Macouri and then drawing his own very large pistol. It looked exactly like a large caliber projectile sidearm of the approved sort, but in reality it was a powerful tight-beam ray device that could burn a hole in a hippo at short range. Its only drawback was that its power was quite limited by the need for imitation; although he had more powerpacks in his jacket, he would have only a few seconds of sustained shooting before he'd have to manually eject the dying cartridge and insert a new one.

Georgi Macouri stared in the direction of the steadily increasing sounds and vibration and shouted over the rising noise, "Magda, what would happen if a dozen full-grown elephants hit that outer fence?"

She looked suddenly at a loss and shook her head. "I don't know. It wasn't designed for an entire herd. More worrisome is the inner grid. At that speed, while the lead couple may well be barbecued, it might displace the connector foundations and bring the whole thing down!"

Macouri looked over at Joshua. "Get most everybody out here, *now*! Leave somebody to look over the guests, but otherwise, emergency! And call in the aerobus!"

The sound and vibration were almost unbearable now, and there was, in addition, the cracking noises and shaking of trees just beyond their direct view, telling them that whatever was coming was almost here. They almost wished that whatever it was, in fact *was* already here. The suspense was worse than fighting off a threat.

A half-dozen burly gunmen burst from the lodge and began fanning out along the porch, heavy weapons in hand. They were huge brutes, heavily tattooed from head to foot, mostly dressed in work pants and sleeveless undershirts. They looked like nothing so much as a cartoon of someone's vision of an old pirate crew; one or two even had nasty-looking side swords to complement their much more modern laser pistols.

Macouri felt better just seeing them there. Any one of them could blow a couple of rampaging elephants to the next planet.

Magda Schwartz looked very nervous now, waiting for the attack to come at any moment. "Oh, and it was *such* a *pretty* morning!" she said, mostly to herself.

Joshua, the clear leader of the staff and guards, frowned suspiciously as he looked out at the trembling bush. "There's something bloody strange here," he said loudly.

"What?" Macouri shouted over the increasing din.

"I said that something's not right here, sir!" the big man shouted. "Nobody controls elephants like that except they be ridden by experts! Particularly not through that bloody swamp! It's a trick of some kind, I swear!"

At that moment, they were all knocked over as a huge blast seemed to strike the lodge from the rear, followed quickly by a series of small, sharp explosions. Instantly, a circular arc of bluish energy was formed by the security grid and seemed to pour to the rear, and there was an incredibly loud clap of thunder and the smell of ozone.

Macouri tried to pick himself off the porch and find where he'd dropped his gun. "All of you! Up and to the back!"

"No!" Schwartz screamed at them as the din of charging elephants continued. "That was the grid shorting out! We've got no security fence!"

That got everybody's attention. "Good god! We're sitting ducks out here, then!" their boss said loudly but as much to himself as to them. Finding his shotgun, he got to his feet. "Everybody spread out! Joshua! You and Spilver to the rear to see what happened! The rest of you stay at your post and be prepared to shoot anything that approaches!" He ran over and helped Schwartz to her feet. "As for us, my dear, I think we'd better retreat inside!"

She looked a bit dazed and shaken, but managed to nod, and with the help of his arm made it back inside the large lodge doors.

At the back, Joshua and the scruffier-looking but equally imposing Spilver made it to the back by opposite routes at almost the same time, weapons drawn and ready. There was nobody obviously there, but *something* clearly had happened. The whole rear grounds had been scoured almost as if a meteor had struck.

Going to the railing and looking down, the two guards saw a massive black basalt rock that had to weigh a ton or more sticking half in and half out of the earth. It had clearly had no problems with the outer fence and had been flung in by someone or something with enough force that it had come to rest on the anchor of the grid, and had gouged enough ground to take out the whole circular base for the entire width of the great rock. It looked scarred and now had several deep fractures, the result of both the landing and the massive energy that had come in and concentrated on it just after it had broken the plane, but it had done its job.

Joshua looked over at Spilver. "Get inside to the security console and cut the exterior power on this thing! Otherwise it could flare up at any moment and fry any of us!"

"Aye, sir!"

"And make sure the internal controls are still viable!" the big security chief added.

As Spilver ran to do his assignment, Joshua got to work with the old-fashioned kind of duty he felt most comfortable about. Calling the security people together, he positioned them around the entire lodge but on the porch, warning them not to step off until Spilver reported that it was safe to do so, and placing them in such a way that each one could see the man or woman on each side of them all the way around. Somebody had gone to a lot of trouble with this, but so far they hadn't taken advantage of it. Well, let 'em come! He felt confident that his people could take anybody else human one on one, and most of them preferred it that way anyway.

Off to the east, someone quite deliberately and somewhat mockingly killed the noises of a herd of charging elephants in such a way that the sounds slowed to a stop, betraying their phony origin.

Joshua fingered his weapon and looked out at the bush. *Okay*, he silently called to whoever it was, *you want to come to me now, come on! Even on elephants!*

"Got both ferrets in," Broz reported. "One of them went in the front door with those two characters! They never looked up! Talk about roughing it! The damned lodge is even air conditioned!"

"They've still got power, then?" Maslovic asked.

"Yes, sir. Full power and water on. They've got internal security systems, too, but with all those people there they have to be on minimum."

"Still, best not to disregard them," the team leader said, both to himself and as a reminder to the others. "They're almost certainly keyed to anybody not in their data banks."

"I wouldn't worry about them *too* much," Broz responded. "They haven't spotted either ferret yet and they had to be easily updatable if the girls are in there, let alone anybody else." She whistled. "Quite a place in there. Not a lot of privacy, but lots of atmosphere. I'll feed it to you."

It *was* luxurious, all apparent hardwoods and polished floors and walls. The main living area was a single great room entered from the massive front doors, filled with antique but comfortable-looking furniture, faux wicker tables and settees, a formal dining area that could seat at least twelve, a big central fireplace that looked real but was betrayed as a simulator by the lack of an outside chimney and, along the walls, the stuffed heads of all sorts of exotic wild beasts, mounted on ornate plaques. Although large, the great room clearly wasn't as big internally as the lodge itself, and there were openings at strategic intervals for entryways into a series of surrounding rooms. Most had push-away netting over their doors, but one near the rear and behind the dining table was a true hinged double door, and next to it a window opening and ledge. Clearly that was the kitchen.

On either side of the central fireplace there were curved stairs leading to a second floor and, up there, a balcony and entrances to what must have been modest-sized but ample bedrooms.

Maslovic did a mental count. Let's see, ten guard-staff personnel, eight of which were now around the exterior of the place, Magda and Georgi, of course, at least two more guards inside, including the big fellow who was clearly the chief bodyguard, the three girls and at least one other referred to when they came out who, it appeared, was a tough-looking woman with fiery snake tattoos on both arms and maybe different subjects on other places as well, acting as a chief cook and personal waiter to anyone inside. She didn't look all that old, but a big mane of woolly hair was almost snow white, and there were visible scars on her face, arms, and back. She'd lived a hard life, no matter if it had been a long one or not, and it showed.

"Have one of the ferrets get a peek in each of those rooms, up and down," Maslovic ordered. "I want to know where those girls are, if they're here, and if they're the only ones we haven't accounted for yet. I don't want any surprises if we bust into the place."

"Will do."

It didn't seem large enough for there to be any more unaccounted-for staff or guests, but the place was larger than it looked and the downstairs staff rooms were quads, four hammocks to a room, and could easily have handled another four or more staff people. Behind the incredibly realistic simulated fireplace was the full cooking kitchen, complete with a small but adequate walk-in refrigerator and a full replicator unit of the type the navy people recognized from their own ship—but much, much fancier. At the far end was a huge single wooden door with a vacuum-style handle on it. It might have been some security door, but it seemed more likely that it was a small wine cellar.

The girls that had brought them all there were also not hard to find. Irish O'Brian was sitting in one of the plush chairs in the great room thumbing through pictures of some sort and looking nervous. Mary Margaret McBride was pacing around near the front door, even more nervous. Only the quiet and somewhat flaky Brigit Moran was out of sight, possibly upstairs.

What was most noticeable about the two they *could* see was that both seemed in excellent health and strength, neither seemed a prisoner and, most astounding of all, neither looked pregnant.

"Doesn't make sense," Murphy said from the control van. "Even if they're better healers with superhuman strength, where's the babies? A crash like we give 'em shoulda woke the little darlin's up into a screechin' frenzy. It ain't normal, I tell you!"

Darch, the overall technical manager for the team, shrugged. "Can you tell me just what *is* normal about these people? *Any* of them? Not just your girls."

"I get your point."

Broz studied the two they could see. "At least they're not prisoners or unwilling participants. Look at those faces. As someone with a lot of experience in these kind of operations, Captain, I'd say that if you walked in there now they wouldn't exactly greet you with hugs and kisses. More likely they'd blow you away without a thought."

As much as he hated to admit it and only partly believed it, looking at those two in the viewscreen, it seemed very close to the truth.

"Well, no apparent sacrificial altars and the like," Maslovic noted from his point of view in the trees just beyond the compound. "This isn't a rescue mission."

"Praise be for that much!" Murphy muttered to himself.

Darch wasn't in such a good mood. "Look, it took half the night and more than half the energy pods in this thing to pick up and fling that rock and then get back out of the way. We fooled 'em last time with some jungle terror but they won't be suckers like that again, and I don't dare risk bringing this thing in close again. Not to mention that none of you have the power packs to be able to clear this region without us. Either we take 'em, and soon, or they're going to have somebody in close that will pick them up and we're off to do this all over again someplace else. Both that big fella before and now our two subjects are on the horn to *somebody*. Either we're gonna have a friggin' army show up, or they're getting a lift. Better decide and quick."

"How much notice can you give us?"

"At best, maybe ten minutes, maybe less. There are busses and vans and shuttles flying all over here at all sorts of altitudes. It's the only way to get in or out of these places. They don't have to come from one of the cities or the small freebooter towns here. They can divert at any moment," Darch reminded him.

Maslovic thought it over for a moment, then sighed. "Okay, so we take them. I don't want any chances with the ones outside. They *all* go down. No exceptions. Knock them cold for an hour or kill them if we have to. But inside, stun grenade and heavy stun shots, *no* lethal force. We need them alive if we can manage it. You see any of those gems on them, you take them. Rip them off with whatever force and by whatever means you need to. Put them in the secure sample pouches and close up tight. You remember what those girls did on the ship. If they get half a chance with us, we're all dead."

That's eight defendin' against you just outside, Murphy thought. *Cocky bald-headed bastards, aren't they?*

Maslovic acted as the spotter. "Okay, everybody, no use for a countdown here. When I give the word, I want each of you to drill the sentry closest to you. Ideally, it'll be when the other two aren't looking, but we all know how *that* drill goes. Sanchez, as soon as you hit yours, cover your left. Rosen, you do right,

Ndulu, left, Nasser, right. And don't shoot each other! I'll cover from here as best I can and when we get them all, we converge on the main doors but don't enter. Repeat, do *not* enter until I join you. The odds are, the first person through without the magic password dies, got it? Okay, the ones outside are beginning to look bored and a couple are just staring out into the jungle waiting for us and wishing we'd attack. Let's oblige . . . *now!*"

One of the guards near the back thought he heard something in the trees and looked up, bringing his weapon up as he did so. At that instant a part of the wooden lodge wall behind him shimmered and seemed to move, and before the sentry knew what hit him there was a sharp electronic *thwang!* and he got a rough shove over the railing and onto the ground five meters below.

The moment this happened, a female sentry, sensing movement and hearing the report, turned to check on her companion. At that split second, Sanchez whirled left and shot her full in the chest as Rosen emerged from the wall and fired a wide spread on the same hapless sentry from the other side. Even as the woman went down, an expression of total bewilderment on her face, her hands still clutching the rifle, Sanchez was to her, kicking away the weapon and joining Rosen in a near simultaneous firing on the next sentry who was just now turning to see what the hell was going on.

Ndulu and Nasser had the same good fortune on their side of the porch, but the next one in line was able to yell out a warning and even get off a shot before being brought down. The noise of the shot was deafening and unexpected; it had been a long time since any of the marines had heard a real concussion and projectile firing.

Ndulu was forced backwards by the power of the shot, and her left hand went to her right shoulder and came back with blood. "I'm all right! Left-handed! Let's get the rest of the bastards!" she yelled, and she and Nasser opened continuous fire on the next one in line on their side.

They were now down to three foes on the porch, and the trio weren't waiting to be picked off. One each crouched on either side of the door, using the porch furniture as shields, while the third, the smallest and most acrobatic of the guards, ran partly down the steps to the ground and then turned and crouched there, able to cover either of her companions or shoot in either direction.

None of them had spotted Maslovic above them and in the trees. "They're waiting for you on both sides," he warned them. "I'll take the one on the stairs."

Without even thinking about it, Sanchez on one side and Nasser on the other leaped over the railing and landed with rolls on the ground below, then got up and made their way out from the building and then forward, just ahead of their companions still on the porch but at just enough distance to be able to shoot anything that presented itself.

"No good, everybody stop!" Maslovic ordered. "Now, at my command, I'm going to take the stair shooter and I want the two on the ground to use their floater packs, go up and shoot low and wide on either side of the front door. Got it? Darch, you come forward as soon as you hear our shots and finish them off. Okay . . . *Now!*"

It was almost a textbook exercise. Although neither of the marines on the ground could see the nearly prone ambushers above, both could see the door and simply rose up and squeezed off an energy clip towards the lowest point on the porch. Maslovic fired as soon as he'd given the order, hitting the woman on the stairs squarely in the back before she even realized he was there. Nasser nailed one on the porch but did not put him completely out of action; the other sensed Sanchez and rolled on the porch as she came up to it. They both fired nearly at once, and both hit their marks. Sanchez dropped like a stone, but the man on the porch was going nowhere, either.

Rosen and Ndulu could see each other as the wounded but still dangerous last guard started firing in wide bursts. He barely missed Nasser but the marine was forced to drop back below the porch line. Shooting out, though, made the guard a perfect target for the two marines closing on his position, and in a double burst he was nearly fried.

As soon as all the opposition was clear, the discipline of the team showed as Ndulu and Rosen kept the door in their sights allowing Nasser and Maslovic to rush to Sanchez. Maslovic kneeled down, checked his companion, and saw that she was still breathing, although shallowly. The shot had been a lethal charge but had been mostly absorbed by the combat suit. It was pretty well shorted out, though, and that meant just insuring that Sanchez didn't suddenly die from shock. He gave her an injection that would help but didn't try the stimulants to bring her around. Without the suit capabilities and having taken that kind of shot, she'd be more a danger to herself than a help to the team if she came around right now.

"Darch, bring the van in closer but keep it out of visual range of the lodge. We still don't know if they have any nasty surprises in there," Maslovic called. "Sanchez is down on the ground to the west of the exterior stairs. She is out but will recover. Pick her up as soon as I call you in. Got that?"

"Aye, sir," Darch responded.

Broz immediately began the report from the ferret camera. "The cook and chief bodyguard inside are on either side of the door ready to blast anyone who comes in, but Schwartz is just sitting, apparently unarmed, on one of the big sofas there and Macouri has that gun in his hands but it's being held in a more or less relaxed position. He doesn't look very confident and may be deciding what to do. The two younger women have backed off to the kitchen area but appear to be just looking nervously back at the door waiting to see what will happen."

"Can you risk exposing a ferret?" Maslovic asked.

"I think so. I wouldn't want to expose the wide-camera one I'm looking at now, but the recon one's expendable if necessary. There's no obvious sound system to broadcast into that's on, but I could probably get the internal speaker levels loud enough to be heard. I think now's the time or they might take a stand. You want to do it or should I?"

"You go ahead. You can see what's going on in there better than I can. I don't want to obscure vision out here now. You never know when something's going to pop up."

"Very well. I'm going to try and position it for maximum effect and minimum target, up and to one side of the fireplace. The acoustics with that high ceiling should do, although I wish that damned ceiling fan was off."

"Just do it!"

Broz cleared her throat. "Attention! You inside! We are a marine field-strike team. All of your support outside has been neutralized."

Everybody inside jumped and began looking around to see where the sound was coming from. It wasn't booming or threatening, rather it was thin and distant, but they definitely could hear and understand it.

"By whose authority do you invade my property and wantonly kill my people?" Macouri shouted out, defiance in his tone.

"We are a special force unit under the command of Captain Kim of the naval cruiser *Thermopylae*," Broz responded. "Your—guests—can tell you more about it if they already haven't. You are engaged in illegal commerce with unknown alien forces."

"Alien! *Poppycock!* I deal in no forces that mankind hasn't been familiar with since its very beginning! You have no right to do this!"

"We have every right under our commission from the Earth System Combine, also known as the Confederacy of United Worlds."

"The Confederacy is dead! You are nothing but a bunch of pirates and thugs!" Georgi Macouri shouted, still looking up and around, trying to locate the speaker but being defeated by the diffuseness given to sound by the great room's design.

Got you there! thought Captain Murphy, watching the whole thing from the van.

"I am not going to argue with you, sir," Broz responded to the outburst. "We are in position. You have one minute. We may move at any time after that. If we continue military action we will continue it to its end. You will not be permitted to cause us harm and then give up. You understand that? I see that you do. No more debate. Your choice. Your free minute begins . . . *now*."

"Now, wait a minute . . ." Macouri began, but he suddenly realized that the point of no return was upon him. He looked over at his remaining guardians. "Joshua? What do you think?"

"We can take a few of 'em with us, sir!" the big man responded confidently.

"Perhaps, but a fat lot of good that does us." He was sweating in spite of the air conditioning, and his face showed real anguish. He turned to his companion on the sofa. "Magda?"

"What can they do, darling? Let them play soldier, then we'll buy them another spaceship or something to play with and everybody will be happy."

His teeth clenched, Macouri hissed, "Yes," although he clearly didn't like the choice. He turned around and looked at the ceiling again. "All right! All right! Resources are the better part of valor and all that! Joshua, Natasha—just put down your guns and stand by. I'm putting mine on the floor."

Joshua looked almost disappointed. "Whatever you say, sir," he responded, and both he and the hard-bitten cook put down their rifles and knives as instructed and walked over and stood behind their boss.

"I think you can go in now," Broz told Maslovic. "They look like they've given up."

Even with all that, the sergeant opened the door as if the ambush was still waiting, and Nasser and Rosen flanked either side of the double doors, weapons at the ready.

Maslovic took a deep breath and walked in. The two on either side followed him, still at the ready, and Ndulu, who was still bleeding but not badly from her earlier wound, brought up the rear directly in back of him.

"Ndulu, think you can collect the weapons and still be okay? That's not a good-looking wound," the sergeant asked, concerned.

"I'll manage."

The drill was then to cover those standing and sitting in front of them while the other two took the sides and explored the rooms, then went up both stairs and did the same upstairs to insure that there were no ugly surprises waiting for them there that the ferrets had somehow overlooked.

Nasser emerged from the far room on the right and said, "Clear!" Rosen was only a few seconds behind on the left. They started for the nearest stairs, but at just that moment Brigit Moran emerged from one of the rooms, yawned, then looked down into the great room and the scene below.

She looked puzzled for a moment, then spotted and recognized Maslovic. "Oh, *hi!*" she called out, sounding very friendly. She even gave him a little wave. "Can we play with your spaceship some more?"

IX:
OF CABBAGES AND KINGS

"Inventory?" Lieutenant Commander Mohr still wasn't sure if he was happy or panicked to have the girls back on board, let alone the others. Maybe both.

"Thirty-two of the so-called Magi stones, all of which are secured, all recovered from the bush lodge area," Lieutenant Chung reported. "None of the subjects has been allowed near them, and they are in a secured vault."

"I find it interesting that none of the stones were being worn by the principals when they were taken."

"No, sir. They were carefully stored like precious objects. There may be many more at the city compound, but we felt it prudent not to return there, and particularly not to allow Macouri, Schwartz, or the two employees to return there. There is simply no telling what sort of mischief they could cause if they were able to get to controls that we could not."

"I see. Yes, that's probably best for now. You remained with the van after modifying it?"

"Yes, sir. That is my function, after all, in this sort of team."

"But you were the one who surveyed the entire compound after it was secure and the principals moved?"

"Sir?"

"What I'm asking, Lieutenant, is for anything you might have found that you would not have expected to be there."

"Nothing, sir. Oh. You mean, like . . . babies?"

"Or something like that."

"No, sir. Nothing. Haven't the young women told you what happened?"

"No, as a matter of fact they haven't. Nor have the others. Nor has our hospital unit."

"Sir?"

"Lieutenant, if we can believe the incredibly thorough going-over that they've gotten, then, except for the obvious stretch marks, there is no sign that any of the three were ever pregnant. Even their breasts, while large, are not engorged or overly distended as the medics say should be the case in such well advanced pregnancies."

"What do *they* say, sir? Or can't I ask?"

"You can indeed. They look rather blank, if you must know, and all our sensor readings indicate that the feeling is genuine. They simply don't remember."

"What happened to the children?"

"No, being pregnant. I should think that would be difficult to forget, yet it's a hole. Our psych people say that they've never seen such a perfect selective mindworm."

"A what, sir?"

"Mindworm. Psychs use it all the time. It's quite similar to the ones used on computers and other positronic devices when they have problems. And, in our business both for long-term psychological health and occasionally for security purposes, there are things that simply shouldn't be recalled, even subconsciously. High pressures, bitter memories, breaking points. But using them always leaves gaps, things that you can find and pin down if you really dwell on them. Not these three. They have a perfectly consistent memory of the entire period with Murphy and with us and down there, and it simply isn't the one we know and saw. It's quite frightening, really."

"Frightening?"

"Consider that whatever did that with them also was in our own main computers and memory banks and even had access to the Admiralty in a limited way. Suppose that power also rewrote or redid some things there? We would never know. Our original medical scans when they were first aboard *do* say that they were all three undergoing normal pregnancies, but now it's not absolute that those scans were or remain correct."

"Well, sir, I'm sure Maslovic and the others can tell you that they were as distended when they left the town house as they were here, so whatever happened happened in a relatively short time after that. And we were out there doing reconnaissance within hours of their arrival."

"And that is the mystery, Commander. The physical evidence we have says that they were pregnant when they were here and when they got out there, and the stretch marks confirm it to a fair degree. Yet not just their memories but their physical state and even their hormonal balances say that they were not. And that leaves us with the big question."

"Sir?"

"If they were not carrying children, then just what the hell *were* they carrying?"

"I still believe that you are acting in a most uncivilized and brutish manner not even to allow me to send for my clothing!" Georgi Macouri said almost petulantly.

Maslovic gave him a wicked smile, remembering the blood on that altar or whatever it was inside the town house.

"Well, you see, Mister Macouri, we're military. We're not *personally* or *individually* brutish, but we're *professionally* brutish. Nothing personal, you understand."

"Yes, but to force me into this loutish, crinkly *uniform*, and these ill-fitting skivvies. *That*, sir, is going too far!"

Maslovic leaned back and took another look at the man opposite him. Macouri wasn't a particularly impressive figure. He wasn't handsome or charming or debonair like the people in commercial dramas, and he had a particularly irritating way of saying everything through his nose in a relatively high-pitched tenor. He had nothing that would mark him as brilliant or dangerous, nothing charismatic that would draw any attention to him. That, of course, was the case with all the best agents and spies in history, but Georgi Macouri wasn't particularly interested in blending in or not being noticed. He had money and he flaunted it. It was, in a sense, his only real attraction, but it was more than enough, apparently.

"Civilized simply means living in cities," the intelligence man pointed out. "You are, right now, in a rather good-sized city in space and it functions. Hence, we are civilized. *More* civilized than most. We have no crime here, and nobody wants more than they have or can have. Everything is provided, including a skilled job that is perfectly suited to them. The competition they *do* have is friendly and meretricious. Improve your skills, do it better, advance in rank which means not only position but respect. That's the only currency here. Respect. We save our violence for training and for the occasionally necessary missions. You can search all you wish on this vast ship, and you won't find a single solitary altar nor sacrifices to *any* deity. We believe in what we see, what we know, what we can smell and touch and measure, and we don't mind that. We don't *need* any altars."

"Bull! *Everybody* needs something greater than themselves!" Macouri snapped, showing Maslovic that he'd finally hit a rare nerve. "Why, I bet you have more shrines aboard this tub than they have on Vaticanus. Not to Saint this or that, but statues of past great military types, memorial plaques, honors lists of military achievers, and so on. Your own uniforms have these little marker things and I suspect that each one means something. Service someplace dangerous, perhaps, or best shot, or something for bravery and valor. They're all shrines. And the larger and more lasting ones are almost temples. It's simply a matter of culture in how you label or approach these things. I've never seen a military of any size that didn't do it that way."

"Point taken. But you know it's not the same."

"It's *precisely* the same! As for blood, well, what's the thing that all combat types like you value most and are taught to value most? Self-sacrifice. Taking the bullet for your comrade. *That's* who gets the biggest shrines and is talked about in all the classes to the young to inspire them. Who shed the most blood. It must be ten, a hundred times more important in this sort of setting when most of you spend your whole lives as nothing more than glorified tax collectors."

"And what do *you* believe in, Mister Macouri?"

The rich man gave a self-satisfied smile. "The same thing as you do, Sergeant. Power. In my culture money can be the means to power, and I use it, but it's not everything. But all religious beliefs come down to a worship of power, sir! Your superiors have power over you. You have power over your specialists. Your organization has a certain kind of power over the remaining world governments, until at least they collapse. The Hindus among others worship many gods because each represents a certain aspect of power. The god of Abraham, whether it be Christian or Moslem or Jew or whatever, represents the ultimate power. That's what makes the old boy God, isn't it? All that guff about love thy neighbor and charity and all that is mere window dressing. You accept and live by the Seven Pillars or you go to Hell. You obey the Law and the Commandments or God will strike you down. Accept Jesus as the Son of God or roast forever in the Lake of Fire. Eat a hamburger and be reincarnated as a flea. Do it the military way or you'll wind up in the brig or worse. It's all the same."

"And you feed your own power god with innocent blood."

"Nobody is innocent! And one can always look on those others as having been destined for just such a role. None that we have ever selected has ever had a higher purpose, or much of *any* purpose, until we gave them meaning. Poor, ignorant, backward, at best mercilessly exploited, at worst forgotten and ignored. They're born, abandoned, manage to survive for a relatively short life doing nothing but scrounging to stay alive, and then they die in squalor and are cremated and dumped in a nameless grave kept out of sight and out of town just for that purpose. *Your* kind doesn't care about them, nor does anyone else. But *we* care. Oh, don't look so shocked! The military of humankind has a history as well as a present day incarnation. How many innocent civilians have died in bombings, strafings, shellings, and for just being in the way of military operations? You justify them as mistakes, or, my favorite, 'collateral damage.' If you get the chance, you say a little prayer for them or apologize to the survivors but you push them out of your mind. Unavoidable. Accidental. As if guns shoot themselves. We *never* treat people like that. No, Sergeant, it won't do. You'll hang me and hold your nose and categorically refuse to accept that there's really not a blade of grass difference between us in the end."

"And those three young women? Were they going to be sacrifices?"

Macouri shrugged. "Possibly. Probably not. They have other potential."

"What was in their bellies, Macouri? If not babies, then what?"

The little man gave him almost a smirk in return. "You wouldn't believe me if I told you, nor would it matter very much. But it wasn't any natural breeding project like I suspect you all believed at the start. No, no. Nothing as crass as that. We would hardly need the girls to do that now, would we?"

Maslovic decided that he'd had about enough for now. "Let's take a break, Georgi old pal. We'll see if the others had anything more to say."

Macouri yawned and stretched. "Capital idea, old boy. But you'll get nothing out of them. The girls don't really know much, and the others would never give it voluntarily and we've all had our little heads wired so that you can't dig it out. And you won't be able to cajole them, either. You see, they are much more frightened of what happens if they tell than of anything, even death, that you might threaten them with. And we've already demonstrated, I believe, that we're hardly helpless even in this monster ship of yours."

"We'll see. But nobody's going to get close to those crystal devices, not this time," the intelligence man warned him. "And thanks to that demonstration, your money's worthless here. It's not a game any more, 'old boy.' The very *best* you can hope for here is to live the most unremittingly boring and lonely life imaginable. Lonely, but never alone."

Macouri laughed. "Rather melodramatic of you, I think. Would it surprise you to be told that all of us, at least all but the young guests, can get out of here any time we choose? And it's beyond your power to stop us?"

"I know you could trigger that little bomb in your brain. It so happens I have a somewhat similar device in mine, just in case," Maslovic responded. "But I won't unless there is absolutely no hope, nor will you."

"My dear boy! If I triggered it now, it would join me to the greatest power in the universe!"

"You're no martyr. Deep down, at the very bottom core of your being, is a highly educated man who can not rid himself of that one last shred of doubt. And if I'm wrong about that, well, then, if you're going to tell me nothing, then you are nothing but a burden and a waste. Killing yourself would be just fine with me, and would simplify the paperwork. You see, you've finally done it, Georgi my lad. You've put yourself in a place and situation by your actions where you can't possibly win. You're either here, like this, forever, or you cease to exist. I'll see you in a bit. Have a bland lunch."

And, with that, the sergeant got up and walked out of the room, making sure that the brig's first security door closed with as much sound and finality as it could muster.

Within a few minutes his intelligence team, along with Murphy, were in fact eating a bland lunch together.

Murphy wasn't complaining about it simply because Maslovic had insured that he could still get that very, very good stout.

"Okay," the sergeant said between bites of a large sandwich, "did anybody get *anything*?"

"Pretty much the same stuff, only not as good speechmaking as you report your boy had," Chung told him. She had taken Magda. "The old girl was a lot more belligerent, a lot threatening of dire consequences from her employer and maybe supernatural or alien sources unstated but implied, and she could drop names like mad. It *is* true that a lot of our own security stuff came from the firm where she's a senior vice president. We should keep an extra close watch on her for that reason alone."

"Done. And the two employees?"

"The cook's nothing more than a thug with a ton of loyalty and no other morals whatsoever," Broz reported. "I'd swear to that."

"There's more to this Joshua than that, but I can't give you anything concrete," Darch told Maslovic. "We've run him through all sorts of databases and tried remote colonial files using tight beam and nothing really comes up. I think he's a good man in a fight, and had some sort of military training or background even if not in our sort of culture."

"Colonial defense, maybe? Many of them went freelance or pirate over the years. Still do. And they shouldn't be underestimated," Maslovic noted.

"Could be. If so, he's not under any of the usual colonial records. Doesn't mean much."

"Any luck on figuring out the girls' role in this?" the sergeant asked them.

One by one they shook their heads. Nobody had given the slightest clue, although all but the cook who, if she knew, probably hadn't paid attention and didn't give a damn now, seemed to be amused by the constant questioning about that.

Finally, there was near silence as each of them thought over the reports of the others and reflected on how little it had profited them.

Finally, Captain Murphy took a last drain of stout, put down the makeshift mug, and said, "Wheelbarrows."

All the other heads suddenly turned in his direction. "Wheelbarrows?" Maslovic repeated.

"Sure. You know what a wheelbarrow is?"

"Not exactly."

"It's a device for manual labor haulin' and such. One wheel in the front, two stands and two handles in the back so one man can get behind it, lift it up on the wheel, and rush it and its contents to wherever it's needed. There's an ancient joke, origins unknown, about a fellow who was known to be a smuggler on some world and there was this security perimeter or somesuch which you had to pass and who was lookin' for blokes what might try to sneak things over. And every day this laborer who worked on one side would come up to the guards with a wheelbarrow full of dirt. Now, they *knew* the fellow was sneakin' somethin' by 'em, but they didn't know what.

"They did him a full scan, analyzed every bit of dirt, did a full inside-and-out analysis of the wheelbarrow, you name it. Never found nothin', so they had to let him through. Did this for months, he did. Finally he quit, and was ready to make his exit with some money that was a lot more than he'd made as a laborer. Guard sees him, knows he's leavin', and begs the fellow to tell him what he was smugglin'. Promises no penalty. So, finally, the smuggler, he smiles and says, 'I was smugglin' wheelbarrows, of course.'"

They all looked at him blankly. Finally, Darch asked,

"But why would he need to pass wheelbarrows through security?"

Murphy raised his eyes towards heaven and sighed. "It ain't worth explainin' a joke. The point is, you can do it with container modules on a space freighter. Fellow keeps bringin' in empty ones, and it's only later that they figure out he was smugglin' in the containers themselves to folks that needed 'em but couldn't buy 'em cheap where they was. You see? The point is, what was bein' smuggled was in plain sight. The container *was* the booty!"

Maslovic thought it over. "But under that logic, the girls themselves would be the object of the exercise. But there are lots of young women down there on Barnum's World and, in fact, the one thing we don't have any shortages of are people. So why smuggle them in? What possible value could they have?"

"I been thinkin' about that, and I come up with a theory. Maybe them girls got a talent. They sure ain't got a lot of education, and I ain't sure how much brains they're hidin' or if they're hidin' any a-tall, but you don't need to be a mental wizard if you got a useful talent. Somethin' you're just better at, or somethin' you're born with. I been tryin' to figure out what the hell Tara Hibernius had that would be worth this kind of trouble to smuggle someplace in that little an amount and I can't come up with nothin'. But pregnant girls—hell, they're the most helpless, least threatenin' folks you'll ever find. Nobody's gonna be scared of 'em but they're gonna be a lot safer travelin' out in the real world. It may even be just some kind of tricky gizmo or substance that made even *them* believe it, which would give 'em real reasons like I told you that first time to make 'em want to run like hell and get on an old tub with an old reprobate like me."

Maslovic thought it over. "You know, Macouri said

something like that. He said that the way you insure people's absolute faithfulness is to have them be scared of something so awful that even death and torture are preferable. So if those three were really put in danger of their lives, in fear of even staying among their own people, it would make it far easier for them to turn their backs on family, friends, the only land they ever knew. Makes sense. And you said that young girls weren't the usual travelers?"

"Nope. Mostly men. Some women, but not *them* type."

"Then that has to be it. Which begs the next question: what makes those three unique enough and valuable enough to go to all that trouble and expense?"

Chung looked over at the sergeant. "You did the research on those weird alien stones?"

"Enough, after I got the captain's lead," Maslovic told her. "Why?"

"Any reports of people with them coming up with strange powers? Any revolutions or crimes of the century? Any major suicides or murders, for that matter, out of statistical norms?"

"No. None that I can think of. Darch, you did a lot of that. Anything?"

"Nothing."

"We're all ears, then, Lieutenant."

She shifted in her seat, a loner unused to this kind of central role. "I am, as much as anything, more than just a human. I'm a human cyborg interface module. I am only truly whole and one when I'm united with a ship or other piece of piloted hardware like the van. But if we put those controls on any of you, even with extensive training, the best you'd do would be okay. You would never combine as one with the machines as I do almost as a matter of course. You would simply use the interface to give orders faster, to *control* the machinery. The captain, I think, knows what I mean if you all do not."

The old man nodded. "Aye. I've handled them things now and then but I don't like 'em."

"Well, aren't there a fair number of rich people like Macouri with those stones? Some sort of status symbol?"

"Yes, okay."

"And even more, I bet, in the hands of government and scientific researchers. Brilliant people, I'm talking about. And not a one of them, or any three of them, could take over and control a naval cruiser's main computer. A computer using proprietary languages and codes, impossibly complex, and a device for which they'd have no knowledge of nor understanding of how it worked. And these three illiterate farm girls from nowhere just do it like it's second nature. You see what I mean? Even *I* would have a lot of trouble handling that kind of complex interface, not to mention disabling all the protections, breaking through all those complex firewalls and security traps. Only the Admiralty together manage that, and *they* knew what it is and how it works and all the codes and bypasses."

"Power," Maslovic muttered aloud, thinking.

"Huh?"

"That's what old Georgi said it was all about. Power. I wonder how they found out that these girls had that kind of gift?"

Murphy had an idea. "You got plenty of money in this devil cult, and you felt that *presence*, that whatever it is, slowly emerge when you studied the stones. So did I. It's so real, so scary, you could easily see demons and build a cult out of it. So their recruiters bring one or even a few with 'em, all paid for with the rich leadership's money, and they go to the strictest, most fundamentalist, socially repressive places in the colonies. Why, hell, they'd have no trouble finding converts among the young malcontents and with that effect from them stones, well, you see what happens and how it goes. And maybe one gets left with the leader of the cult or coven or whatever they call it so they'll always have their own demon."

"Sounds reasonable," Maslovic said. "Go on. You're doing fine."

"And along come these three unhappy farm girls, probably gonna be forced into arranged marriages and break their backs with work and havin' babies and all, and for some reason the stones react to them and them to the stones in a way nobody's seen before. Maybe they have, but I bet it's really rare. Power they can't tap in these not terribly bright but terribly unhappy young lasses. But the recruiters, the leaders, *they* know what it's all about. You stumble on the ultimate weapon, but the thing's on automatic and just fires randomly in all directions. Dangerous to all. But if you pick it up and treat it good and point it careful like, then it's *your* weapon. Sarge, you give most of the prisoners a whole bag of them stones and I bet not much happens. But you give one each to the three, and you put 'em together in the same room so they can act as one, and I think you got, well, some kind of biological amplifier. Now your three young ladies, under your control, can take over whole damned planets."

"Okay, but why Barnum's World?"

"Well, possibly just because Macouri was livin' there and already had a lot of influence and knew the lay of the land and who in the authorities can be counted on to look the other way. And when you got a city maintained by central automated computers, much like a ship like this one is, it's a wonderful test. Let's take over and reprogram the computers. Let's become the sole authority and power in Port Bainbridge. If it works, then you go on. Lots more worlds out there with far more people."

"Then why get them out of town so quickly?" Broz asked him. "It seems to me you'd want them there."

"Not until you had them under your control, and with *them* three I think it would take a while for *anybody* to get 'em under control. Until then, you risk tippin' your hand early, like discoverin' who it was that was chargin' all sorts of fancy stuff on invalid but accepted credit accounts. Their power's so natural they hardly even realized they was doin' it. No use in alerting the smart boys in authority until you were ready to take over their city. But you get 'em off in the swamps with folks like the woman in charge of much of the computer security for New Bainbridge, and you practice. Now you can spread your filthy religion and your naked power in a nice, safe, controlled progression. It *was* wheelbarrows they had me smugglin'. You put it to 'em. Macouri and his gang, that is. I bet they'll give it away if it's *you* tellin' *them*."

Maslovic looked at the others. "What do you think? Honest answers, please. If we put this to them, it'll have to be from total conviction. We want them to believe that one of the others cracked and bragged so they'll feel free to fill in the blanks. Darch?"

"Smacks a lot of mysticism to me," the tech responded. "All my life I been hearing friend-of-a-friend stories about telepaths and telekinesis and all sorts of psychic powers. Never actually met one myself, nor seen a convincing demonstration. The idea that three stupid little twits can just waltz in to where one of these stones is and suddenly cause it to be the amplifier to enormous power . . . I don't know."

"But you've seen it! We *all* saw it!" Broz pointed out. "Right here. It took our best efforts for days to execute a parallel system switch without crashing the ship. Otherwise who knows what nasty little worms they might have left in our main computers. And Captain

Murphy said it, too—that a city like that one back there isn't much different than a ship like this."

"But the kind of specialized knowledge and skills needed to hack the system are way beyond what I can accept as intuitive. Nobody gets *that* kind of information from evolution," Darch maintained. "Those systems are so complex they're designed by computers even larger and more complex than the ones they build. If not a conscious plot against us, where did it come from?"

"Possibly from the devices, for that's almost certainly what they really are," Maslovic replied. "Or from the intelligence that made them. Possibly more machine than animal itself. Not from Hell, which I am not at all sure exists, but from someone, somewhere. Too faint to be more than a jolt to us. Our brains interpret the attempt at feeding into us, controlling us, as some kind of presence, some kind of powerful and, yes, *evil* presence, but no more. It shows up randomly and it looks back at you, or at least that's what it feels like it's doing. Something in the girls' brains, maybe only when they're all together, is more sensitive. It can amplify what's coming through. And thus the 'demon' connects in the same way the lieutenant here connects to her ship. Where do they get it from there? Who knows? Possibly from us. Possibly from our machines, constantly communicating through the very air and empty space we occupy. I don't know how those things work, but whoever or whatever is behind them has been waiting for the likes of those three for some time. Magic, mystical stones of power made in a way we can't duplicate even now. Magic is science we haven't figured out yet."

"So what now?" the lieutenant asked.

"I'll have to feed this through higher command," the sergeant replied, "but it seems that there can't be but one possible answer to this, and one response. The question is, do these people know what we need to know?"

"And that is?"

"These stones, these—*things*—first showed up on a derelict spaceship. More, according to records, have appeared in wrecks mostly connected to this Three Kings legend. We saw the displays and pictures in Macouri's place back in New Bainbridge. If they weren't the Three Kings I can't imagine what they might be. It all comes down to the legend of the Three Kings. People go there but none come back. Their *ships* occasionally do, but they're ghost ships running on automatic or wrecks. How convenient that we keep finding them, considering how impossible this place is alleged to be."

"You think they exist, then?" Chung asked him. "And that the answers, the ones behind this, are operating from there?"

"The evidence is pointing that way. And who do the records identify as going there over the past couple of hundred years? Visionaries and missionaries and greedy mercenaries. Not the kind of people best suited for facing a potentially hostile alien force using them to probe and possibly control us, bit by bit."

"I agree, Chief, the Three Kings is where the answers lie," Broz put in. "So let's go there and see."

"Slight problem with that, isn't there?" Chung responded. "I mean, if there were any maps to that route, it would have been overrun by now. We don't know where they are or how to find them."

Maslovic gave a wry smile. "But I have a sneaking suspicion that at least one of our new guests here does. This might get to be very interesting and profitable after all."

And, with that, he got up and headed back for a second round with Georgi Macouri.

✧   ✧   ✧

"Tell me about the Three Kings, Georgi," said Maslovic.

Macouri laughed. "A superstition by an outdated religion that won't go away."

"You know what I'm talking about. You have portraits of them in your house, surrounding your happy devil."

The little man seemed surprised and irritated. "You were in the building? You *saw* all that?"

"How else did I know of the blood sacrifices?"

"True, true. Hadn't connected the two. There are other ways to find that out if you really want to look. Not prove it, mind, but find it out. How do you like the looks of my god, Sergeant? Does he look like the Lord of Terror?"

"I couldn't care less. It's what frames his statue that I want to know about. Those huge pictures."

"Well, you must know something of the history in order to recognize them at all. Those aren't artist renderings or educated guesses, you know. They're exquisite digital blowups of actual frames. Those are in fact the Three Kings. Not exactly the worlds of everybody's dreams, are they?" He chuckled some more.

"If that's so, how did you get hold of them? They're not supposedly available to the public, although I have no idea who has the originals at this point."

"Oh, my family got them back. I assume you know the legend?"

"I didn't, but I do now," Maslovic told him.

"Couldn't do much about the names, but my grandfather was quite the explorer in his time. His hobby was going into unknown areas and mapping and charting them. He was certain that, somewhere out here, there just *had* to be some creatures, some civilization, if not contemporaneous to us at least one or more that had been here long ago, and he was going to find it. He wasn't crazy. That was his chosen field, and he did it in style. Made some really major discoveries in that super luxury yacht of his. Then he got this data that convinced him that he could locate the legendary and missing Three Kings. Something in that old fool of a priest's truncated survey caught my grandfather's eye and he was convinced that there might well be traces of ancient alien civilizations there. He went off, and he found them. The pictures prove that, as does some of the survey information that survived. You know the rest, though. The yacht came back but not any human or AI device that could tell us anything about it. Worse, no trace of how to find those three worlds or what my grandfather discovered. But inside—inside that perfectly good, working luxury spacecraft were the pictures, the strange little artifacts like nothing ever seen before and, of course, what came to be horribly misnamed as the Magi stones. I think you're aware of them and their peculiar, shall we say, properties?"

Maslovic nodded. It was all finally falling into place. "And because it was your family's property, when all was analyzed and said and done much of it came back to the Macouris. Your father put the artifacts in traveling shows and gave many of the stones out to rich and influential people as the ultimate status symbols. And he let some get sold at auction by the finest art houses, didn't he?"

"You're smarter than you should be," Georgi Macouri told him, in the closest thing to a compliment he could muster. "I'm impressed. We didn't need the money, of course, but the *legend* that went with them, *that* was the important thing. That silly El Dorado stuff. My father was convinced that somewhere, someone had my grandfather's papers, his research and calculations, that would give away the location of the Three Kings. What better way to find it, when the best detectives in the known universe couldn't, but to make it a contest, a quest for the Holy Grail, the magical place of dreams. And good legends really help sell status symbols, you know, and they grow in the retelling. We never did get the pictures back, and a lot of the data recordings, but we got copies of the interesting stuff. There was still a semblance of interstellar government then; it hadn't begun to break down. I assume that just as this ship and its crew are all leftover relics of that past time, somewhere out here there's still a bunch of folks who think they're the intelligence service of some big, monolithic government who are still classifying everything Top Secret and pretending that the Silence never happened. It doesn't matter."

"Odd that after all that, and such a clever plan, nobody ever found the stuff, though," the sergeant commented. "You'd think something would leak after all this time."

"Oh, it *has*. Your pitiful pretense at being part of some vast navy has blinded you to subsequent history in many areas. I think there's been a slow but steady progression of people and ships out there as the location turned up. I've traced many. The trouble is, just like my grandfather, nobody who goes comes back. Or, if they do, they come back very, very dead."

Maslovic sat up very straight. "You *do* know where the Three Kings are, then, don't you?"

Georgi Macouri gave his Cheshire Cat smile. "Who? Me?"

"But you haven't ever gone out looking. Your father's great dream, and his clever plan uncovered the coordinates, yet you never used them. Why not?"

"You assume too much not in evidence," the little man responded. "Why, just a few years ago a group of brave men and women got the address from a third party and went off to mine the riches and return. They haven't yet. Nothing. Not even a trace of their ship, either, although its wreckage, perhaps in tiny pieces, may be all over a half a light-year-wide region out there."

"But you never made the try."

Macouri shrugged. "Sergeant, I inherited everything. The money, the power, the influence, the excellent wine cellars, you name it. I even enjoy the thrill of risk. I bathe in it sometimes. But if it's not to be even odds, then the odds must be on my side. I seem to lack the recklessness."

"So you just have manipulated and sent others over and over, and to no avail."

"Oh, there's been some profit. Some of the wrecks that made it back—and not all do—have some goodies in them. Magi stones in several varieties and types, enough to depress the market if anybody else knew. Soil samples including tons of those funny little enigmatic machined thingies, too. Stuff like that. Stuff that survives being twisted and flattened and turned inside out inside a wild wormhole. No, Sergeant, I've gotten some things back. Not this last batch, but half the time. Why should I risk it until I can speak with someone who's made the return trip?"

It was Maslovic's turn to smile. "So I was right about you, you see. Deep down, there's that hollow spot in your brain, that secret place called Doubt. As deep as you can go, you really don't have faith in your religion. It's just a game. Otherwise, you'd be overjoyed with the idea of going off to meet your masters at the Three Kings and you'd not even worry about a return. And if by some stretch you really *do* believe in them, then you don't really trust them. Not a good position for somebody serving a god, is it?"

Macouri didn't like this direction, and his face showed it. "I think we end this for now. It's not any fun any more."

"You can't end it until I say we end it," Maslovic pointed out. "You're stuck here, Georgi, as long as we want you. Now we've established a new level, though, that may be working to your advantage."

"Indeed?"

"Now it's not just that I have you. Now you, in fact, have something I want. For the first time, there is a basis for negotiation."

Macouri sat up and stared at the big, bald man in uniform sitting there across the table from him. "And what do I have that you truly want, Sergeant?"

"We want the Three Kings. We want the address and anything else you might have on them."

"And if I give them to you? What do *I* get?"

"Out of here. Off this ship. As a permanent prisoner here, you're a liability. You consume but do not contribute. But you must believe this, Georgi: If we don't get what we want, if you don't *give* us what we want freely and accurately and willingly, then you *will* stay here. For years. For decades. For what will pass for forever to you. And you'll do it in a padded room, a little box, with nothing even to write with or do yourself or us harm. Alone. Forever."

Maslovic got up and started towards the security door, his back to the prisoner. He had delivered his ultimatum and now it was up to the other man.

"Sergeant?"

Maslovic stopped but didn't turn around. "Yes?"

"Your word. On the official record, endorsed by all your superiors. You will not take this information and then just discard me or throw me back in the hole?"

"I guarantee you that you'll not die here, and that we're not going to do you harm. If you want off this ship, that is the only way."

"And the others?"

Maslovic turned around and faced the little man who

was still sitting at the table. "I don't see any grounds for holding the cook, and I'm going to allow this Joshua of yours to make his own choice. The three girls aren't your worry or responsibility any more. That's basically it."

"Why do you want to go there? You won't get back, you know. I understand that much now."

"Well, we can say we're looking for a little payback for what was done to our own operations here," the intelligence man said. "Or maybe we think there might be answers to questions out there that can stop this drift of humanity into oblivion. At least we might find out the answer to the greatest philosophical question of our time."

"Yes?"

"Whether or not we were locked *out* or locked *in*," Maslovic told him.

"I—I shall have to think on this somewhat," Macouri said after a pause. "There may be the basis of an arrangement here."

"Take your time. We're not going anywhere off the schedule right now and, as for me, I'm home."

With that, Maslovic walked out through the security doors and back down the hall to get a drink and wait for the others to reassemble. Still, unlike before, he felt quite good at this point.

Maybe someday soon he would gaze into one of those damned crystals and that thing, whatever it was, would eventually show up to peer back at him as before. Only this time, that creature would discover that Maslovic would be standing right behind him. . . .

"So, Sergeant, what do you plan to do if he *does* give you the key to the front door?" Captain Murphy asked.

"I plan to go through it, kicking it down if I have to, and see what this is all about."

"Might be a real letdown," Darch put in. "The remnants of some machine doing its automated thing, or maybe even just some kind of broadcast into areas of the brain common to most organic life-forms. You might wind up standing there, freezing or boiling, with nowhere to go and nothing to do."

Maslovic grinned and looked around at them. "Well, I might have some company. Or would you prefer to break up this happy group?"

"And who else would be with us?"

Maslovic grinned. "The biggest damned ship in the fleet that the Admiralty will allow us to take, of course, with all hands. I want power behind me when I go in if possible. I want to know that, if we can't take control of the planet, well, then at least we can blow it up."

"But you're talking a wild hole!" Murphy noted. "Hell, man, that's tricky enough under the best of conditions with a small ship designed for the task. The records don't show any ship comin' back that's of any size. Biggest is that yacht his grandpa had. We know from the record that some pretty large ships went in, but none of 'em ever came back, and the biggest not even in pieces!"

"Nevertheless, if they allow me to risk such a ship I'm going to take it. What about it, Lieutenant? Think you could run a wild hole with something the size of, oh, the *Agrippa*?"

She nodded. "I do not see anything against it. The principles of physics are quite different inside a hole, wild or not, than here, but they are still pretty well predictable and their characteristics known. A wild hole is incredibly dangerous, but a competent pilot should be able to get even a large ship through. That is why I believe that some agency interfered with the return of some of the ones on record as having vanished after going. Nothing comes back intact larger than that yacht, which is no larger than one of our shuttles. That is the only danger I would feel threatened by. A good pilot can do that job, but we do not know what we will be up against once there."

"Well, Murphy here and I have been looking over the archives," Broz told them, "and we can't find any military ship on the list. Mostly research and exploration ships, freighters, and similar craft. Even one interstellar small city devoted to Christian evangelism, of all things. I feel confident that if we can keep them out of our control computers, we can handle the rest."

"Then as soon as I get the coordinates I will put the proposal to the Admiralty directly," Maslovic told them. "We will probably be approved with the limitation that we take only volunteers and then only the minimum human crew to do the job."

"And the girls? What of them?" Murphy asked him.

"That's up to the Admiralty. I know that if I had my own choice I'd bring them along. They may be the best, perhaps the only way of getting into direct one-on-one contact with this alien presence, and they have nowhere else to go. Of course, the Admiralty may feel that it would not be just to take them along at their age and experience. We'll see. You, Captain, will be allowed to depart with our thanks."

"The *devil* I will!" Patrick Murphy snapped. "I ain't come this far to turn and run now, maybe never knowin' what the hell it's all about. No, no. You're stuck with me, Maslovic. Nobody but nobody is gonna keep Patrick Xavier Aloysius Murphy from settin' his old eyes on the Three Kings themselves!"

"Then it's a done deal. I'll go run it past the higher-ups and see what they'll give us."

It took almost a day to get everyone on board. The main points of disagreement were whether or not to try it with the full task force or to send just one element.

Maslovic argued for real power, which meant one of the destroyers at the least, but after the Admiralty became concerned that, if everyone wasn't going, there was the likelihood of a one-way trip judging from the evidence, it was decided that the force should be as minimal as possible while still sufficient to get the job done.

Maslovic would get his destroyer, with full weapons, but minimal crew. It would be stripped of all but one fighter squadron, put on as full automation as possible, and full discretion would be handed to the special captain appointed for the mission and to the ground force under Maslovic.

Both would also have the code strings for auto-destruct.

By the time the group assembled again, Maslovic had the full set of details.

"Lieutenant Chung, you will take command of *Agrippa*," he told her, watching her face light up. She was suddenly now, at least with a brevet promotion, about twenty years advanced beyond where she would expect to be. "I am mission commander, and, yes, you can call me Sarge, Chief, Commander, or Hey you! Makes no difference. Captain Murphy, I'm going to put you in charge of your three girls."

"You're takin' 'em along, then?"

"Got nowhere else to put them, and in a pinch they may be our avenue of communication with whatever's out there. We're pretty sure we understand now how whatever it is hacked into the system and that avenue's forestalled. That doesn't mean they might not surprise us, but the captain and I will have personal control of weapons and similar systems outside the primary. No matter what, I feel certain we can blow them to hell if need be. Darch and Broz will handle our involuntary guests. Feel free to call on the rest of the team if need be."

Broz had a wicked smile on her face. "They been told yet?"

"I rather think we'll let old Georgi know just before we jump, in case he's fed us the wrong coordinates or is setting a trap. Until then, both he and his alter ego Joshua are to be given the impression that they are being taken back to a colonial world as part of the bargain. Clear?"

Murphy looked Maslovic straight in the eyes. "It's not much for this kind of thing."

"It's what we've got. Now, let's go do it!"

X:
THE THREE KINGS

"You can't do this to me! You gave me your word!"

Maslovic grinned at the little man, who had been going back and forth about this for most of the trip.

"What's the matter, Macouri? You know we made a deal. I thought you were the agent of the devil here. Isn't that the devil's trademark? Finding the loopholes and sneaking in the fine print? You're not so good at it on the receiving end, are you?"

"But you said—"

"I promised you that you would be off the *Thermopylae* for good if you gave me what I wanted to know, and you are. This is *Agrippa*, and it's a much smaller ship, comparatively speaking. And while you are under ship's security, you are no longer a prisoner and are free to mix with the others, walk the decks, you name it. Just be aware that if you or anyone else without the proper security codes tries to, oh, disengage a lifeboat or raid a weapons locker or something of that sort they will get a nasty and *very* painful experience and will, from that point, be locked away in a padded cell in the brig wearing nothing but a smile."

"But I could have gone at any time! I don't *wish* to go!"

"Nevertheless, you are going. We are lining up on your coordinates even as we speak. And if we don't come out the other end at the Three Kings, you will have more than a little explaining to do. It is one of the major reasons you're here. If you have anything to tell me that we don't know about what's on the other end and what might be expected or not, you'd better tell us soon, because whatever happens to us from this point on also happens to you."

"This is beyond even your powers! I demand to be returned at once!"

"Remember our weighty conversation? Power is everything, isn't it? Your money means nothing here, nothing to me anyway, or the others. You might be able to buy Murphy, but he can't drive this ship."

They had kept it from him until just now, when they lay off the region of wild holes waiting for the correct mathematical match to pop in. That could be any time, and at that point Chung would have to instantly commit or abort. Wild holes were unstable; they popped in and out like soap bubbles and lasted in most cases only fractions of a second before "bursting," closing up and ceasing to exist once more. Only by putting a ship and its energy field into that hole at precisely the moment it was open could they stabilize it. Once inside, they could ride through it to the other end even as it closed itself back down. Not only space, but time itself, would be bent and twisted. It was why the route to the Three Kings had been so difficult to find even if you knew in what region to look for the entrance on the human end, and why it was as hard or harder to find your way back if you made it.

"I—I don't know if the numbers work! They're the right numbers!" Macouri insisted. "They're the ones everybody else used. Who knows *where* they actually go? I—I—Oh, god! Don't make me go in one of those!"

Maslovic grinned, feeling no sympathy for the murdering little fart. "Did I hear you just call on God? That might not be the best way to go there, I wouldn't think. Not if you meet your old master on the other side."

It was too much for the little man. He stood up and tried to look his captor straight in the eyes while getting his blood pressure down enough so he wasn't totally beet red. It didn't happen.

"*I am Georgi Macouri!*" he thundered, as authoritative as anyone could sound. "*You can't do this to me!*"

"You're the same mix of a few cheap chemicals and water, born little different than anyone else and destined to die like all of us and go back to those components," Maslovic shot back. "You have the same value to me as those girls you slaughtered had to you. How's it feel now, Georgi? What the hell ever gave you the idea that *you* were somehow immune?"

There was dead silence for a moment as the reality of that seeped into Macouri's brain. While it was still percolating, Chung's voice came over the public address.

"Attention! Please be seated at a secure station. Strap yourselves in if possible or hold on. The mathematical progression of hole formations is following the correct formula we were given. I will sound the alarm. At any point after that, we may have to go in fast and hard."

Macouri's mind suddenly shifted to the imminent. "How many times has she jumped through a wild hole in a ship this size?" he asked nervously.

"Never, as far as I know, except in simulation the past few days. Relax. Size doesn't matter as much on this one, I'm told, and the ship's own systems know what to do. I'm belting in. You should do the same."

Almost at the end of his sentence the warning klaxon sounded throughout the ship. Almost everyone else was already lying down and secured or belted in a proper jump chair.

"*NEVER???*" Georgi Macouri's voice sounded even as the ship suddenly accelerated from a near coast to fantastic speeds and headed for what the Macouri formula said would be the wild hole to the Three Kings.

"Definitely not what I expected," Darch commented. Although his primary job was security on this mission, he was also the de facto head of the entire science department aboard the ship. In fact, except for the computerized labs and research programs, he *was* the entire science department. "In fact, what I am seeing not only I but all our science computers say is damned near impossible."

They were lying several million kilometers back from the mini system, far enough outsystem that they could see both the strange dense star and the close-in massive gas giant as well. The visible-light screen view was impressive; it was almost as if they were looking at two suns, one on fire, the other not.

"Science is not my strong point," Maslovic told him. "In fact, I believe it because the folks who know it tell me about it."

"This kind of system is unprecedented, and for good reason," Darch explained, not just to his boss but to all of them. "The kind of gravitational forces I'm reading show that there is simply no way this system can be in this kind of stable formation. This is a system that should be at war, pulling things apart, pulling others in for incineration. That kind of star shouldn't even *have* planets. The turbulence on the big gas giant is an indicator of just how nasty things should be. These kinds of forces are why that wild hole field is where it is." He exhaled and shook his head. "No, I don't even envy the captain keeping us in any kind of stable orbit anywhere around here. No wonder almost nobody came back. Anybody who came along here who wasn't the best would have been sucked in or flung down and crashed. This kind of system makes no sense. It can't exist like this if physics is to be believed. There has to be a third force here, something not showing up on our instruments, that acts as the stabilizing constant between the warring sides. Otherwise it's voodoo, Chief. It's magic."

"I knew it! I knew it!" Macouri muttered. "This is Hell! The seat of the Powers of Darkness! Oh, my! Oh, my!"

Maslovic totally ignored him. "Any idea of the force?"

"Well, in one sense our quaking friend here is right. In a good simulator I might well be able to *build* this thing. Sure, this is the universe. Anything's possible out here, or so it seems, but it would be a lot easier to build it than to wait to find it, maybe, naturally, including some mysterious third force we haven't seen anywhere else."

Maslovic turned and looked at him. "And you could create a third force?"

"Maybe. It wouldn't probably work here, or be much like here, but I could kludge it. *This*, now—*this* is no kludge. This was *designed*. This was *engineered*. I'd bet anything I had that this whole damned place was *built*."

"Well, *we* sure couldn't build it," Broz noted.

"Irrelevant," Maslovic told her.

"Huh?"

"If it was built, and I defer to the experts on that, then the question isn't *how*, not unless you want to build another and I have no desire to do that. The question is *why*."

"Beg your pardon," he heard Murphy's voice behind him. "Sure'n it's obvious, I would think."

"More of your wheelbarrows, Captain?"

"No, not exactly. But the same analogy. On at least twenty worlds that I know of there exist plants, or what serves for plants, that don't eat sunlight and minerals or the usual. They got confused somewhere after creation, poor things, and decided to eat meat instead. There's a ton of them types back on Barnum's World. They keep the insect population down to that dull roar, or help to."

"Yes? So?"

"That's what that is, don't you see? It's a giant fly-catcher. And we're the flies."

"He might be right," Darch commented. "Hold on. Let me do a hypothetical here." His tone changed and he adjusted something on his control panel, then said, "Computer, assume for problem that the data read in represents an intelligent construct."

"Postulating," the computer responded.

"Now, give me a visible representation of the missing energy force X that would be required by a builder to maintain the system at stasis."

On the screen, superimposed on the actual view, was a series of translucent spidery webs connecting the various parts of the inner solar system and particularly the secondary system around the gas giant. Primary energy flowed not from the moons or sun as expected but from the gas giant.

"Interesting. They're using the very instability of the system that's causing the tremendous storms and volatility on the planet to give them the power they need to stabilize the inner system," Darch noted. "There's no perfect stability, however. Eventually sufficient energy will be lost in the exchange to weaken the planet. Not much, but the tolerances here are very slight. It will slow, begin falling inward taking everything with it, and collide with the sun. The result will be a monstrous explosion and possibly the formation of a small singularity. We don't want to be anywhere around when that happens."

"How far away would be safe?" Maslovic asked him.

"Um, how about a hundred and fifty or so light-years minimum? No, when this goes, it's going to take the evidence with it."

"How long until that happens?"

"Hard to say. Remember, what you're seeing is presupposing an artificial construct with forces we can't measure or understand and which, if they exist, have been fairly stable for centuries, maybe longer. However, there is very small slippage, measurable slippage, of the big guy in system. Whatever process is going on, it's begun. Still, I don't think we're talking tomorrow or next week or even next year, but when it goes, it's going to go really quick."

"Which of those three big moons in the life tolerances zone around the big boy would be most likely to harbor the builders?"

Darch chuckled. "Oh, none of 'em. Whoever did this, assuming somebody did, wasn't from around here any more than we are. But, boy! Is that technology impressive!"

Maslovic thought a moment, then asked, "So, Darch, if they have that kind of power, could we blow it up if we have to?"

"All else being even, I'd say yes," the tech chief replied. "Depends on whether or not they deployed defenses at the same level as their building projects. I'd walk real careful on this one, Chief. If we *could* blow it, we'd almost certainly be killed in the same attempt, since it would destabilize everything. Wouldn't be much of an escape route."

"Have you done a lifescan of the big three moons there?"

"No sweat. Now, understand, there's a *ton* of moons around this baby, but only three that could sustain our kind of carbon-based life. That and the Macouri pictures identify those three as the Kings. They're not all resort spots, but I can tell you that all three are just teeming with life. The one that gives the weirdest readings is the little cold one. I'm not sure that the majority life-form there is carbon-based, but it's within our biological understanding. If there are any devils or even angels around, then they're made of something our sensors don't know about."

"What about humans?"

"I don't get any signs of our folks on any one except the middle one. Not real surprising, I don't think, if we're the smart ones. A land of milk and honey. Rich atmosphere, mostly warm to hot on all the land masses, vegetable life that might well produce stuff we can eat, all that. We're by no means the majority population there, but there's a *lot* of our kind. I don't get *any* close matches on the other two, which means that if any of us are there we're in numbers too small to register. Just what *is* there, well, we'll have to go and see, I guess. Not human. Not consistent types, either. I'd say at least twenty different major life-forms on the big volcanic one alone, and a couple on the little cold one, although in that case one really stands out. I think, though, Chief, we've broken the old puzzle. I don't know how intelligent they'll turn out to be, but I'll bet you pretty good that we've got not one but several thinking alien types out there."

"Well," Murphy muttered, "there goes the neighborhood."

"Let's go see," Darch suggested.

Maslovic wasn't quite as eager. "We aren't the first ship from our species to make it this far," he reminded them all. "And none of them got back. Murphy may be right. That may be a gigantic flytrap. It's definitely well baited."

"But we can't just *sit* here," Darch noted.

"True, but we may be able to take a bit of a lesser risk. Captain Chung! I believe it's time to tighten up all security at all points," he said in a particularly loud voice. "And then you and I will get some of the jewels out of the vault."

"What are you going to do?" Murphy asked, still feeling a bit protective of his wards.

"They, whoever they are out there, came and looked us over uninvited and without saying a word. Macouri seemed to think that the girls were a unique conduit to whatever's here. Let's see."

They were delighted to get their "jewels" back. Maslovic was careful to match each girl with the color of the stone she'd been wearing in the earlier encounter so that things would be replicated as much as possible. He did hope, though, that they wouldn't have to go through a long and boring ceremony painting their naked bodies and chanting over a pentagram. Nothing he'd seen indicated that what people like Macouri and his group had come up with or interpolated into this business had anything to do with what was really going on. He was, however, prepared to gather together Macouri and his bodyguard Joshua with the girls if he had to and endure almost anything.

Right away the girls all seemed to notice something different and tried to figure it out.

"They're talkin' to us, like as always," Irish O'Brian noted, and the others nodded. "Kind of funny, though."

"Yeah," Mary Margaret McBride responded. "None of the ceremonies done, and you can still sort of hear 'em. Like tiny voices."

Maslovic looked over at Darch who shook his head briskly in the negative. Nothing was being picked up on the instruments, although if his "simulation" was correct about the third stabilizing force in the system, then by now they were well within its range and influence.

Darch in particular seemed somewhat relieved by this. The observable phenomena were consistent with his model even if he had no way to actually detect this third force, and things like physics and practical sense didn't seem all that violated, either. These might well be some kind of alien transceivers, but they were of very limited range and power. He had theorized, though, that somehow there was an exponential power growth when these stones were combined. If so, this trio should be able to get increasingly clearer signals. They might well even be overwhelmed and dominated by whatever was out there, as had happened to a degree back on the *Thermopylae*.

"There's somebody talkin', or tryin' to," McBride commented. "Only they're still so far away I can't make out what they're sayin'."

"It's speaking in English, then, or Gaelic, or what?" Murphy asked them.

They all shrugged. "It's inside your head, y'see," O'Brian tried to explain. "It's like talkin' only it ain't. I don't think what tongue they use would have anything to do with what I understood, if that makes any sense."

"Telepathy?" Maslovic asked his people.

"I don't think so," Broz told him. "At least not the way we think of it. It really is more like radio. The earliest radios were created with crystal sets, and could be made simply by poor people even without any local source of power for reception. Like this, reception wasn't very good, but you had it if the transmitter had enough power to vibrate that crystal from far off. We all build one as part of our training classes. In this case, though, acting as both receiver and amplifier, the transmission isn't through vibration of the air but of something inside the brain. The question is how they have enough power from this end to send back from that area, but I think they do. In some ways, it's the old basic crystal radio principle. In others, it is to us what a hyperspacial tight-beam com signal would be to those early crystal set people who were our ancestors. It's close enough that I can understand what it's doing, but far enough ahead of our technology that I can't for a moment imagine how it's doing it."

"They ain't talkin' to us!" Brigit Moran muttered, sounding disappointed. "It's some guy and some girl talkin'."

Maslovic was suddenly doubly interested. "They're definitely people? Like us? You can tell that?"

"Yeah, sure'n she's right," O'Brian agreed. "It's a kind of gab fest. And from the few words I can make out, it ain't even dirty or romantic."

"Do they know you're listening in?"

All three shook their heads. "Don't seem to," Mary Margaret told them. "It's like we're just eavesdroppin' on the extension."

"What about our mysterious friend who always seems to lurk around the other side in those gems? Any sign of *him*?"

"What? You mean the demon? He don't usually show up for a while. Sometimes he don't show up at all," O'Brian said. "I don't get much sense of him yet, at least not in this stuff. I don't think he's in the same place as the talkers. Come to think on it, it don't seem like these two are anywhere near close, either. That'd make sense, though. If they was close, why would they need these to talk?"

Maslovic looked up at the main screen, which showed the subsystem view and highlighted the three huge planet-sized moons that had life-sustaining atmospheres. "Now, let's see. Kaspar, Melchior, and Balshazzar?"

"You have the last two backwards," Broz told him. "Kaspar's the small cold one, all right, but the pretty one in the middle is Balshazzar, the one in and belching smoke into warm oceans is Melchior. If your guess is right, and the controlling force or group or whatever is on Kaspar, then maybe these two aren't. Best bet is that they're on separate continents on Balshazzar, since that's where the people are."

"Them three worlds, they're the Kings?" Mary Margaret asked, looking at the same picture.

Maslovic nodded. "Yes. You saw their pictures at Macouri's big place in the city."

"Yeah, I remember. I can tell you, and I dunno why, that the guy I'm hearin' is on the one in the middle and the girl's on the big one closest in. That help?"

"On Melchior! Yes, that *does* help. Darch?"

"I don't get any human readings for the world, but that doesn't mean there aren't a few or even a few hundred down there. That small a signature would be lost in that sea of alien life."

"Okay, okay. So we have people on at least two of them, and they can contact each other. Now, if our watchers are on Kaspar, that could mean that they don't even pay attention to that kind of local traffic."

"No," Captain Murphy said, thinking in his usual bent way. "But you and I both know, Sarge, that they'd be lookin' at us right this moment."

Maslovic nodded. "I agree. Girls, still no sign of your mysterious friend?"

"Shush!" responded Brigit Moran. "We're tryin' to put ourselves together so we can *really* eavesdrop!"

The marine put his finger to his lips and made sure the others in the room saw it. If the girls wanted to chant a little and hold hands and get in sync to boost their power, that was exactly what he wanted this time.

The girls, as usual, started off in anything but unison, but within a few minutes the chanting—not just the words, which were mostly nonsense, but the pitch and meter—seemed to come together, first as a sort of harmony, and finally as if a single voice, even though the three voices were very different normally. All three had their eyes closed and seemed lost in a world of their own.

This was the most dangerous time for the experiment, they all knew. The last time these three had achieved this level of unity they'd managed to almost literally take over a starship.

Maslovic decided they were far enough into their self-induced hypnotic trance that speaking was no longer a problem, although he kept his voice quiet and low.

"Anything, Captain?"

"I felt several weak probes of my systems," Chung responded, keeping that quiet tone and localizing it as much as possible on the science control panel. "Nothing threatening at all, though. They're casting out, but it's strictly one-way. Nobody or nothing's yet trying to come through them at me or us."

"Stay alert. It might come in the twinkling of a star and those folks know their system a lot better than we know how to stop it."

"I'll let you know. If they do break through, at least I feel confident at this point that I could warn you about it."

Maslovic turned and looked over at Murphy. "Cap,

you want to give it a try? They still seem to trust you, for some reason."

The old man shrugged. "Well, I'll give it me best. The big problem may be gettin' through to 'em."

He walked over to where the three had stopped chanting now but were standing together holding hands with eyes closed.

"Hello, darlin's, this is Captain Murphy. Can you hear me?"

No response.

"C'mon, darlin's! Speak to the old captain, now."

Still no reaction. He was just about to give it up as a bad bet when all three voices as one said, "Captain?"

There was something in the way they said it that made the hair on the back of his neck stand up. It didn't sound like them or anybody else he knew at all.

"Yes? And who might ye be?"

"You have an accent. It is hard to make it out."

"I doubt if it's me accent that's the problem. Just who might I be speakin' to through these girls?"

"I had no idea you were speaking through others. Are you on Balshazzar?"

"Goodness, no! I'm on a ship in space."

There was no reaction for a moment, then the voice said, "You are in a spaceship? From the colonial sector?"

"Yes. We're just comin' insystem now."

Maslovic gave him a frown at that, but he figured that any possible enemy around who hadn't noticed a naval destroyer approaching inbound by this time wasn't much of a threat.

"How about you?" he asked the voice. "Are *you* human, or one of them peek-a-books from the stones?"

"I'm human. Just barely any more. It's been very hard here."

"Looked like Balshazzar wasn't that bad a place to be stuck," he noted.

"We—we're not on Balshazzar. We're on Melchior."

That caused some consternation among everybody on the *Agrippa*.

"Melchior! Ain't supposed to be no folks like me there!"

"There's not many. Four of us are left. We were marooned when the salvage freighter *Stanley* deserted us. No way to get off. No human population, no alien population that we can trust."

"How is it you're talkin' to me like this, then?"

"The stones. We can use them like communicators. They grow here. Millions of them, probably. Too many around and they'll drive you insane, but you can handle a few. Large population of us on Balshazzar. We can talk through these. For God's sake, if you can come and get us, please do so! Don't try Balshazzar. Something will let you land but won't let you leave."

"Names," Maslovic hissed. "We need names!"

"Just who are ye, then? Kinda hard to make out when you're hearin' yourself this way."

"I am Doctor Randi Queson, sort of science jack-of-all-trades. With me are engineer Jerry Nagel, shuttle pilot Gail Cross, and team leader An Li. Li suffered a breakdown or seizure or something partly due to the stones and hasn't been anything but child-like since. We have minimal food we've been able to gather, too much water, no supplies."

Murphy thought a moment. "You say somethin' keeps folks from leavin' Balshazzar? What about where you are?"

"Should not be a problem. We went back and forth to the *Stanley*. My head is killing me now. This only works for short periods. Got to stop or I'll pass out."

"Wait! Is there any way we could locate you? That's a mighty big world down there!"

"We have nothing. Lost everything now in the storms and quakes and always moving. Big oceans, lots of dust and islands. Oh, God! This close! I don't know how . . ."

"Do you think you could link up with me girls here again via these alien stones?"

"I dunno! Got to quit! I—"

It was clear from the total slack in the faces of the three young women that there was no longer any contact.

Darch threw his arms up in a gesture of helplessness. "Damn! If we had a conventional signal, *anything*, I could trace it, but sending and receiving via the brains of morons helps not a bit! How do I find four humans who could be anywhere on a world bigger than the one we left not long ago? It's impossible!"

"We have time, I think," Maslovic said. "They've survived this long, they can make it another couple of days, and we have a valuable heads-up on Balshazzar. The prettiest one's always the biggest trap. That's probably why all the humans are there. Weird, though, that these stones would be formed on a hellhole like Melchior." He sighed. "Okay, people! We got a couple of days to work out a way to locate these folks. No question we can use some locals aboard, particularly if they're adults who can use these things without us having to go into chanting rituals and who don't think everything is magic."

"Of course, we hav'ta make sure that they're actually rescued, too," Murphy noted. "Just gettin' 'em off there ain't gonna do much good if we wind up stuck someplace else."

Murphy looked over at the still-entranced girls. "So what do we do with them for now?"

"I'm not going to sit around and wait for somebody

to wake up out there, notice them, and try and take this ship," Maslovic commented. "I think we get some of the squad up here and strip those stones off them again. *That* should break the circle."

But before he could even call down via the ship's intercom, the trio, as one, suddenly swayed, let go of one another, and collapsed in a heap on the deck.

Maslovic and Broz were there before Murphy could even move a step, quickly taking the necklaces holding the stones off their necks. That done, Maslovic called down for Rosen and Sanchez to come up and take the girls back to their quarters, carrying them if need be. Sanchez still wasn't a hundred percent back, but she was more than up to this sort of thing.

Now they could settle back and try and figure out how to locate and extract four humans from a moon almost fifty-six thousand kilometers around at the equator and teeming with hundreds of thousands of representatives of unknown alien life-forms.

"Why do you still serve this man, Joshua?" Maslovic asked the big bodyguard who had chosen to come with them of his own free will.

"I have sworn a blood oath," Joshua replied. "I shall follow him into Hell if need be."

"You might not be far from doing just that," Maslovic pointed out. "But why? What kind of oath would hold a man like you?"

Joshua turned and looked straight at the intelligence man. "What, precisely, is 'a man like me'? Do you think I am nothing but a pirate? That I have no honor?"

"It is difficult to tell someone's innermost self at the best of times. In your case, the only way I have of judging your sincerity and honor is by the company you keep. Tell me this, then: do you believe what he believes? Is that a part of it as well? That is, do you believe that there are actually demons out there, and that we are moving towards them?"

"I believe in evil," the big man responded without hesitation. "Who commits it or who has it is the only question. I also believe in good. In an evil universe that is crumbling around us all, honor is the only thing one can cling to. That is my code and I cannot vary it. To do so would leave me with nothing at all."

"You know he's insane, don't you? That he hears voices and sees visions no one else does and that he acts upon them without a second thought, even if they are random acts of violence?"

"He saved my life once, and the life of my extended family. Sane or not, I am bound to him."

"Was it a Faustian bargain, then?" Captain Murphy put in. "Did you sell him your soul in exchange for them services that saved the others?"

"No. I appreciate that you are both attempting to understand what can only be understood in my personal context. To have sold him my soul would have been easy. He buys many, and is generous to those who sell. But as I do not believe in souls, I could not sell him mine. It would be meaningless. No. We were on a far colonial outpost. Most of my family was barely making ends meet. We were attacked by pirates, and Mister Macouri happened to be nearby doing some more normal business. He answered our call, and asked me what I would give for salvation, since his own beliefs preclude charity involving risk. I offered my humble services for soever long as he needed them, and my unquestioned obedience in life. He accepted, and hired local mercenaries to rescue us. He then put a reward on each pirate head, and they were tracked down and their heads delivered to his representative for payment. I had the will but not the resources to do that. Does that answer your question?"

Maslovic nodded. "I believe so. I'm not sure, though, that you won't have to make a choice that is as ugly as any you've made before."

"Why are you so disturbed, Maslovic? We are the same," Joshua said to him.

"I beg your pardon?"

"We are the same. Your code—it says you obey orders. That you serve your mission as given by your superiors regardless of whether or not you, personally, believe it is right or wrong. You do it for family, for personal honor, and because it is your function in life. The rest do the same, except, perhaps, for the man Murphy here, who *may* do what is right and honorable, or not, depending on how he feels that moment, and those young women."

Maslovic didn't want to travel that road. "What about Magda Schwartz?"

"She is in highly profitable sales. Security equipment and all the peripherals that are needed. Most of her clients might be considered insane in one way or another. Great fortune and no responsibility does that more than not I have learned. She makes them happy and does not judge them. When she makes them happy, they give her big orders that make her rich by commissions. She, too, thinks that our part of the universe is falling apart. Her solution to it is to amass sufficient money so that she can at least be very comfortable until it ends or she dies happy. It is not something I would like to do, but I can understand it."

"As can I, Joshua. As can I. Tell me, though— Macouri's beliefs? Did he come by them himself, or did he get something through those stones?"

"I do not use the stones. He does. I do not think he gets any messages, but he does get the effects. They excite him and conform to his cosmology. But I believe he envies the young women. *They* can speak and understand. They have no need of cosmology."

"And they couldn't pronounce it anyway," Murphy noted.

"Then why is he so frightened to be here?" Maslovic asked the bodyguard.

"Mister Macouri is a powerful man. He places power where I place honor and you place duty. That is more than sufficient where we live. But here, in *their* part of the universe, what is he? Without his power he is nothing. Without his power *he* is the potential victim."

"Well, go on back and help him prop himself up," the marine said. "We may yet need him."

After Joshua had left, Maslovic turned to Murphy. "You've been around more than I have with these types. What do you think?"

"I dunno. If honor is so important that you promise to obey every command and the bastard commands you to strangle children, are you honorable? I don't trust folks like that. They got no questions. This is a man who will unhesitatingly butcher the innocent because he promised a madman he'd do whatever the madman asked. Them's the kind that put women and children in ovens and turned on the gas in past history. They give me the creeps."

"Point taken."

"You better watch it yourself, though, Sarge. Your own folk have a history of openin' up on innocent kids if some crazy general or admiral says to. You got the real rock and a hard place. You expect your team to obey instantly, to die for you if need be, 'cause if they don't it could be too late for everybody. That don't make your kind evil like that fellow—he has a choice and he already decided it—but it does open up the same result. None of you are no better than the folks what give you the orders. That's why I'm me own man. 'Cause everything I do is my responsibility, my decision, and I'm the only one what decides if I sleep good nights or not."

"You continue to amaze me, Murphy. I thought you were just a drunken old sot."

"Oh, I *am*. But there's worst things to be. If I was real smart I'd be rich and retired with scantily clad girls peelin' and feedin' me grapes while I reclined in me garden. But I'm clever enough to have done somethin' that most folks in me line of work rarely get to do."

"Yes?"

"I'm old, Sergeant. I got old and I'm still here."

The computers were of little help in figuring out a method of isolating and picking up the *Stanley* survivors, and they soon realized that the only hope they had was the same sort of contact system they'd used to speak in the first place. Somehow the waves or particles or whatever sort of energy linked all the Magi stones would have to lead them to one another.

"We're going to have to use the shuttle, not any of the fighters, to have any sort of chance here," Broz said. "That means making contact while inside, and hoping that we can somehow use that link to ride the beam, as it were, down to the people."

"No probes?" the sergeant asked.

"Many probes, sure, and I still got some good ferrets, too, but what good do they do? *They* can't identify and latch on to this broadcast connection, and they can't be one end of it, either. It seems to work only with a brain at each end."

"I don't like it. That means taking the girls, who seem to need to be all together on this. Add a pilot and a couple of people to aid in getting the survivors aboard, and we've got a significant group of exposed personnel. What if it's a trick? What if nobody's down there and they nail our people? We'd have no practical way to rescue them, considering how stripped the old girl is here." Maslovic shook his head. "I don't like it."

"Still and all, we got to try," Murphy said flatly.

The sergeant sighed. "Yes, we do. The girls okay?"

"Yep. Don't remember a thing 'cept that for a while they felt hotter'n Hell and everything smelled bad. Got to smell like sulphur down there, and if they're in the mid latitudes, north or south, what'd we figure? Forty-five, forty-six degrees Celsius? They felt and smelled what the speaker told 'em. Kinda sounds like what you'd expect from a demon at that, don't it?"

"Don't *you* start on that! They willing to try it?"

"Sure. It's somethin' to do, and it gets them their pretty baubles. They're still pissed we took 'em back before they woke up."

"Okay, then. Cap, you with the girls. We'll let Sanchez and Nasser handle the rescue, and Broz, you fly it manually. No merging, you're just not trained for it."

"Got it, Boss," she said. "Don't worry. If we can get the coordinates, we'll get them. Man! Is that one *ugly* place down there, though! I'd take breathers."

Everyone was nervous except the girls, who thought it was a big adventure. As far as the others were concerned, once the people on the surface were located, it was going to be quick in and out just as fast as possible.

The shuttle was launched from high orbit, and Broz decided to take it in a broad series of spirals covering as much of the northern hemisphere as possible from a decent altitude. If they found nothing, she was prepared to climb and do the same at the south.

"You gals ready to get into your magic circle or whatever?" Murphy asked them.

"Don't need to," Irish O'Brian told him. "I can almost smell 'em now."

"Me, too!" piped up Brigit Moran. "And they don't smell good, neither!"

"Well, I hope they're away from them seaside colonies," Murphy commented. "You see the sucker mouths on them things? I don't think I want to introduce meself to them right now."

"They're not near the big ocean," Mary Margaret McBride said. "Oh, I wish I could really *see* down there! I can *feel* 'em when we get close!"

"Take your time," Broz told them. "You tell me when we're close and when we're going away. I'll try and narrow it down."

It took much of the day to do it the hard way, but finally they were able to zero in on one particularly large and active island whose interior had a series of jungle outcrops amidst what seemed to be blowing dust and steaming ground.

"There! Right down there!" McBride announced. "Oh! You're goin' past 'em again!"

Broz slowed to a crawl and then backtracked a bit. All sensors were deployed now, and they were at such a low altitude that she felt sure she could locate individuals if they got close enough. The trouble was, they were getting pretty exposed to whatever other hostile elements might be down there, including the creatures Murphy had christened the Big Suckers. Still, this location made sense if you wanted to avoid that kind of contact. The Suckers weren't averse to going in the ocean, but they didn't seem to stray more than a few kilometers inland.

"Got 'em!" Broz announced. "I have absolutely no idea how we just did this, but we got 'em! Right down there, just ahead and below us to the right. And they see us!"

Murphy and Sanchez checked the screens. "I only see three of 'em," the marine noted.

"Well, we're not staying around here long. I'm putting down. Cap, you and the girls come forward into the pilot's compartment. I'm going to seal us off and keep us pressurized here, so we won't have to eat that dust. Sanchez and Nasser will have the suits and breathers, and medical kits as well."

The people who came out to meet the shuttle were burned black by the sun, but their hair had turned almost snow white. They were all thin enough to count ribs from afar, but still they looked in reasonably good shape. It was in their eyes that you saw the length and depth of their ordeal. These people had been camping out in Hell for several lifetimes.

Even with the breather and the protective suit it was no place the others, even the marines, wanted to linger. The air was thick with volcanic dust and gasses, there seemed tremors that vibrated everything and everybody coming every minute or two, and with just breathers on there was no way to completely avoid the stench.

The girls hadn't been joking. Hot as hell and it stank.

It was only when the marines were helping the castaways aboard that they could see the signs of injuries on the leatherlike skin: scars and missing or chipped teeth, and places where they'd been both punctured and sandblasted with nothing in a kit to help.

Nonetheless, the one man in the group carried something in a kind of sack made from the leaves of one of the jungle outcrop tree fronds.

Over the howls of the wind outside, Sanchez yelled at him, "Where's the fourth person? We can't stay!"

"We don't know! She's around! We haven't had much of a way to control her!" Jerry Nagel shouted back.

"Well, we'll give her a few minutes. Otherwise we'll just mark the spot and see if we can come back later."

"Li! For God's sake! Get in here!" the smaller and older of the women yelled.

Suddenly, from the thick brush beyond, a tiny figure raced for the shuttle and almost jumped on board.

Nasser hit the bay door closed the second she'd cleared it, and even before it was all the way shut, Broz had begun to lift off. The wind and coming storm were actually buffeting the shuttle, and she wanted up and out of there as quickly as possible. The moment the aft compartment was sealed and pressurized, she took it up at full speed.

Most of their new passengers were out cold the moment they hit the deck inside, but one, a nearly skeletonlike figure of an older woman, kept looking around at them and muttering, over and over, "Thank God! Thank God!"

XI:
INVITATION TO THE DARK

The Voices were there and they spoke to him in the same soothing, cajoling, wondrous way that they'd first reached out to his mind. He was afraid he'd lost them, or that they no longer needed him once they were here, in *their* domain, but they had not let him down in the end.

It was all so . . . *simple*. He'd never demonstrated any special powers to the others, so they had been content to keep a ship's watch on him and restrict him to an area where they thought he couldn't cause any trouble. Little did *they* know!

Now, though, the demons had come again to him, and spake unto him, and this time they had unfolded his destiny.

They already knew how to fool these primitive ship's

systems. It had been so simple and, of course, they'd had the download from the minds of those simpleton girls. Now, though, it was time to put away childish pettiness and fulfill his dreams.

He had been limited here because of the lack of sufficient stones, but now there were enough, more than enough. That was why the others had to be rescued. He understood that now. But he saw that they had brought him not only sufficient stones for him to commune and transfer the vast power they offered him, but they had brought him his sacrifice as well. They had kept the useless thing alive so long, under such miserable conditions, until she could be bled out alive to their greater glory.

Now it was time.

"Joshua!" he whispered, shaking the big man slightly so as to awaken him without startling him.

"Huh? Uh . . . Sir?"

"Joshua, you are to proceed to the shuttle and do a systems check," Georgi Macouri instructed. "I shall be along shortly. I have someone special to collect."

"The shuttle? But that's going to be under full security, sir!" the big man whispered back, awake now.

"They will not see you nor notice you. You will be as if invisible to them. Trust me. We are both called to glory this time, and this time no one shall interfere!"

Joshua had no faith, but his code required obedience in these matters. He had seen enough in his service of his master that he was prepared to accept almost anything as possible, yet he didn't believe that this was more than delusion. It didn't matter.

"Do you have a chronograph?"

"I have a watch, sir. Three thirty-seven ship time."

"Good, good. I will synchronize. Yes. Are you awake enough to go now? I do believe we must operate within a window here."

"Yes, sir. As you wish. Anyone else accompanying us?"

"How I would like it to be so! But, no, the voices have instructed that we carry only one, the one who fits the situation of sacrifice. Leave her to me."

Joshua rubbed his eyes and got as awake as he could, then stood up. "As you wish, sir."

Macouri went to the door, his eyes glowing with the vision of the fanatic. "This is Destiny. My family, now me. This is the climax to my life and the reason all of us have been born. I feel ashamed to have doubted it, but I shall never doubt again!"

In another part of the ship, a far different scene was taking place.

"You should be asleep," Maslovic told Randi Queson.

"Yeah, I should, but, the fact is, I did more of that than anything else. I'm now beginning to feel some energy come back into me. Hope will do that. I looked at myself in the face, though. I was never much of a beauty and it's been a long time since I was a child, but I truly look *ancient*."

"It will pass, or much of it will. You just need to get some weight back on and get a solid reconstruction medical program going. The same with the others."

"Lucky—that's Cross, the other woman like me— she might actually come out of this ahead. She weighed over a hundred and sixty kilos at standard one gravity, which is why she spent so much time in low gravity situations. Now—well, she was always tall, but she's as skinny as me. I know she never gave a damn about her own looks, but I suspect that if she doesn't thoroughly relapse she's going to look radically different and that'll change some of her future life." She paused. "Um, we *have* a future life, I assume?"

"Hard to say. Your ship never made it back, either. Just like the others."

She nodded. "I heard someone say that. Hell, maybe we won't be *able* to go back. We may wind up enlisting or whatever it is you do to join the services."

"Nobody joins the services anymore," Maslovic told her. "You are born into it, period. We have changed just enough from you that it's no longer possible—or necessary."

Someone else entered the wardroom and they turned. It was Jerry Nagel, looking over the spartan machinery for a snack.

"You get pretty much what it decides, rather than you," Maslovic called to him. "This is the navy, after all."

Nagel took what he fervently hoped was some coffee and a rectangular bar of the nearly tasteless vitamin cakes that were kind of standard fare here and came over to them. "Hello," he said, more to Queson than to Maslovic. "I'm surprised you can still get coffee."

"Synthetic, like everything else," the sergeant responded. "But it's traditional. There is *always* coffee in all wardrooms."

"After God knows how long eating leaves and tasteless fruit and berries and drinking mostly water, I can tell you that even *this* helps."

Queson turned the conversation towards the practical. "So what are you going to do now?"

"You've been asleep the better part of several days, and under the medical computer's treatment. During that time, we've taken a closer look at the problem of Balshazzar."

"Give me a few of those stones and we can talk," she told him, "but that's about it. They taught me a lot. It was going back and forth with them that kept us close to sane, or at least gave us hope. They were a huge Christian religious commune of some kind and they somehow managed to keep their own values. I was raised Catholic, but the nuns never taught anything like *that*."

"Being a secular Jew I had a bit less taste for the theology," Nagel told him, "but they never pushed it. Some of them were pretty damned smart, too, in a lot of areas. Their guru or whatever was a missionary and a former astrophysicist if you can believe it. Some had military backgrounds. Maybe from the old days before you had a more closed society. All I know is that one of them who called himself Cromwell had done something really nasty in his past and had turned to religion as, I guess, some kind of penance. But you could tell just talking to him that he wasn't as changed as he liked to think himself. The old whoever he was wasn't far below the surface. It was still conversation, though, not mind reading, even if we were using funny little stones across a distance of almost a half-million kilometers."

"They at least said it was a peaceful world there. That several intelligent species of vastly different biologies and cultures managed to get along or at least tolerate each other without going into battle. That's something," Queson noted.

"I'd be interested in knowing more about those creatures," Maslovic told them, "and about the rest as well. We looked up the names in the computer history files here. Karl Woodward's group was one of the largest ever to vanish while hunting for the Three Kings, but that was a very long time ago and he was already an old man. If he's still alive, he has to be truly ancient. Your Cromwell—well, we know who *he* is. He would have been right at home with some of our more disreputable guests. He had the blood of millions, perhaps more, on his head. Our records show him as long dead, but that's often the case when someone is cast out. Normally he would have been executed for such breaches, but he was a general. Unfortunately, that's how things work here."

"Really? I've never seen a lieutenant defer to a sergeant anywhere else," Nagel noted.

Maslovic chuckled. "Well, technically she does outrank me. In terms of official stuff I'm actually a chief warrant officer. That's below lieutenant and above everybody else. But sergeants and chiefs have really run the military since time immemorial, and I find it more comfortable this way. In a way, even in a small society, I'm like an actor. I change my face, my name, my rank, I'm a different person. It hardly matters so long as my team knows who's boss and I have the backing of higher-ups."

"So what now?" Nagel asked him.

"Now we try to set up some contact with your friends on Balshazzar. I need to know as much as possible before heading for Kaspar."

"You think then that whoever is behind this is there?"

"I think that their equivalent of Sergeant Maslovic and his team are there, at least. The ones running this operation. I want them. Hopefully, since they know so much about us and we're still around, they'll eventually make some kind of pact with us, but me and my superiors are always leery when somebody sneaks out in your back yard and doesn't tell you about it, and even more suspicious of somebody whose technology is enough ahead of ours that eventually they may decide we're their inferiors or lab experiment or something. I think that's the running theory, anyway. Lab experiment."

"If that's right, they could take us out the same as they've taken everybody else out," Nagel said worriedly. "There are a lot of crash-landed creatures, human and nonhuman, on these world-moons, and nobody yet makes it back alive."

"We will see. At least if this power decides to crash us it will be off Balshazzar. A lot nicer place than you were in recently," Maslovic pointed out.

"I'm beginning to wonder if *any place* that could sustain us was worse than there," Queson responded. "What an awful existence. I still can't sleep on the bed upstairs, or tolerate wearing very much. It's just been so long and it no longer feels comfortable."

"I can understand. Let me ask—you haven't spoken about the small girl. She's deranged, or injured in the mind?"

"Injured in the mind may be a good way to put it," Randi Queson agreed. "She used to be tough as nails. She was the head of our company and expedition, and she saw nothing but profits and didn't give a damn about people unless she needed them. I think she'd had a hell of a hard life before she ever got into salvage but she never spoke of it to us, and it was too removed from any sort of polite society to be easily looked up."

"You tried?"

"At the start. You want to know who you're trusting your life to before taking a job out on the frontier. All I got was past salvage experience, but that was enough."

"And she is . . . How do I put this?"

"No longer home," Nagel finished for him. "Not since we made a serious mistake the first time to camp out on Melchior right in the middle of a massive mountain of these damned Magi stones. The cumulative power is enormous. It disrupts, it maddens. You get terrible visions and, with that, become an unreasoning beast. One of our people, a big, tough, muscular type, was butchered during that period, and it blew Li's mind out. She's never gotten any better, but the only rational part of her has been her refusal to get near any deposit of

those stones. She remembers something, deep down."
He suddenly frowned and then gave what could almost
be taken as a snort. "Huh. Funny. I just remembered.
When we ran for the shuttle, I grabbed a stash of the
stones. Old instincts, I guess. But I passed out in there
and came to here. Did you take them and lock them
away?"

Maslovic turned and called out to the air, "Chung,
did you see to the securing of a bundle of the stones
from the shuttle? Did anybody?"

"No, Chief. Sorry," came Chung's voice. "I'll run a
search pattern and see. I—*what the hell?*"

"What's the matter?"

"It's impossible! I am constantly monitoring everything and everybody! *It can't be!*"

"*What* can't be?" Maslovic demanded to know, getting to his feet.

"The shuttle! It's *gone!*"

"*Gone!* How could that happen?"

"I—I don't know. It *couldn't*! The security was fail-
safe!"

"Personnel check! Fast!"

"Uh-oh. Three missing. Macouri, Joshua, and that
girl we picked up on Melchior."

"You mean Lucky Cross?" Queson asked. "She's a
damned good shuttle and tug pilot. . . ."

"No, no! Cross is asleep! The little one! An Li!"

"Full alert!" Maslovic ordered. "I'm heading for the
command center. I want Darch and Broz there on the
double!" He looked at the two others in the wardroom.
"Come along, too, if you want."

"Yeah, I think we will," Jerry Nagel said.

"Cheer up! At least it's only a shuttle!" Randi Queson
noted. "Last time we went through this we had the
shuttle fine, but they stole the whole damned mother
ship!"

❖   ❖   ❖

Even Joshua was astonished at the ease of their escape. "Where to, sir? We are approaching Balshazzar now."

Georgi Macouri looked at the viewing screen and made his adjustments. "Beautiful. It is the Garden! And the serpent is always the master of the Garden, is it not? Park in a stationary orbit over the center of human habitation, Joshua. If we go down there now we will be simply two among them. We must prepare the way before achieving the scepter of rule from our Master!"

He went aft where An Li lay on the floor, tied-up hands and feet like some kind of animal, her mouth sealed with medical tape.

She saw him, and writhed, trying to get loose, but he was too much the expert at this sort of thing. Not that someone as tiny as her could have done all that much against even a man of Macouri's modest size, let alone Joshua's massive bulk.

"Well, little one! The Master saved you for us!" Macouri told her, as she tried to wriggle from his grasp and found herself far too bound for that. "Now we shall give you to Him and make meaningful your miserable, worthless life and, with your blood, open the Way to my ascension! The die is cast! The time has come!"

Most medicine for centuries now had been via computers and specialized machines, but on a shuttle or similar small craft where all the wonders of modern medicine could not be expected to be carried, there was still a basic old-fashioned medical kit. He found it, opened it on the cushions, and came up with several small surgical knives that were intended to be used in minor emergencies. They were never intended for what he had in mind, but they would do just fine.

There were quite a number of drug capsules for the injectors, and a portable diagnostic computer, but he ignored them. She had to be awake, to feel and therefore radiate the pain, in order to make the sacrifice worthwhile. It would be her screams, along with her blood, that would consecrate the sacrament, not her miserable worthless life.

He reached around and looked on the floor and under things and eventually came up with a large, almost meter-long sack made of tree growths from Melchior. They had whispered that it would be here, told him to hunt for it, and now he had it. Confirmation!

Although resembling purplish palm fronds, the leaf turned out to be a bulblike affair useful for carrying things. He forced open one end and poured the inside contents onto the couch seat.

Stones! Perhaps a hundred or more! He couldn't believe how many there were in one spot, or how great the variety of colors. And they all pulsed with energy, with *life* of a sort. These were not the ancient souvenirs sold as objects d'art to the rich back home; these were fresh, pulsing in the same way as the girl's heart now pulsed, waiting, waiting for her blood to be poured over them still warm.

He laid out all the things he needed, then stripped naked, so that there would be nothing between him and *them*, him and *her*. . . .

Her innocent eyes showed fear, and he drank it in and let it wash over him like a luxurious aphrodisiac. He was already turned on, harder and more irresistibly than he'd ever been, and it was time to begin.

"I am going to free you now," he told her in a soft, almost erotic tone. "You must lie there and stay like I put you. Do you understand that? If you do not, if you kick me, I will break your legs. If you hit or fight me, I will twist your arms out of their sockets. If you just lie there, and do *exactly* what I say, and let me do what I want, then nothing bad will happen to you. Do you understand?"

She looked absolutely scared to death, but she managed to nod.

"There is nowhere you can run, nowhere you can hide, so just relax. Yes, that's a good girl. Lovely, just *lovely*!"

She lay there, legs spread, arms stretched out on either side of her head, with all the Magi stones placed around her on the big mat, and then he approached her for what had to be the first part of the ritual, the part that established him once and for all as the master. She lay quite well for this, like she knew what was to come, and she made no effort to resist him as he slid on top of her and into her.

It was a violent but sublime rape, the best of the countless number he'd had, and the kind he had despaired of ever doing again. Now, even as he gave of himself to her, he reached out for the twin knives, one on each side of her just above her head, and, as he did, he touched the plane of the Magi stone outline he had created.

There was a sudden, sharp, violent shock running through him, knocking him almost senseless, and she acted quickly, wrapping herself around him. The shock immobilized him; he could not move, even as she seemed to grow larger somehow, to grow and grow and wrap herself around him and engulf him. She now was holding *him*, and he felt as much confusion as fear. He had somehow lost control of the situation, and he did not know what to do next nor how to do it.

He felt her physically and yet he also felt her mentally; not the feeble, retarded figure but one of great power, someone or something that simply had not been there before. It held his mind as well as his body, and it was filled with a kind of fury and power that he could never even have dreamed of. He fought against it, suddenly terrified, as it wrapped around him, and within him, inside of him, and attacked, as if it were trying to drive him out of his own body.

"JOSHUA!" he managed finally to scream, but it was one last scream, a scream that came from the primordial self he would never have thought was there, and it was answered by a sense of falling, falling, falling *through* the mat, *through* the very shell of the ship and out into the vacuum of space, and then down, down, towards the pretty blue planet below at a speed and violence that was surely fatal.

Joshua heard the scream, a scream like no other he could remember, beyond even the terror of his own loved ones dying at the hands of those long ago pirates, and he immediately unhooked himself, put the shuttle on auto, and rushed back to help his master.

What he saw was not too different from what he expected to see, with a few startling differences.

There was blood all over. There always was. The place had the look and feel and stench of a slaughterhouse. The difference was that there were two bodies covered in blood and excrement in the center of the cabin, and it was Georgi Macouri who was on the bottom, clearly dead, the look of abject terror in his wide open but unblinking eyes and on what was left of his face giving no doubt. The small girl had seemed dead on top of him, her long hair caked with blood and her tiny form covered with it, but, slowly, carefully, she backed off and away from Macouri's dead form and sat back in a kneeling position. Her face was all too intelligent, and all too filled with a look of pleasure. It was as if, as if . . .

As if it was the face of someone possessed by demons.

The two surgical knives she'd used to make such a

mess of Georgi Macouri were in each hand, held the way one would hold them before stabbing a victim.

An Li was no more than a hundred and fifty centimeters high and, combined with the weathering and semistarvation of the months on Melchior, she could not have weighed more than thirty-five kilograms or so, yet there was an energy and force inside her that made her seem like a giant to the nearly two-meter-tall muscular man, who easily had a hundred kilos on her, and who now stood there gaping at this sight.

"You need to clean up this mess," she said with a firm tone. "Or would you join him now?"

"He is dead. There seems no point to joining him," Joshua commented. "I pledged my service to him, not to his causes."

"Will you pledge yourself to me, now?"

"I do not know who I am addressing," he told her. "If it is for my life, I would prefer to simply die quickly."

"You are many times my size. Do you think I can do it to you?"

"He was larger than you as well. I suspect that you might. You are not the girl we brought here."

"No, I am not. I am going to clean this body up in the back while you do what you can here. Once we have tended to the basics, turn this thing around and head back for the destroyer. I have much business there."

"I will do it," Joshua told him. "Not out of fear, but out of respect." And perhaps a bit of curiosity as well, he added to himself. If the soul did exist, he had long ago forfeited his. If this indeed was who held claim to it, then it was time they got to know each other.

"Very well. And collect the stones. Don't worry, they won't do much to you if you just collect them and put them out of the way."

Joshua nodded and gave a slight bow. It was going to take a *lot* more than he had to make this cabin presentable, but he would do the best he could.

The creature in An Li's body went back to the showers and took a look at herself in the mirrored reflection before beginning what was obviously going to be quite a chore washing this stuff off. Well-toned, superior reflexes, but *this* was going to take some getting used to.

As it turned out, it wouldn't be much of a trip back to the *Agrippa*. As soon as the missing shuttle was discovered, Chung had initiated a close-in search of the immediate vicinity and had no trouble finding it parked in orbit around Balshazzar. It was a curious thing to do, after all this time and trouble, but she lost no time in pursuing it with the intent of bringing it back aboard or shooting it if need be.

Maslovic didn't want it damaged, since after the stripping it was the only space-capable vehicle that could handle more than two people, but neither was it any good to him in enemy hands.

They approached cautiously, but saw no signs of the shuttle building up power or taking any action at all.

"I don't like it," Darch commented. "Macouri's crazy, but why steal it and get away, however the hell he managed it, and then just *park*? He's a sitting duck."

"Could be a trap," Maslovic warned. "You never know." He was very much concerned with the fact that Macouri now had a defenseless young woman with him. The little man had only one history with that kind of person.

Randi shook her head. "Somehow, I just don't think so. It's hard to explain, but when you've been practically saturated by those stones for so long you get a kind of sense of them. Something's wrong. Not for us. For them. I can sense it."

Before they could close to capture range, Darch turned and called, "We're being hailed!"

"Put it on."

"This is Joshua. I am bringing the craft back and will dock. Do not fire on us, please," came the somewhat familiar voice of the big man.

"Joshua, where is Macouri? Put him on."

There was a pause. "I don't think that's possible, sir. In fact, I doubt if that will ever be possible again, unless he is correct about an afterlife."

"He's dead?"

"Yes, sir. It is difficult to explain. Far easier for me to just bring the craft back. I simply cannot imagine how I personally could clean this up. It will have to be your ship's maintenance systems."

Randi was suddenly alarmed. "What about An Li? Did he hurt her?"

"No, ma'am. Not that he didn't try. It is simply going to be much easier to show you. There is no threat here that I can determine, except for an incredible number of those execrable stones."

"Shit! The portable stash! I don't even know why I bothered," Jerry Nagel said, mostly to himself. "I'd forgotten all about them."

Maslovic wasn't buying anything until he had the full story. "Sanchez, Nasser. Cover the shuttle when it docks in Bay One. Take no guff from anybody. Understand?"

The truth was, neither they nor he *did* understand. Why quit and give up when you walked through security and a cyberlinked ship without being noticed? Did Joshua kill Macouri? Had they misjudged him? Or what?

The truth, such as it was, was soon plain when the shuttle docked and the hatches hissed and then opened.

Joshua emerged first, and was clearly both unarmed and no threat. In fact, he looked to the marines as if he had suddenly grown very tired and very old and beyond any of this.

Nasser gestured for Sanchez to keep a watch on Joshua and went inside. He wasn't gone long, and when he emerged he had a look that no marine had shown for a very long time.

"It's a butchery in there," he told his partner and by extension the others waiting above. "I've been in a few nasty fights, but I've never seen anything like that."

Behind him, a tiny figure emerged, dark, weathered like the others of Melchior and, like them, almost a stick figure in spite of long and still messy-looking matted hair trailing down its back.

The one who was once An Li looked neither shocked nor traumatized in any way, although she did have a little bit of that pissed-off look she'd had from the start.

"I may have to get used to this for a while," she said, "but I don't have to sacrifice. Anybody on this tub smoke cigars?"

"That's not Li," Nagel commented. "It may be her body, but that's not her. Not even before. The face, the walk, the movements, all different."

"Wake Murphy up and get him up here," Maslovic instructed Broz. "We may just be making a first contact here and, if so, this is definitely right up his alley."

The one in An Li's body sat there in the ward room looking at the rest and somewhat enjoying it. Even Murphy hadn't been able to come up with a cigar, but he *did* have some Irish-style whiskey that the little one seemed to find very much to her liking.

"Well, I see you all gathered round and hovering like scavengers over dead meat, so we might as well get this over with," she said. "I admit right now I expected to feel a lot better than I do. I think I've got bruises in places where until not long ago I didn't have places."

"Needless to say, you are not An Li," Randi Queson attempted a more casual beginning.

"No, hardly. But I'm not the folks I suspect you're looking for, either. Let's just say I'm from Balshazzar, or at least I've been there a very long time. This is a trick we'd discovered and practiced quite often down there over the years, although it's no mean trick to do, let me tell you, even face-to-face, and from surface to orbit—well, I'm surprised it worked. Whether I'm pleased I don't rightly know. I'm not used to being this, well, *diminutive*, let's say, or to be assembled in quite this fashion. However, when the watchers below observed the ship and zeroed in on it and immediately saw what was about to go on in it, we just had to do something. Much good came of that decision, which was made in quite a hurry. Karl Woodward, the founder of the group below, was dying, and dying ugly. By millimeters. Slow and painful. Mostly it was age, together with a lot of things that we carry with us. He could have used this method. Young people were willing to give their bodies to save him, but he wouldn't have it. Now he's got one. Not as young as it should be, but younger, and in better overall condition. And I have performed an excellent operation and surgically removed an extremely evil man from this plane of existence. Karl would be shocked to hear me say that, particularly in that manner, but it's true nonetheless."

"And An Li? What of her?" Randi asked.

"I don't know. There was precious little home when I moved in, I can tell you that, and it had noplace to go so it's still here. I can access it, and there really isn't anything there. You thought it was trauma, but I think the old An Li was too tough for that. I think you all went to bed in that mountain of Magi stones and in the mental seizures it caused, she either was wiped clean or, maybe like me being here inside this shell, she went somewhere else. Where? Who knows? But it gives me some peace that I didn't destroy or force a cohabitation with anyone to pull this off." She looked around. "Pretty small crew for a ship this size."

"We're the suicide brigade," Maslovic told her. "Mostly automated. A shuttle couldn't have made it, and it was too risky to bring through the fleet. That left us." Quickly, he introduced everyone. "And you are . . . ?"

She thought a moment. "The old one was Li, so let's just call me Ann. I think maybe it's best that way. There's no going back, and I'm not sure I could ever get up the emotion and total commitment it took to do this sort of thing again. I can tell you though, seeing, feeling that terror and that evil I had no hesitation whatsoever. The moment he thought he was in complete control and cut her bonds, I moved. Even then, without all those stones all heaped up and arranged around the rapist's bed, I wouldn't have had the power. As it was, it just happened. That's what we have found gives the most power with these things. Pure emotion. You don't think, you act. I suspect that's why we're going to stay second-tier citizens. I think *they* can control the power through reason and will. We need rage or lust or something equally base to really do the impossible."

"Were you one of the ministers there in the cul— religious commune?" Randi pressed.

"Please! No more! Who I was I will never be again and that is for the best. That person is now dead. Who this person was," tapping her chest, "is the same, or so I suspect. If she shows up again and demands it, I couldn't deny her entry, but I suspect that she and

I will never meet in this life. I suspect that Doctor Woodward will tell you the same. On the other hand, here I am, off Balshazzar. That's something nobody has managed to do before in *any* incarnation."

"Why do they keep you there, but not us on Melchior?" Nagel wondered aloud. "I've been trying to figure that out since the start."

"We're huge down there, and we multiply. The other races down there are about as alien as you can imagine, but in many ways they're the same. Breeders, high technology types, who got snared here just like we did. *They* are all threats, or maybe just enough to gum up the works a bit, and all are from civilizations that would come swarming in here. You, you were a few stranded prospectors nobody would miss. Nothing personal. And none of the other races on Melchior seem sensitized to the stones." She looked straight up at Maslovic. "You know what you have to do."

The sergeant, who had a mild suspicion that he might have indirectly known the person now in the tiny woman's body but who decided not to press it, nodded. "We have to go to Kaspar."

Murphy sighed. "The one pretty one in the bunch and we got to go to the cold, dark place."

"We're still here, Captain," Maslovic responded. "It appears that, of all the ones who have come here before, for any and all reasons, we have been invited."

It must have been odd, Randi thought, to look through the stones and see yourself somewhere else down there on the planet, but that's what Ann was doing.

The figure that appeared in their minds as they spoke with the leader on Balshazzar was of a huge man in a pink robe and a tremendous gray-white beard and long flowing hair, the very picture of a prophet or perhaps Moses getting the Ten Commandments.

"I am still getting used to this," Karl Woodward said. "You are all right with all this, my old friend?"

"It is actually quite practical," Ann assured him. "And it beats the DNA makeover that never really did the full job which you have now inherited. It is you who have the really difficult job now, Karl. You have to continue to sit there and lead. I, on the other hand, get to finally go where common sense should have told us to go so long ago."

"It was Kaspar who always traveled, says the legend, with a finely hewn box of the most exquisite mahogany," Woodward reminded him. "And all who saw it marvelled at the box and wondered what great mystical treasures it contained. And when the baby Jesus reached out to the box, only then did they discover that inside was where the old astrologer kept his candy. You won't find candy in Kaspar's box this time, you know."

"I know. But perhaps we will find truth, old friend. If we can get back the word, we will do so."

"Take care. Go with God, and keep the temper in check until it's necessary."

"But give 'em Hell when required," Ann responded, completing some private joke of theirs. "Yes, I remember. Perhaps not yet farewell, but it is time."

"I agree. It is time."

Ann broke contact, and Chung prepared to secure the ship and break orbit. Randi Queson wandered back to the wardroom and sank down in a chair next to Jerry, Murphy, and Broz.

"You are worried," Nagel said. "I'm worried, too, but I expected to be dead and done to a turn back there by now, so at least we're going to go in full steam and of our own free will. Who knows what we're going to find?"

"I know, I know. But with all that, I keep going back to the nightmare."

Nagel nodded. "I know. I can't get it out of my mind, either." Randi, Jerry, and even the less sociable Cross, had all used the stones to share the nightmare with the others, a nightmare they had experienced only once, yet could not forget.

She had been flying, flying through some strange, alien greenish sky with pink and yellow clouds.

Although it had clearly been a point in some kind of atmosphere, she could see through it to the stars beyond, the whole starfield laid out before her, not in the usual visual spectrum but through some other means. It was almost as if she were viewing some kind of photographic negative of the sky, an alien sky she'd never seen before filled with all the stars and formations of a globular cluster, but where light was dark and black was a kind of bright, soft pink.

Looking below, she saw a vast world that was heavily developed but long past its prime. Great domed cities stretched in uncounted number to the horizon, encapsulating ancient and dying masses whose shape and other details could not be determined from this height.

It would have been awesome if she hadn't felt permeated with a sense of awful hopelessness, a feeling that all those billions plus billions down there were in total despair, creating so much unhappiness that it collected and beamed from every individual and every dome and perhaps every centimeter of the planet, and beyond, going to and right through Randi Queson. She felt tremendous sorrow for them, all the more because she knew that she could not help them in any way, only watch their decline into despair and death.

The others were all with her. She could feel them, sense them in a hundred inexpressible ways, yet she could not see her companions. They were wraiths, flying over a planet of the dead, but they were still wraiths, as helpless as any spectre.

And now they were off the world, and into the strangely inverted and bizarrely colored void.

There were others out here as well. Many others, but wraiths just like themselves, able to witness but only to witness, as they went from world to world, system to system, in a flash of darkness, instantly going from world to world and finding only the feelings of horror, despair, and death.

There were Others, as well, on some of those worlds, and going between them. It was no more possible to tell anything else about them than it had been to tell details of the first and subsequent civilizations, but this was a different realm, a different sort of sensory perception, and they were clear as could be.

These were the Bringers of Despair, hatching from the dark, hidden places and wrapping themselves around the worlds they found and helplessly sucking the life out of them. The ones the Others attacked wanted to fight back, wanted to push back this horror, but they could not. Once attacked, they progressively lacked the energy to push against this overwhelming darkness, a darkness that seemed both infinitely collective and yet of one mind and attitude.

They veered off, swallowing pride, running for their lives, flying through holes and folds in space one after the other, throwing off the pursuer or pursuers. All thought was gone; there was suddenly only panic, only fear, and a sense that they must return together.

And then it was all emotions, rising up like a giant wave and crashing down, washing over them, bathing them in a range so intense they could not bear it.

"Are the ones we head to the Bringers of Despair or those who fight and flee them?" Ann asked her.

"I don't know. I can't know. I certainly hope it isn't

the Bringers. If they're real, and I deep down believe that they *must* be, then we're doomed. Ones who sterilize the universe behind their waves of aimed cosmic ray storms . . . It's too horrible!"

"Let's go see," said Ann, even as Maslovic gave the command from the center to break the ship out of orbit and head towards the small, dark moon of mystery.

XII:
KASPAR'S BOX

At one hundred and eighty kilometers above the planet-sized moon, the instrumentation and cameras could do an excellent job. If somebody had stopped off there and left graffiti on a rock, they could read it. The trick was noticing the rock in the first place.

It was a forbidding-looking place in any event. The residual heat from the big and still officially unnamed mother planet plus pressure deep under its oceans, freezing around the coasts but still liquid for most of their expanse, allowed it to maintain a barely habitable temperature during its long semi-night, but it just gave an even more eerie look to the place.

"Not any signs of glaciation," Nagel noted, feeling a sense of *deja vu* as he looked once more on the forbidding little world and said much the same to a new but at least more appreciative audience. "It must melt pretty good on the sunward leg. Lots of erosion in the regions against the mountains, but the main land masses have been so chewed up they're just cold powdery desert. Those dunes and that wind would make it even nastier. And we thought that overrun colony's choice of worlds was bad!"

"Atmospheric content?" Maslovic asked.

Darch checked the figures. "Very cold at the moment and dry as a bone, but the oxygen and hydrogen mix is within limits. I wouldn't like to do it without a breather just to keep the grit from choking you, but the air would be okay. I don't know what we'd eat, though, and any fresh water in those big lakes would take a fission reactor to properly melt for use. It's probably as ugly but very different on the solar traverse. No way to tell until we can see it, and that's still almost fifteen standard days, I think."

"The subsurface scan will show you what we found," Nagel told him. "Nobody's dumb enough to live up here, but that's not the only place to live."

"It's honeycombed, a vast cavernous system down there," Darch noted. "Most of the interior caverns, some of which seem to go *way* down, appear to be relatively dry, and those figures there just *might* indicate some running water even at this point. That's how you survive the cold cycle. Ten to one the caves maintain an above freezing temperature that's either constant or nearly so. The surface is only comfortable half the year. Odd, though."

"I'm sure you've already seen what we saw in the makeup there," Nagel commented, kind of needling the tech.

"Yes, I see what you mean," Darch responded, oblivious to the dig. "Caverns of that signature tend to be sedimentary rock, easily eroded away over time by the underground rivers and streams, and certainly all the makings are there for a classic setup. Note, though, that there are *no* such caverns within a hundred or more kilometers of the coastlines. They're away from the oceans and in the highlands no matter where you look. There doesn't seem to be a major change in bedrock composition in most of those cases that would explain it. The planet's got a heavy but mostly solid core that's maintained the gravity and kept the atmosphere, but a lot of the underground water doesn't seem to obey the laws all that well. It's probably scrambled data from all this interference, but on the face of it, it seems like as many of those deep rivers are flowing upward as are flowing downslope."

"Yeah, I noticed the uphill flow when we were first here," Nagel told him. "We never did figure it out. Li thought it was caused by pressure, using some of the caverns like pipes."

"Interesting. Plumbing for a race driven from the surface? Fascinating concept, but we're getting heavy organics but nothing that would suggest a civilization or even a big colony that would justify building works like that. If our master aliens are down there, then they're probably long dead or reduced to a primitive existence. This is a planet you can *survive* on, it's not one you ever want to try and live and work on if you don't have to."

"That's why we thought the place wasn't as interesting as it first looked."

"Perhaps, but the fact is that the entire Three Kings is an artificial construct." Darch saw their stares. "Somebody built them, and this whole thing, and is maintaining it. That's more than enough down there for a maintenance base."

"We're coming up on the wreck," Randi Queson put in. "We were all excited by it, I remember, since we hadn't seen all the life on the other two yet. It's still impressive, though. There! See?"

It *did* look very much like an artificial structure, but not for humans. It also gave off virtually no power signatures, meaning that it either used a power system unknown to them and therefore unmeasurable or, more likely, it was a derelict from times long past, covered and then uncovered by the shifting sands.

It was a huge ball shape, perhaps three hundred meters across, sticking out of the sand. It was light gray in color, and all over its surface it had short probelike protrusions. A close-up didn't reveal much more about it, but it *did* reveal at least one clear breach of the hull or exterior or whatever it was. A jagged hole, half in the sand and possibly anchoring it there.

"That's been down there a while," Darch noted. "You can *smell* it as a long-term derelict, an ancient shipwreck. Sure, you wonder if any of 'em survived and, if so, did they manage to set up something permanent down there, but it's a long shot. More telling is that it's there at all, and that there's good evidence it's been buried by the sands and winds several times, and maybe baked and thawed as well on the sunward side. Good bait, though, for the curious."

"Not a bad spot to visit, either, if they've gotten the shuttle cleaned up," Maslovic noted. "If they're putting that thing there to attract visitors, why not, well, visit?"

"Maybe because it could be a trap?" Murphy suggested.

"Could be. Let's see . . . I've got full suits for my team, and most of you can fit into them, but Ann, it's going to be a *very* loose fit."

"I've had your computerized shops working on modifications as we approached," the strange woman responded. "I think you'll find there's one that's just my size."

Maslovic was now positive who he had aboard. Now all he had to do was decide whether or not he liked it. Certainly he felt as if he could handle it.

"Okay, then. Surface team . . . Might as well make this a political thing; it sure doesn't seem like we're going to do battle down there, or that it would do us much good if we could. That makes it me in the lead, Ann of Balshazzar, Cap if you want to try it, and Nagel and Queson of Melchior. Bring one of the stones each but we won't distribute until we're away from the ship. The rest stay locked and secure so our little girls won't have the run of the place while we're gone."

"I would like to come as well," Joshua put in.

Maslovic was surprised. "You joining the team?"

"I am in the service of the one who killed Macouri," he told them. "Besides, I have nowhere else to go."

"Okay. That makes a pretty awful military team but a good science and muscle blend. Draw your suits and check your equipment, suit up, and be outside Bay One in an hour. My own team, who are showing really nasty looks at me at the moment, will be backup. We're not going in blasting here. I have a feeling that this is pretty close to the group whoever it is down there would want invited."

"Not at all by the book," Ann muttered. "About what I'd expect of an intelligence man."

The fit for the suits, including Ann's, was quite good. Nobody there would have to face the elements, nor go in cold. All also had sidearm weapons, but it was understood that those were a last resort and Maslovic had a cutoff. If anyone got too nervous, he could stop them from shooting.

They decided on the alien spaceship simply because it was so prominent. Anyone who actually landed would be almost forced to check it out and, for that reason alone, it seemed to be the logical place to start.

Nobody said much on the way down. Joshua took it slow and easy on manual and put it down about a hundred meters from the alien wreck, which seemed even more ghostly and bizarre close up.

"Okay, you can expose your stones to the outside," Maslovic told them. "Let's see if they act as old Kaspar's candy and bring the natives for a treat."

"Yeah, *us*," Murphy said gloomily. It was too dark, too barren, and too alien for him.

Queson and Nagel finally got to examine the wreck close up. It was gigantic, and much of the interior that had stayed intact didn't make a lot of sense, but clearly it was what it appeared to be. What had come in it? How long had it been since they'd crashed here, and where were they or their descendants now? These questions had no obvious answers.

After several hours of surveying the wreck and the surrounding area, though, it appeared that they had guessed wrong.

"We're going to have to pack it up and move, folks," Maslovic told them, gathering them around him against the eerie backdrop of the ruined ship. "This is getting us nowhere. I propose we try one of the low cave entrances. There appears to be illumination just inside, so maybe we'll have to go knocking."

They all agreed, turned to go back to the shuttle for the move, and stopped dead in their tracks.

How long the creatures had been there it was impossible to say. They didn't show up as a recognized lifeform on any of the instruments, yet they had something of a familiar look. And, Ann noted, they were even smaller than she was.

There were six of them, one for each of the humans it was supposed, and they looked identical.

In one sense, they were humanoid. Less than a meter tall, they stood on two thick trunklike legs with massively oversized feet and they had two arms ending in equally outsized hands, three fingers and an opposable thumb that extended opposite the index finger rather than at the end of the hand. Their heads were hairless balls, with two big, round black dots for eyes flanking either side of what seemed to be a massive nose that began almost at the top of the head and extended down and out to the waist, sausage-shaped but with a number of tiny pits at the end rather than a single large pair of openings. Two outsized floppy ears, one on each side of the head, completed the look, as well as earth-tone tunics and pants, leatherlike floppy boots, and light brown gloves.

Most important, each wore a ring on the middle finger that clearly contained one of the Magi stones.

"Silica based," Nagel commented, checking his readings. "Definitely not the natives here."

One of the little creatures stepped out from the others and looked at each of the humans in turn. The huge round eyes captured and reflected the pale light, but there was no question that it was examining each of them in turn. Finally, it raised one oversized gloved hand and, with its index finger, it pointed in turn to several of them. Ann, and Maslovic, Queson and Nagel, and then, after a thoughtful pause, it pointed to Joshua and to Murphy. With a dismissive wave, it made absolutely clear that those were the only ones it wanted, period.

"I wonder what would happen if the squad followed us, no matter what the big-nosed bastard wants?" Maslovic mused aloud.

"I don't think they'd get very far," Ann responded matter-of-factly. "Any group or power that can keep several high-tech masses on a world by negating their technology and who can play the kind of games they've played so far isn't likely to be overcome by a show of force. These things, or whoever or whatever they serve, most likely built these three worlds and rearranged the furniture of this less than hospitable solar system to maintain it. I don't know about the other worlds, but you have no idea how advanced one of the other alien colonies is on Balshazzar. They were nonetheless as helpless as we were."

"*Are*," Randi Queson reminded her. "I feel about as empowered at the moment as I did sealed in the control room of our salvage station on a different world far from here, hoping that something very alien couldn't find a crack to ooze through. I have this nasty feeling that I've been here before."

Although the surveys had shown a vast network of caves beneath the surface and some wide entrances to them, the little gnome surprised them by simply going over to what seemed to be a barren rocky knob, which proved to be an artificial hatch of some sort that began to open, first with a hissing sound, then a rush of steam. When the steam floated off into the cold atmosphere of Kaspar, they discovered that it had emerged from a steep set of stairs going down beyond their point of view into the heart of Kaspar. The stairway seemed carved or fabricated out of a single unbroken rock wall and was also scaled better for the gnome than for the much larger party of visitors, but it was manageable. The gnome had no hesitation and jumped in, taking the stairs at a good clip. The humans were much slower, but, one by one, they managed to get down into the hole and, with the aid of a suddenly visible thin but sturdy hand rail, were able to make it, single file.

The top of the stair was also icy, which they hadn't expected, but the condition didn't last long and caused only minor discomfort in spite of the depth of the passage. When the last of the party had descended below the surface, the hatch closed behind them and there was another hissing sound as if sealing an airlock, followed by a deep rumble from far below and a rush of much warmer air into the stairwell.

"Temperature's going up," Jerry Nagel noted. "This may be comfortable in a little while." It was already in the mid-twenties Celsius, and the humidity level was going from moist to tropical in a hurry.

"Maybe uncomfortable in a few minutes more," Ann noted. "I think these little people like hot and wet. I am already thinking of Dante's *Inferno*." Sensing that nobody else seemed to understand the reference, she added, "He was the author of an account, widely believed at the time, of his walking trip to Hell. It went from dull and boring to boiling and beyond."

"Ah, that's what I thought you might be thinkin' of," Captain Murphy responded, already beginning to sound tired and breathing a little heavily. "And the devil himself was at the bottom, as I recall, chewin' on the worst sinner of all."

"Well," Ann responded, "let us hope that the similarities don't end there. Dante, after all, walked out of the place safe and sound."

"I'm just wondering if these little people built all this, or are the natives here?" Nagel said. "They don't look like planet builders."

"Looks can be deceiving," Ann cautioned. "On Melchior we met some creatures that seemed incapable of much at all, yet they were as smart or smarter than we, had built and flown their own spaceships here, and had created quite advanced colonies. One of them saved my life. That in spite of their having lost any belief system they might have had long before they were stuck there, and being pretty cynical. Doctor Woodward is a challenge for them. They have been trying to argue him out of his faith and he's been trying to convince them of the reality of his for decades now."

"Any progress?" Queson asked, curious, but also pleased to have something to take her mind off the fact that they were rapidly descending into a place that might not allow them out.

"He has them very worried," Ann told her. "But they are aliens in more ways than we can imagine. Not even humanoids like these little creatures here. Before you can successfully argue you have to be very clear as to the terminology you can use, and that what you think you are saying is what the other is receiving. We all think that is what's been going on here as well. The ones behind the Three Kings want to get to know all of us very well."

"The question there is to what end?" Maslovic noted.

Funny, Randi Queson thought after the exchange. *None of us have even considered the idea that these funny little creatures might be the masters. I wonder what that says about all of us?*

They reached, if not bottom, at least the bottom of the passage after a few minutes and looked out on a vast cave complex that seemed to stretch and branch in so many directions it was hard to understand how the surface of the moon kept itself from caving in. There was little wonder why the surface had resembled Swiss cheese in the survey scans. The odd-shaped pillars seemed too thin and flimsy to support the whole structure, yet they had to be doing so.

The caverns certainly weren't dark, either. The whole place had a kind of fluid texture, as if it were wet and glistening, yet to the touch it was merely cool and somewhat smooth in feel. Randi thought of it as "soapy," although she couldn't quite say why.

It was, however, a radiator of ghostly light, mostly a dull yellow but occasionally almost lime green or light red. There were spots where the light seemed to run in threads, or veins, creating eerie abstract patterns on the walls, floor, and ceiling, yet visibility was never poor.

They encountered large numbers of the gnomes now, off on some mysterious errand or another; it wasn't clear what they did, or why. They moved with little sound in the caverns even though noise tended to amplify and echo, and not once had any of them uttered a word or so much as a sound.

Once they came upon one of their villages, and it seemed like something out of an old human fairy story; gumdrop houses, not a consistent straight line or quite identical building, yet all made out of the same kind of rock as the caves and either mined or carved from them. There were small rivers through the area, leading into fresh water pools in some cases, and, for the first time, there was vegetation as well—growths of some sort of plants that resembled mosses and lichen but which also echoed the colors of the minerals in the walls, often contrasting with whatever they were against. Seas of yellow clung to walls of strawberry red, and light blue growths seemed to crawl up or down lime-green or lemon-yellow walls. Now and then one of the little people would go up to some of the growths, tear off a small strip, and stuff it into its tiny mouth nearly hidden behind the huge nose. Clearly this was the food source, although it didn't seem to need much if any care; there were at times a lot of the gnomes around yet little sign of large gaps in the surrounding growths.

"Constant temperature down here, plenty of food and water, lots of easy building materials," Maslovic noted. "Looks like a pretty comfortable life for such a bleak world."

"Yes, but what do they *do*?" Ann wondered.

As they went through chamber after chamber the mystery didn't seem ready to be solved. Still, now they came across monstrous side caverns in which were sitting what had to be monstrous machines of unknown purpose and design.

"They do *somethin'* " the old captain noted, impressed by the sheer scale of the things.

"Or they did, or somebody did," Nagel responded. "They're mostly overgrown with the mosses and there's little sign they've moved in ages. They were used once, but not in a long, long time I don't think. I wonder if these little people were the operators, or the descendants of the operators? Hard to say." There were what looked like mounds covered in blue and purple lichen all around, and, on impulse, he reached down into one of them and brought up a handful of what at first looked like gravel.

"I'll be damned," he said, looking at the material as he continued the slow walking pace behind the lead gnome. "Take a look, Randi. Familiar?"

She took some of it and looked it over. It wasn't gravel at all, but a mass of those mysterious little shavings and small remnants they'd found in concentrations all over their area on Melchior. Ann took a look and said, "Yes, we've seen a lot of that on Balshazzar."

"Those are some of the holy artifacts of the Macouris," Joshua said, breaking what had been a long silence. "They were brought back along with the Magi stones by the ship of the First Emissary. No one could divine what they were."

"Machine poop," Captain Murphy commented. "I'll be damned! It's the leftovers from the innards of them damned giant playthings there!"

"Probably some kind of byproduct," Nagel agreed. "The stuff was formed by the ton, that's for sure. They probably used it to help shape and maintain certain essential land features. Over time, it would have been eroded and show up, even in a volcanic hell like Melchior. We may never know for sure, but apparently the machines just can't not make *something* out of anything they have on hand, even if it's just miniatures of whatever they were doing. In a way you're right, Captain. Giant machine shit." He chuckled. "And so are the icons of the gods exposed."

"I have a feeling that we're at the end of this journey," Maslovic said, looking ahead. "You feel it?"

He didn't have to elaborate; they could all feel it. That horrible eerie sense of uncaring power that the Magi stones exuded, magnified now over and over again. And, too, a sense of something, perhaps *someone* else, waiting just ahead.

"It's a bit colder," Randi Queson pointed out. "And there's a bit of movement in the air. There's something pretty big just around that bend."

"That's an odd sound, too," Maslovic added.

It was impossible to describe; an alien thing, yet a pulsing tone that seemed to go very deep and wash in a steady series of waves right through them, body and mind, in a machinelike rhythmic perfection. It got no louder as they entered the final chamber, but it seemed all around them, all pervasive.

"Oh, my god!" Randi Queson breathed.

"I believe we are here," Maslovic said simply, looking around in a mixture of awe and fascination as they walked out onto a bridge that seemed to go on forever, spanning a round pit easily kilometers wide and going both up and down to what seemed infinity in both directions. If it was false perspective, as surely the gap above them had to be, it was perfectly staged.

The bridge was perhaps four meters wide and polished so smoothly that they could see themselves clearly reflected in it as they walked. It looked so pristine that it seemed unimaginable that anyone had ever walked on it before, yet they themselves were making no mark, their boots giving no trace of scuffing or wear.

"You feel the presence?" Randi whispered to Jerry Nagel.

He nodded. *"He's* here," he replied, and none of them had to be told what he meant. That unseen presence, who always crashed the party and stole the wonder from the Magi stones after a while, was most certainly present.

Murphy frowned. "Hey! Where's our wee one?"

They had all been so busy gaping as they'd walked out onto the bridge that they hadn't seen the gnome make an exit, but exit it had. They were alone, six tiny figures in a grandiose pulsating shaft of some kind.

"Ouch! Suddenly me head's poundin' like a son of a bitch!" Murphy exclaimed.

They were all feeling it now, increasingly intense headaches that were not at all helped by the deep and inexorable sonic two note.

"Look at the walls!" Ann almost screamed at them. "Good Lord! No wonder . . . !"

As throbbingly painful as the headaches were, they all managed to look and saw immediately what Ann meant.

Magi stones. . . . Hundreds . . . thousands . . . *Billions* of them! The entire shaft was either made of them or coated with them, each with a tiny solitary light that came on from within to illuminate the chamber so brightly it was as hard to see suddenly as it was to think through that pounding.

Silica based, that's what the gnomes had been. And not just the gnomes. These stones weren't just baubles, gems to amuse the rich and famous and befuddle the geologists and physicists, no. *These stones were alive!*

"I believe I can adjust your responses to allow you some comfort here," a voice said, a voice both coldly alien yet somehow familiar to them. As the headache seemed to retreat to a low throb fairly easy to endure

and the light level became a bright but not unbearable glow, they were finally able to think.

"Li? Is that you?" Randi Queson managed.

"All that An Li was and knew is a part of me, except, of course, for the physical body. I am others, too, if you would prefer someone else."

"It doesn't matter," Nagel told the voice. Still, he couldn't help thinking, *Great! The alien wanted an idea of what we were like and winds up picking Li! Boy is this gonna be a tough first contact!*

"Please do not be concerned, Mister Nagel," the voice responded as if he'd said rather than merely thought the comment. *"We are well aware of the differences in your people. We have been analyzing them for quite a while now. Your variety at this level of maturity is unusual, but hardly complex."*

"I should have known you could read minds in here with this gathering of stones," the engineer commented, mostly to let the others know the context of what was going on. "Considering I've seen somebody else move into the body Li left."

"Surface thoughts only. To read everything, even of the small samples on this and the other two moons, would be more confusing than useful if they could not be tuned. We get a sufficient sample from those who, you might say, overdose on the wave amplification effects that are a byproduct of what you call the Magi stones, and the sample is more useful because it is random. Had we not uploaded An Li at the point we did she would have had an embolism and died taking all her life's experience with her. What a waste that would have been."

"You grow those stones on all three worlds, don't you? That's what you're doing here," Maslovic said to it.

"Of course, Maslovic. In the same way as your

birthing machinery creates new and well fitted and designed soldiers, we must replicate ourselves. As should be obvious, though, we do not have the innate mobility of your people. We have power you cannot dream of, yet we need others for the simplest of things. It is our curse, an evolutionary curse of sorts, which has caused much misery and despair. It keeps us always hiding, always fearful, never able to stop what threatens our long existence, yet which also destroys countless civilizations who die in total ignorance and bewilderment of why they are being extinguished."

Maslovic seemed to be the first one to understand. "Our people are silent for a reason, aren't they? We're not cut off from them. They aren't there any more."

"Always the military man must correctly analyze the tactical situation," the voice responded, a voice which, they now all realized, was only in their minds, but radiating from the tiny creatures within the walls themselves, perhaps collectively, perhaps selectively.

All the Magi stones were alive. The ones here, the ones back home, the ones on the other moons. Each contained that tiny spark of life, perhaps pure energy encased in a physical shell, that made up an almost imperceptible part of the vast intellect represented here. *That* was who you saw when you gazed too long into the stone. You began to sense the tiny living being within, and, eventually, the infinitely greater whole that it was somehow linked to. No wonder it seemed both alien and scary.

"What do you mean by them not bein' there?" Murphy asked the sergeant.

It was Ann who gestured with a wave at the huge alien population all around them and explained, "They aren't scouting us. And with the kind of knowledge they've absorbed from their long history and with the help of a few other groups of creatures, they don't need us or anything from us." She looked around at the multitude. "You're hiding here, aren't you? You're hiding here from whoever or whatever it was that killed seventy percent of humanity. You're not spying *on* us, you're spying *through* us. My God! What in *hell* can be hunting *you*, who can create whole solar systems and keep them stable?"

"We ain't gonna like this answer, right?" the old captain asked with a sigh.

"There is another race as ancient as we," the voice said slowly, even a bit wistfully. *"Their names do not matter any more than ours do. They are, however, quite different. Your Doctor Woodward would call them a race born without souls. They have great power as well, but are mobile as we are not, and are not part of a greater whole as we are, but more in some ways like you might become, as some of your past cultures became. They are a race capable of any greatness you might imagine, but they can not imagine greatness. Their motivating factor is fear."*

"You speak of demons," Joshua noted. "Why would demons fear you or anything?"

"Demons. Not a bad concept, but perhaps too mystical. Just imagine this one concept. It is by no means all of the story, but it is enough, and is something easily grasped. Imagine if you were a god. Imagine if you had the powers of a god, to rule, to create, to destroy at your command. The absolute command of all you survey. And now imagine one more thing. It is not something as common as you might imagine, nor is it easy to achieve, but it is something that does happen often enough that you know that it can happen to you.

"Imagine you are a god who can die."

"These—others . . . They can die?" Randi Queson asked, mostly to confirm the bizarre concept they had been given.

"*They can die. They have physical form and no direct continuity. They can upload their consciousnesses to new or artificial bodies, but they are still each alone, and they can be caught by the accidents of the universe or in a few ways by deliberate entrapment.*"

"These demons hunt you because you can kill them?" Joshua asked.

"*No. They know we could never get them all, that we are both too few and bound in some ways not to exterminate. No, they might have fought us forever because of our power, but not in this single urge to sterilize the universe. They would merely enslave it and play with it as toys. No, you misunderstand the depths of their fear and paranoia. They will kill us all, our race and your race and tens of thousands of other races, a few of which are represented here in what you call the Three Kings. They have tried without success to kill us many times. Now they are going about it differently. Since we cannot do anything on our own but think, they will wipe out any race that might be our arms and legs, you might say. It is not hard for them to do it once they find it. A few unstable stars coerced into monstrous explosions, gamma ray showers so intense that nothing at all of any sort of life of use to us could survive it.*"

"And that's what happened to our people? That's the Great Silence?" Maslovic asked.

"*Yes. But as with others over the eons they did not get everyone. It is a brute force approach. But, sooner or later, they will find your people, or, accidentally, your people will find them. That is why the route to the Three Kings was kept so secret after we were accidentally discovered. When a second expedition found us, we knew that our safe haven here could not last forever. So we sent back some of us as sentinels, as listeners, and we used the fringe, the cults,*"

*to minimize our obvious presence. We needed our
arms and legs as usual, so that if and when the others
come the secret yet findable route here can be sealed
and our sentinels recalled. It will give us time to move
again."*

"There's *nothing* we can do to stop them?" Maslovic
asked. "I mean, you said they were mortal. If they're
mortal . . ."

*"We know what you are thinking, but you would not
get the chance. We have been working the problem now
for two billion years. It is not hopeless, but it has not
yet been solved. Until then, we hide, and we move."*

"Then at least let us return to try and prepare our
people, even if *you* won't help in a defense," the sergeant almost pleaded.

*"We are sorry, but no. You are in the Three Kings.
You must remain. The passage is deliberately controlled.
In a word, you know too much to be allowed to fall
back into the hands of the coming enemy."*

"But you just told us there was hope!" Randi pro-
tested.

Ann sighed. "Don't you get it, Doctor? They've all
but come out and told us why the others hate them
so much, will destroy the universe rather than let them
be. It's the corollary of the fact that they are like gods
but can die. Get it now?"

"Well, I sure don't," Murphy grumped.

"Consider what happened to me, Captain," Ann
prompted. "I was on Balshazzar, watching a horror
through these very transceivers, unable to help and
wanting desperately to do so. They allowed it. With
pride, I thought Doc and I had figured it out and managed it on our own, but we'd never done anything like
that before. Not loading consciousness into another body
somewhere else, let alone him into my old one. We just
thought we did. *These* people did it. Or, they understood

what we desperately wanted, made a decision to help, and it was done. The result was that I not only changed my gender I also lost almost a century and a half in age. A century and a half, Captain. You understand it now?"

"Jesus, Mary, and Joseph! I'm an old con man, lass! I ain't no brain!"

"They're immortal," Randi said, almost too soft to hear. "These people simply grow something new and move in, probably automatically. The memories, the intellect, who knows what? It all keeps." She turned to the wall. "That's it, isn't it? They might have been able to stomach a limited rival in power, but the only thing worse than them being able to die is to discover that you don't!"

There was no immediate reply, and it allowed the stunned others to recover somewhat.

"I got an inkling right off, when they said that everything that Li was was still there," she went on. "I'm right, aren't I?"

"Yes," came the answer at last. *"And it is a limited gift that can be shared. Those who help us and work with us can have it if they want it. Not everyone does."*

"Sweet Jesus! Me three empty-headed darlin's can dance till Doomsday?" Murphy muttered.

"My people are still stuck on Balshazzar," Ann pointed out. "What good will they do you?"

"They are stuck because at least one of the races there is not only not inclined to help but is inclined to hinder. Something will have to be done about it, but your Doctor and your people are already trying to win them. In the end, they will be left but your people will not, and all by their own choice. We have more than enough people. We do not have enough good people."

Joshua suddenly roared and reached into his utility pack and pulled out a very nasty laser pistol. *"No!"*

he screamed, his voice echoing in the shaft. *"You are the angels of control! I swore to serve the demons of freedom!"*

Maslovic, nearest the big man, went into action almost reflexively, bringing up a leg and kicking hard into Joshua's backside. Not expecting it, the big man fell slightly forward, taking several steps nearer the edge of the bridge, but not losing his grip on the pistol or completely losing his balance. He managed to put out his other hand and stop his forward motion a good meter short of the edge, and it was clear he was going to make it, turn, and begin firing. He did not, however, decide to go down on his knees and turn and fire, a movement that they might not have been able to counter, but instead struggled unsteadily back to full erectness.

Patrick Murphy raised his leg and pushed it right into the big man's groin. Joshua yelled again and took several steps backward, trying to bring the pistol up and aim it first at the one who'd just kicked him. He stepped back one step, two steps, three steps.

He didn't have three steps.

With a look less of madness than total bewilderment, Joshua plunged into the seemingly bottomless chasm, his roars of defiance fading quickly.

Murphy smiled. "I didn't know I had it in me!"

"I never did understand why we brought him along," Maslovic commented.

Jerry Nagel looked up at the wall. "I assume your folks can lead us out of here? At least for now?"

"We had to bring you here. You represent all the factions of your race. You can be our ambassadors to them now."

Randi Queson looked at where Joshua had gone over into oblivion. "He made his choice. Now we get to make ours."

The gnome was suddenly there, gesturing for them to follow.

As soon as they cleared the bridge, Murphy reached into his own pouch and brought out a flask. He drank a good deep belt, then offered it to the rest, including the gnome, who sniffed with that huge nose and then made it clear that it was to be nowhere near him.

Ann took a slug herself, then handed it back. "I wonder if we can perhaps help them to win this thing? Or at least believe that they can."

"Maybe, maybe not," Maslovic responded. "But now at least we know the score. It's always the challenge that makes life worth living, isn't it?"

"I can see that you will have to learn a bit more about being human," Ann responded. "It took me a very long while myself. Still, there's great power here, and opportunity, and none of us have anyone left back in the colonial systems to worry or worry about."

"You're going to have to start introducing him to some philosophy," Randi Queson noted.

"You don't go back to Balshazzar for that," Jerry Nagel put in. "I think we start with the captain, there."

"Aye, lad! I think this will be a heavy time. I think maybe I can weather it, with me whiskey here, and maybe some good cigars someplace, and with three beautiful girls. The rest of you can think the deep thoughts and save worthless humanity. Maybe you just might. I think of meself as keepin' the home fires burnin'. . . ."